FAILURE TO APPEAR

Other works by J. A. Jance:

Hour of the Hunter

J. P. Beaumont Mysteries

Until Proven Guilty
Injustice for All
Trial by Fury
Taking the Fifth
Improbable Cause
A More Perfect Union
Dismissed with Prejudice
Minor in Possession
Payment in Kind
Without Due Process

Joanna Brady Mysteries

Desert Heat

FAILURE TO APPEAR

A J. P. Beaumont Mystery

■

J. A. Jance

William Morrow and Company, Inc.
New York

It is the policy of William Morrow and Company, Inc., and its imprints and affiliates, recognizing the importance of preserving what has been written, to print the books we publish on acid-free paper, and we exert our best efforts to that end.

Library of Congress Cataloging-in-Publication Data

Jance, Judith A.
    Failure to appear : a J. P. Beaumont mystery / J. A. Jance.
        p.   cm.
    ISBN 0-688-12674-X
    1. Beaumont, J. P. (Fictitious characters)—Fiction.   2. Police—
Washington (State)—Seattle—Fiction.   3. Seattle (Wash.)—Fiction.
I. Title.
PS3560.A44F5   1993
813'.54—dc20   93-15558
                                                                         CIP

Printed in the United States of America

1   2   3   4   5   6   7   8   9   10

BOOK DESIGN BY LISA STOKES

First Edition

*To Leah and Florence, two of Ashland's
goodwill ambassadors, and to Lynn K.,
the best "Laredo Kid" ever.
Also, to Steve and Juli, who signed the napkin.*

FAILURE TO APPEAR

Prologue

I hate hospitals. I hate the smell of them and the shiny glow on long, empty-looking corridors. I hate the ominous swish of white clothing that precedes nurses as they bustle down hallways or march unannounced into rooms. But most of all I hate waiting. Even for supposedly tough-guy homicide cops, there's nothing in the world that makes you feel more powerless than cooling your heels in some obnoxious waiting room while a person you love goes under the surgeon's knife.

When I couldn't take it any longer, I escaped outdoors, retreating to the relative safety of a concrete bench next to an overflowing ashtray. There I sat, exiled to the smoker's outdoor dungeon, even though I don't smoke and never have. There was no tree to keep off the worst of southern Oregon's blazing late June sun, but then I wasn't looking for shade. I felt chilled. From the bones out. The 90-odd-degree weather could neither penetrate nor melt the ice floe building up around my heart.

Ralph Ames, my attorney, followed me outside. He glanced in my direction but left me alone. Instead, he walked over to the other pair of worried people, the one made up of Karen, my ex-wife, and her present husband, Dave Livingston. As Ralph spoke to them, I noticed that, periodically, Dave would reach over and pat Karen's shoulder or pull her close and let her lean against him. Karen isn't the "helpless female" type, not by a long shot, but she was taking it hard. Real hard. I was thankful she had Dave there to lean on when she needed it.

I could have had someone with me as well if I hadn't been so damn stubborn. Alexis Downey was willing. In fact, she had offered to come outside with me, but I had sent her back into the waiting room to stay with Jeremy. He needed someone there with him, too, and God knows I wasn't it. How could I possibly comfort him when I could barely stand to look him in the eye?

Ashland Community Hospital. Why did this have to happen here in a little Podunk town like Ashland, Oregon? I fumed for the hundredth time. Why couldn't it have been in a big city like Portland or Seattle? Someplace civilized, where the number of high-tech doctors outnumber high-priced lawyers. Someplace where, in spots like Seattle's Pill Hill, glass-and-concrete hospitals stand cheek by jowl, stuck so close together that you can walk from one to another in a driving rainstorm without ever wetting your feet. I had suggested hiring a helicopter to fly Kelly to Portland, but the doctor nixed that idea. He shook his head and said there wasn't time. Not for either one of them.

Alexis stepped outside then, too. With the highlights in her auburn hair gleaming in the afternoon sun, she walked over to where Ralph Ames stood huddled with Dave and Karen. The murmur of their conferring voices carried through the still, hot air even as far as my standoffish bench. If I had tried, I suppose I could have made out what they were saying, but the way I felt, not knowing was better than knowing. Ignorance may not be bliss, but at least it allowed a slim margin for hope.

I glanced down at my watch. Two-thirty. The minister, a determinedly cheerful woman from the yellow Unity Church, had spent the better part of an hour at the hospital, sticking closer to Jeremy than to anybody else. Now she had gone off to Lithia Park to make sure all the guests knew the wedding had been canceled due to lack of a bride rather than lack of interest.

I saw Alex turn toward me, her eyes questioning, but I ignored her. I didn't want to talk to anybody right then, not even Alex. In my case, misery most definitely does *not* love company. Coward that I am, when she started toward me, I abandoned the bench and beat it down the hill. For what seemed like hours, I wandered aimlessly through Ashland's boiling midday heat, thinking about the unlikely chain of events that had conspired to bring us all here together.

As I walked, I brooded. I wondered if, after all this was over, anything would ever again be the same.

1

It had started only three days earlier, although now that seemed a lifetime ago. It began with a ringing telephone and with me cursing the noisy instrument that I regard as technology's worst blight on the human race. Telephones follow me everywhere. Even in my car. There is no escape.

The blaring phone jarred me to my senses sometime around seven o'clock on a drizzly Saturday morning toward the end of June. Friday night had been a late one. I wasn't nearly ready to rise and shine, but homicide cops at Seattle P.D. are used to unscheduled, early-morning wake-up calls.

Around what locals call the Emerald City, people tend to knock each other off in the middle of the night or in the wee small hours of the morning, especially right after the bars close on weekends. If the work load gets too heavy for the regular night-duty squad to handle, they start calling for reinforcements. Being off-duty doesn't mean you're home free. When your name comes up on the rotation, you're called and you go in, regardless of what you may or may not have been doing the night before. Having a personal life is no excuse.

I figured my early-morning phone call meant it had been another one of those busy Saturday-night-special Friday nights around Seattle P.D.

"Beaumont here," I grumbled into the phone, wishing we could somehow convince the city's crooks—the gangs, the thugs, and the variously affiliated drug dealers—to use each other for target practice during regular daytime eight-hour shifts. "What's up?"

"This is Dave," an unfamiliar male voice replied. "You know, David Livingston?"

I was still muffled in a warm, sleep-induced cocoon, and this joker had me stumped. I could have sworn I didn't know anyone in the whole wide world by the name of David Livingston. The telephone must have passed along my blank silence, because a moment later good ol' Dave gave me a helpful hint.

"You may not remember, but we met once, a while ago, down in Wickenburg, Arizona. I don't think we were ever properly introduced."

Jump-started now, the old brain finally fired and caught hold. Of course! *That* Dave Livingston. My ex-wife's second husband. No wonder I didn't recognize him!

I sat up a little straighter in bed. Of all people, what did Dave Livingston think he was doing calling me up? So early on an otherwise peaceful Saturday morning that I had not yet tasted a single sip of coffee, here was Dave, already up and about and letting his fingers do the walking.

In a universe full of complicated matrimonial merry-go-rounds, second husbands don't often reach out and touch first husbands. By telephone, that is. It isn't done. Not unless it's a dire emergency—a matter of life or death or missing child support. We're all reasonable adults, but there is a limit.

Now, though, I heard Dave, talking to me as calmly as if conversations between us were an everyday occurrence. Since child support has never been a source of controversy, my mind leaped instantly to all the other worst possible conclusions.

"Dave," I croaked. "What is it? Karen?"

He paused a moment and cleared his throat. "No, not Karen."

"The kids then?"

I said "kids" aloud, but even as I said the word, I knew it was a lie. I have fathered two offspring—Scott and Kelly. Scott, my first-born, is as steady and responsible a kid as any parent, good or otherwise, has any right to hope for or expect. He's never given any of us—Dave Livingston included—a moment's trouble.

Kelly is something else, our collective problem child—a wild-haired, pain-in-the-ass-type kid who started wearing makeup and testing limits at the tender age of eleven and has been off the charts ever since. She had run away from her stepfather's home in Cucamonga, California, some four months earlier, disappearing one week shy of her eighteenth birthday and several months short of high school graduation. Once Karen finally saw fit to tell me what was going on, I had hired an L.A.-based private investigator to look into Kelly's disappearance. All he had sent me so far was an outrageous bill.

"Kelly then," I added. "Did you find her?"

"Sort of," Dave Livingston allowed gloomily. "More or less."

For a supposedly hotshot accountant, Dave was being damnably nonspecific. Meanwhile, my homicide cop's mentality was working overtime, filling in the most gruesome kinds of missing-person details—the dry ravines where unsuspecting people sometimes stumble over vulture-scattered human remains. Memories of long-overlooked and rotting corpses loomed in my mind's eye. Unfortunately, cops have chillingly realistic imaginations. We've seen it all. More than once too often.

"Tell me then, for God's sake!" I urged. "What the hell do you mean, 'more or less'? Is she alive or not? And if she's alive, is she all right?"

"I haven't talked to her yet," Dave put in quickly. "Not in person; neither has Karen. As a matter of fact, Karen knows nothing about all this. She was so bent out of shape when Kelly ran away that I didn't exactly tell her I was hiring a detective."

Great minds think alike. So Dave and I had both hired private eyes. His had gotten results. I'd have to fire mine.

"So where is she?" I prompted. "Is she okay?"

"In a little town in southern Oregon. A place called Ashland. Ever heard of it?"

I had heard of it, as a matter of fact. Months earlier, the town of Ashland had been nothing more than a green-and-white freeway exit on I-5, the last stop in Oregon before hitting the California border. Now, thanks to my new friend Alexis Downey, the director of development for the Seattle Repertory Theater and the lady with whom I had spent most of the previous evening, I knew a whole lot more than I would have otherwise.

From listening to Alex, as she likes to be called, I knew that the Oregon Shakespeare Festival in Ashland has, over the last fifty-some-odd years, created a multimillion-dollar business out of doing Shakespearian reruns every summer. In Ashland the Bard of Avon translates into big business. People come from all over the country year after year to see the seven or eight plays that run concurrently in three separate theaters.

Because of increasingly stiff competition for regional arts dollars, Alex Downey keeps a close eye on all the theaters on what she calls "the I-5 route." She had even suggested that we might want to skip down to Ashland for a romantic weekend once over the summer to take in a couple of plays, all in the name of knowing what "everybody else is doing."

At the time Alex mentioned it, a trip to Ashland had sounded like a treat—your basic roll in the hay with a dollop of culture thrown in for good measure. Now, that selfsame Shakespearean weekend didn't seem like nearly such a good idea. The thought of running into my daughter on the streets of Ashland threw a real wet blanket on my fantasies of sexual/cultural adventure.

Call me a prude if you will, but I didn't want to give my already headstrong daughter any bright ideas that she might not think up on her own.

"What's Kelly doing there?" I asked. "Acting?"

When she was little, that's what Kelly always said she wanted to be when she grew up—an actress. In high school she had played major roles in several school productions, but by then her mother and I were divorced. I never actually saw her perform onstage.

My experience with Kelly's acting capability came primarily from being on the receiving end of emotional temper tantrums whenever the two of us wound up in a nose-to-nose confrontation. High-powered theatrics aside, I didn't regard acting as a realistic career choice. All little girls can't become actresses any more than millions of little boys can all grow up to be cops or firemen.

"Hardly," Dave answered. "She's working as a hotel maid and doing some baby-sitting on the side."

Baby-sitting was no surprise. All her life Kelly had been exceptionally good with little kids, but I couldn't imagine her working as a maid. Neither could anyone who had ever seen her room. Incredible irony—that's what Mrs. Reeder, the beautiful woman who taught my senior English class at Ballard High School, would have called it. Kelly is the only person I've ever met who can totally trash any given room within fifteen minutes of entering it. On the odd occasion when she's stayed with me in Seattle, I've watched her make a shambles of my whole apartment in far less time than it takes to say, "When's dinner?"

"Kelly, a maid?" I choked. "You've got to be kidding." I did my best to stifle a relieved chuckle, but Dave Livingston was not amused, and he wasn't laughing, either.

"I'm not kidding," he returned doggedly. "And I'm not making this up. I just found out. She plans to get married sometime early next week."

That got my attention.

"Hold it! Did you say married? She can't do that. She's only eighteen years old, for Chrissakes. And she hasn't done a damn thing about getting her education."

"I know," Dave agreed. "I was hoping you could go down there and maybe talk some sense into her thick skull."

"Karen's way better with her than I am. Has she tried?"

"Like I said," he confessed uneasily. "I haven't exactly told Karen about this. She was upset enough to begin with. When she hears what's going on now, she'll go crazy."

Dave had a point—a good one. Once or twice I've had the misfortune of being in close proximity to Karen Moffit Beaumont

Livingston when she's busy kicking ass. It isn't a pretty sight. Karen is a lady who knows how to indulge in histrionics. By comparison, Kelly is a rank amateur.

Wide awake now, I sat up and groped on the nightstand for pencil and paper. "Who's the boyfriend?" I asked.

"His name's Jeremy Todd Cartwright, the Third," Dave answered.

"Sounds impressive. What does he do?"

"I've got a short bio right here. It says he's a part-time actor and musician. Up in Ashland this season he's in something called the 'Green Show.' He plays a character called 'The Laredo Kid' in a play called *The Majestic Kid*, and he's 'servant' in *Taming of the Shrew*."

I might have known—an actor. Talk about music to a future father-in-law's ears. I could already visualize the flaky son of a bitch. Long, greasy hair. At least one earring. Maybe even a single tasteful diamond chip in one side of his nose. But then I forced myself to look on the bright side. If Dave's bio information came from a current playbill, Kelly's intended was at least working. He had a job. From what I know about actors, that's highly unusual in and of itself.

"Great. Do you have an address for this boy genius?" I asked, sitting there with my bare feet on the carpeted floor and with pencil poised over paper.

"As a matter of fact I do," Dave Livingston answered. "One-forty-six Live Oak Lane—the same as Kelly's."

The pencil lead snapped off as I wrote down the address. I wasn't upset. Not much.

"So will you go see her?" Dave asked, almost pleading. "I need to hear what she has to say for herself before I tell Karen. I'll give you my work number so you can call me here. It's the end of the fiscal year. I'll be working off and on all weekend. If you don't mind, I'd rather Karen didn't find out I've gone behind her back on this."

I can only describe it as one of life's supremely surrealistic moments, finding myself involved in an underhanded plot with my ex-wife's second husband, both of us scheming together behind Karen's back. But then, that's what makes life interesting—those little unforeseeable surprises. I took down Dave's work telephone number at the chicken-raising conglomerate in Rancho Cucamonga where he was the chief financial officer.

"How soon will you go?" Dave asked.

"That depends," I told him, "on how soon I get off the phone."

With that, we hung up. After a quick detour to the kitchen to start a pot of Seattle's Best Coffee in my Krup's coffeepot with its thermal carafe, I headed for the shower. I figured I could go a long way in my little red Porsche on a full tank of gas with a full pot of coffee along for the ride. While I showered, though, reality set in. Alex and I were supposed to have dinner together that evening, and Ralph Ames, my attorney from Phoenix, was scheduled to arrive on Sunday afternoon.

Once out of the shower, I called Ralph first. He's an early riser. Alex isn't. Ralph listened quietly while I brought him up-to-speed. When I finished my tale of familial woe, Ralph's reply was infuriatingly unflappable and lawyerly.

"What's the plan?" he asked.

"What do you think? I'm going to drive down, tell Kelly how the cow ate the cabbage, and put her on the first plane home."

Ames cleared his throat. "That's not exactly realistic, is it, Beau? What if she won't go?"

"Won't go?" I echoed. "Of course she'll go. She's just like me, stubborn as all get-out, but she'll listen to reason. She has to."

"Not necessarily. If she's planning a wedding for next week, she may have decidedly different thoughts on the matter. After all," he added, "she is eighteen, you know."

"I don't care how old she is. She may be eighteen, but she doesn't have the sense God gave little green apples."

Ralph Ames and I have these kinds of disagreements all the time. He came on the scene at approximately the same time that Anne Corley, my second wife, shot through my life like some brilliant, sky-illuminating meteor. The profound impact she had on me is totally out of proportion to the amount of time the two of us actually spent together. When she died, she left me with more money than I know what to do with.

Along with the money came Ralph Ames, who serves as general overseer of not only the money, but also of me. Through the years, and despite our somewhat divergent views, I've come to value both his unwavering friendship and his innate good sense. We argue from time to time, but more often than not I end up paying attention to what he says and doing things his way.

"Don't you still have some use-it-or-lose-it-type vacation time coming to you?" he asked me after a slight pause.

When Ralph asks a question, he usually does so in the same way most good detectives do—knowing, before he ever opens his mouth, exactly what the right answer should be.

"You know I do," I returned irritably. "We talked about it last time you were here."

"So why not take some time off? See if you can schedule vacation for all next week," he suggested. "That way, if it's possible to bring Kelly around, you'll have more time to make it work. If you drive down today and come right back tomorrow, you'll be under a tremendous amount of pressure. So will she."

"And what if I can't make it work?" I growled, tweaked by Ralph's irritating and unreasonable reasonableness.

"Look on the bright side," Ralph returned cheerfully. "That way, you'll be there in time for the wedding."

Count on Ralph to discover some remote silver lining.

"Whatever you decide," he continued, "I'm still planning on coming to Seattle tomorrow. Let me know if there's anything I can do. And say hello to Alex for me when you see her."

"Right," I said. "She's the next person on my list to call. I'll give her your regards."

I waited until I was seated in my leather recliner and drinking coffee before I dialed Alexis Downey's number. Middle-aged dating is hell. First you have to sort through what's out there to see if there's anyone you like who might possibly like you back. Do that, and things become even more complicated.

In the past two months, I had discovered a good deal to like about Alexis Downey. There were also more than a few stumbling blocks—a major one being her huge, man-hating tabby cat named Hector. Another is her bed.

Alex prefers to sleep on one of those crazy futon things, which she folds up into an unusable couch by day and turns into an equally uncomfortable bed by night. She insists my king-size Posturepedic mattress hurts her back. So we spend time together, quite a bit of it, actually—fun, enjoyable time—but one or the other of us is always creeping home to our respective beds in the middle of the night. From a neutral-mattress perspective, a trip to Ashland might have been fun, but not now, not with Kelly living there.

Once I had Alex on the phone, I tried explaining to her exactly why I was on my way to Ashland by myself, why a joint trip seemed totally out of the question. At least to me.

Alexis Downey had her own thoughts on the matter. "Like hell," she declared heatedly. "If you're going, so am I."

"But what will I tell Kelly about you?" I asked.

"What do you think you'll tell her? Your sex life is none of Kelly's damn business, that's what. How soon are we leaving?"

After years of Fuller Brush training, I recognize assumed closes when I hear them even though I'm not always quick-footed enough to dodge out of the way. Alexis didn't ask whether or not she was invited. All she wanted was an estimated time of departure so she'd know how long she had to pack.

"Can you be ready in forty-five minutes?" I returned.

"No problem. I'll farm Hector out with Helen upstairs. Then I'll call my friend Denver down in Ashland and get her working on rustling us up a room and some play tickets. At the last minute, tickets may be damned hard to come by."

"Denver?" I said. "You have a girlfriend named Denver?"

"Denver Holloway. Didn't I ever tell you about her? She's directing at the Festival this year. If anybody can get rush tickets, she can."

Advancing age has increased my ability to give in gracefully. "I'll be there at eight o'clock sharp," I told her.

After that I called Sergeant Watkins, the desk sergeant on the homicide squad, and filled him in. Watty wasn't thrilled by my last-minute scheduling of vacation time, but he understood. He and I share the misfortune of being fathers to troublesome adolescent daughters. His youngest had married some two months earlier. Watty was well aware that I'd been worried about Kelly. He was one of the few people at the department who knew I'd hired a private eye.

"Good luck on straightening Kelly out," he told me, "but I'm betting you won't be able to change her mind one iota. As far as I'm concerned, boys are a hell of a lot easier to raise. With boys, you only have to worry about one penis. With girls, you have to worry about all of them."

His helpful, fatherly comment didn't improve my frame of mind. "Thanks for all the encouragement, Watty. I needed that."

I could hear him grinning into the telephone. "Always glad to be of service," he said.

I slammed down the receiver.

The Automobile Association of America says it's a ten-hour drive from Seattle to Ashland averaging fifty miles an hour. I didn't drive Triple A's recommended fifty. I threw a hastily packed suitcase into the 928, gassed up, and collected Alex from her condo on Queen Anne Hill at eight on the dot. Once on I-5, I tucked the Guard-red Porsche in with the crush of fast-moving southbound traffic and stayed in the middle of the pack.

Fortunately, Alexis Downey isn't a backseat driver. She doesn't have to get out of the car every mile or two, either. With short but necessary pit stops in Portland and Roseburg, we turned off the freeway into Ashland at 4:45 that afternoon.

As we headed south, steady rain gradually gave way first to drizzle and then to occasional showers. While we were passing through the Siskiyous, partly cloudy blue skies appeared overhead. By Medford, it was full-fledged summer, but I didn't notice. I was far too distracted to enjoy what should have been a pleasant, scenic drive. Preoccupied with thoughts about Kelly, I'm sure I wasn't much of a travel companion to Alex.

Kelly had been missing from home for almost four months. I should have been overjoyed that Dave had located her. But I'm a cop in what I call the Nasty Nineties. I've seen what happens to runaways who take to living on the streets for even as short a period of time as a few weeks. I've witnessed the heartbreaking aftermath when anxious parents, thinking they're getting their kid back, come downtown to pick up the pieces. Or else to identify a body. With all the stuff that's out on the streets now—drugs, AIDS, herpes, gang warfare—even if the kid isn't dead, what the parents get back isn't the same person who left home a few days or weeks or months earlier.

Fortunately, Alex is a very patient woman. For most of the way, she left me alone, but finally even she could no longer tolerate the thick, oppressive silence.

"Have you decided what to do?" she asked.

"Murder's out," I replied glumly, "for professional reasons if nothing else."

She laughed. "No. Seriously, Beau, what options do you have?"

"How about offering him a bribe, sort of a reverse dowry? Maybe Jeremy Todd whatever-his-name-is has heard through the grapevine that I'm supposed to be loaded. It wouldn't surprise me if he's only in it for the money. Kelly has lousy taste in men."

"Getting married isn't exactly the end of the world," Alex argued. "Some of the people I went to school with got married right after high school and are still married to each other. Some of them even seem to be happy."

"He's an actor," I said.

"So? Actors are people, too. Besides, what makes you think he's so awful? You haven't met him yet. If he's working for the Festival, he must have something on the ball."

"Being a part-time actor isn't much of a recommendation for a bridegroom," I retorted. "Not much at all."

In downtown Ashland, Alexis hopped out at a stoplight on the main drag, promising to call me on the cellular phone as soon as she knew for sure where we were staying. Despite all the No Vacancy signs we'd seen along the way, she seemed certain that we wouldn't be forced to sleep on the street. In the meantime, I went off on a solitary hunt for Live Oak Lane. Ashland isn't very big, and I figured if I drove around some, I was bound to stumble across it. Finding it might have been easier if I'd broken down and picked up a map.

The tourist guidebooks all say that Ashland is a lovely, picturesque place. Quaint, I believe, is the operative word. The shady tree-lined streets showcase prosperous-looking, newly rehabilitated but authentically Victorian houses of the gingerbread variety. Most of the bigger ones seem to have been converted into bed-and-breakfast establishments.

To an outsider, although there were lots of cars parked on the downtown streets, the whole place seemed almost deserted. Then, suddenly, at five o'clock and for no apparent reason, I found myself stuck in the middle of a traffic jam while the sidewalks bustled with hurrying pedestrians. That's when I finally gave up, played against gender stereotyping, and stopped at a gas station to ask directions.

"Oh," the attendant said. "You mean the co-op. It's not in town at all. It's out in the county on the old Live Oak Farm. A bunch of actors live out there. Cheap rent and all."

It sounded like a damn commune to me. Straight out of the sixties. All the more reason to want Kelly out of there and back home in California where she belonged. Surely, she'd listen to reason, wouldn't she?

Don't bet on it, buster, I told myself sternly. Why would she? After all, she never had before.

2

Following the attendant's detailed directions, I drove out through the end of town, under a freeway, and past a golf course. In the process, as distracted as I was, I couldn't help noticing that this quiet corner of southern Oregon is beautiful country.

The town of Ashland is nestled in a broad valley only a few miles north of the California border. June in Seattle usually carries on gray, rainy, and cold. Here, the atmosphere had a California feel to it—dry and airy. The sky was a clear, untroubled blue.

With the onset of early summer heat, lush grassland had turned gold in sharp contrast to the fringe of the steep oak- and pine-covered hilltops that formed the valley's border. In one fenced field, a single cow stretched her neck to crop scarce but reachable leaves from a few low-hanging branches. That explained why the trees had such a uniform, trimmed appearance. They all looked as if they were subject to constant, loving pruning, and they were—with hungry livestock doing the trimming rather than people.

I turned off the blacktop of a well-maintained county road onto what the sign said was Live Oak Lane. The word "Lane" vastly overstated the case. Live Oak Rut would have been closer to the truth. Some of the potholes were deep enough that I worried about the well-being of my low-slung Porsche. Luckily, I didn't have far to go. The kid at the gas station had assured me that once I made it to Live Oak, I wouldn't miss the house, since the road dead-ended just past Live Oak Farm.

At first glance, when I saw the house winking at me through a grove of trees, I was surprised. Expecting a disreputable, run-down shack, I glimpsed instead an enormous two-story farmhouse. The place probably dated from back in the days of large families when hard-pressed farmers had home-grown all the kids they could manage. Then as now, kids had meant mouths to feed, but back then they had been a steady source of unpaid labor as well. They provided the extra hands to gather in the crops and get all the chores done. Back then kids had meant survival, not hassle.

As I bounced toward it, I wondered how many kids growing up in that old house had longed to run away from it, to escape dull country life for the excitement of the city. Any city. Now that very same house was a haven—a place to run to—for my city-bred daughter. More of Mrs. Reeder's miserable irony.

Eventually, the road turned and crossed a cattle guard. On a leaning fence post dangled a bullet-marred sign saying LIVE OAK FARM. Behind the sign stood a junkyard full of wrecked cars. Another rutted track, this one far narrower and rougher than the first, wound off through the cars toward the house.

The Porsche thumped noisily over a bumpy set of metal rails embedded in the roadway. As I picked my way between potholes, I tried to glance up now and then to get my bearings. Derelict cars—rusted-out wrecks in various stages of decay—stood parked in haphazard rows that meandered off in either direction. Doors sagged open on broken hinges, and ambitious, sun-loving weeds grew up through the shattered windshields and cracked floorboards.

The newest model I recognized was a once-dashing '67 Chrysler New Yorker. The flattened roof and caved-in sides testified that the car had rolled over more than once on its way to this isolated auto graveyard. It was easy to assume that sometime in the seventies whoever had been running the wrecking yard had exhausted his supply of money or enthusiasm or both.

The track turned sharply as I passed the Chrysler. Coming around the corner, I could see that the New Yorker's broad bench seat had been pried loose from the car and positioned on the far side of the vehicle, possibly as someone's idea of low-cost yard furniture.

A young woman, clad in an almost nonexistent bikini, lay on this open-air tanning bench, soaking up some rays and seemingly oblivious to the sun-rotted foam leaking out of the seat beneath her. It crossed my mind that the sun was probably doing the same kind of damage to her skin that it had already done to the car seat, but I didn't bother stopping to point that out. At that stage of life, kids are immortal—in their eyes, anyway.

Beyond the cars and closer to the house, I drove past the grim remains of a recently blown-down barn. Only three feet or so of roof line were still visible above the pile of weather-beaten, termite-ridden wood. The shattered barn made me dread what I'd find once the house came under closer scrutiny, but my worries proved groundless.

When I was close enough to see it in detail, I noticed that indeed the exterior of the house was as mottled and spotty as a Dalmatian dog, but not from rotting wood or peeling paint that had been left to its own devices. Instead, someone was systematically scraping the old paint off, from the topmost gable of the slate-gray roof to the old-fashioned columns on the broad front porch. A line of newly repainted but not-yet-reinstalled shutters marched in close formation across the front exterior wall.

One sagging corner of the porch had been propped back up and was being held in place up by a strategically positioned hydraulic scissors jack. Several uncut lengths of eight-by-twelve lumber lay nearby and were probably intended for permanently shoring up the porch. Another neat stack of two-by-twelves and two-by-fours testified to someone's intention of framing a new set of steps from ground level up to the spacious front deck.

Obviously, someone was hard at work refurbishing the old place. That should have made me feel better, but somehow I couldn't see how Kelly could abandon her comfortable, upscale California nest with her mother and stepfather for this aging Gothic kind of work-in-progress. But still, taking on a complicated renovation project shows a certain amount of initiative, organization, and skill. For the first time, I wondered if maybe the people Kelly was staying with were reasonably okay after all.

I stopped the car, got out, and then found myself stymied. The lumber to rebuild the steps was there, but in the meantime, the stairs themselves were missing altogether. I wondered how visitors were supposed to get close enough to the front door to knock or ring the bell.

Standing only a foot or so away from the porch, I was busy contemplating my predicament when an ugly, gangly yellow dog of indeterminate lineage rose stiff-legged from behind a wooden porch swing. Barking hoarsely, he hobbled toward me. I worried momentarily that the dog might leap off the porch and come after me, but when he got close enough, I could see he was far too old and frail. He stared at me blindly through eyes clouded with cataracts. It seemed to take all the strength he could muster to keep up his croaking but ineffectual bark.

Eventually, the screen door slammed open behind the dog, and a woman marched out onto the porch. "What is it, Sunshine?"

At first I thought the woman was being sarcastic and talking to me, but then I realized she was actually speaking to the dog. She strode over to the edge of the porch, leaned down, and patted the dog soothingly. "It's okay, Sunshine girl," she crooned. "I'm right here."

So Sunshine was a girl. With a strange dog, it's hard to tell that kind of thing from a distance. The woman caught sight of me and frowned, first at me and then at my shiny red Porsche. Since she was so much higher than I was, she appeared to be a giant. Not necessarily a friendly one, either.

"Who are you?" she demanded coldly. "What do you want?"

"My name's Beaumont," I said. "I understand my daughter lives here."

I'm not a particularly good judge of women's ages. She could have been anywhere from her late forties to her early sixties. Her hair, mostly gray, was parted in the middle, braided, and then pulled into some kind of knot at the back of her neck. Wearing boots, jeans, and a man's old dress shirt rolled up to the elbows, she stood on the porch with her arms crossed, staring down at me with the afternoon sun playing off the even planes of her spare, angular features.

I'm not a weight lifter, but I recognize muscle definition when I see it. Since the woman's forearms had plenty of muscle definition, it was safe to assume the rest of her did, too.

"Really. Kelly didn't mention she was expecting visitors," the woman remarked with a coldness that was only one step short of sending me packing.

I wondered what I'd done to merit such open hostility. Before saying anything more, I studied the woman closely. Her face was tan, but without the leathery look that comes from too many years of unrelenting sun. Everything about her was plain except for her eyes. They were a startling shade of violet that hardened to a flinty gray while she gazed down at me.

"It's a surprise," I answered, trying to keep things light. "I was in the neighborhood and thought I'd stop by."

"I'll just bet," the woman returned, not bothering to mute her biting sarcasm.

It wasn't going at all well. If this woman was the designated keeper of the co-op's gate, then I would have to find some way around her if I wanted to speak to Kelly.

"Look," I said, drawing myself up to a full-attention stance. "If you'd just tell my daughter I'm here . . ."

Eyeball-to-eyeball confrontations are just that. The first person to blink loses. My damn car phone rang just then. I lost the glare-down fair and square.

"You'd better go answer your high-priced toy," she jeered.

Trying to maintain my somewhat damaged dignity, I turned and stalked back to the car. Naturally, my caller was Alex. "Did you find Kelly?" she asked.

"I think so."

"You're not sure?"

"Not exactly. I haven't seen her yet. Give me a break, Alex. I just now got here. What gives?"

"Denver found us a room at a place called the Oak Hill Bed-and-Breakfast. We've got tickets to *Romeo and Juliet* in the Bowmer Theatre tonight and to the opening of *Taming of the Shrew* in the Elizabethan tomorrow. Denver's going to try to get us into see *The Majestic Kid* at the Black Swan tomorrow afternoon, and she's invited us to dinner tonight. Meet us in the dining room at the Mark Anthony at six."

"The Mark Anthony?" I repeated. "Where's that?"

"It's a hotel owned by one of Denver's friends. It's back on the main street, near where you dropped me off. You can't miss it. It's the tallest building in town."

When someone giving me out-of-town directions says the words "You can't miss it," I know I can and will. Miss it, that is. "Right," I said. "See you there."

I put down the phone and turned back to where the woman stood watching me from the porch, her lips curled in grim amusement. The dog, exhausted with the effort of barking, had flopped down at her feet and was snoring noisily. From inside the house came the inviting smells of something cooking, soup or a roast perhaps, and the unmistakable aroma of baking bread. But baking her own bread didn't transform the woman in front of me into Homemaker of the Year or make her the least bit friendly, either. Certainly not to me.

"Well," I said, "is Kelly here or not?"

"It depends," the woman answered gravely.

"On what?"

"On what you want with her."

I was tired. My temper frayed around the edges. "Look," I said testily. "My daughter is a runaway. She doesn't even have a high school diploma. I've come to send her back home to her mother where she belongs."

"Kelly is eighteen years old," the woman pointed out. "What if she doesn't want to go?"

I was losing it. "All day long, any number of people have been quick to remind me about how old Kelly is. She happens to be my daughter. I know damn good and well she's eighteen years old. I also know she isn't old enough to be out on her own. I want her to go back home and finish growing up."

Suddenly, with the graceful agility of a cat, the woman hopped off the porch, landing effortlessly in front of me despite the four-foot drop. Her nimble leap both impressed and depressed me at the same time. My ability to jump like that has all but been eliminated by an ever-increasing assortment of middle-aged aches and pains—including incipient arthritis and heel spurs. Whatever this woman's age was, she certainly wasn't acting it.

Now that we were both on the same level, I discovered the woman wasn't that tall, only about five foot eight or so. From the way she glowered at me, though, she didn't find our relative sizes the least bit intimidating.

"Kelly may not be old enough to live on her own in your estimation, Mr. Beaumont, but in the eyes of the law she's an emancipated young woman. She holds a responsible job. Two, in fact. She pays her rent on time and causes no trouble."

"You're telling me you're her landlord?"

"Landlady," the woman corrected firmly. "So don't think you can come in here and push her around."

"I see, Miss ... er ..."

"My name is Connors. Marjorie Connors. *Mrs.* Marjorie Connors."

At least I knew my opponent's name. "Well, Mrs. Connors, I would very much like to see my daughter, if she's home."

"She's out back, playing with Amber."

"Who's Amber?"

"The girl Kelly baby-sits. Amber and her mother live here, too."

"I see. Which way?"

Marjorie Connors didn't move. Her striking eyes never left mine. "You're the policeman, aren't you?"

"Yes. I'm a detective. With Seattle P.D."

"You may be a detective in Seattle," Marjorie Connors said pointedly, "but not here. Understand?"

"What's that supposed to mean?"

"It means that if you try to bully your daughter in any way, I won't hesitate for a moment. I'll call the sheriff. Kelly came here of her own free will. As far as I'm concerned, she's welcome to stay as long as she wants. Do I make myself clear?"

Gorillas have a way of making their wants and desires known. So did Marjorie Connors. "I believe we understand one another, Mrs. Connors. Now, if you don't mind . . ."

"Come with me," she said, moving toward the back of the house. She set off at a brisk pace, with me trailing along behind. We walked around to a side yard and threaded our way through a collection of ladders. Here, the scraping was finished and painting was well under way. Around the corner, on the back of the house, restoration was complete. Fresh paint gleamed in the sun. A spacious, newly built, multilevel deck covered the entire length of the house. Slotted trellis material lined the insides of the rails, making the deck totally child-proof.

"You'll find Kelly in the play area," Marjorie said, pointing down a slight incline to where a small enclosure had been fenced off into a carefully mowed play yard. Inside it I could see a swing set, a small tricycle, and a huge tractor tire filled with sand. The sandbox was shaded by an unfurled Martini and Rossi umbrella that presumably had been liberated from the now-naked table of some unfortunate sidewalk café.

At first, I saw no one but a small red-haired child playing alone in the sand. She was enthusiastically pushing a plastic bulldozer back and forth, building mounds and destroying same.

"Kelly," Mrs. Connors called. "Someone's here to see you."

A pair of suntanned, shorts-clad legs appeared under the umbrella. "Who is it?"

At the sound of Kelly's voice, a hard lump formed in my throat. Dave Livingston hadn't been making it up, I realized in sudden relief. Kelly really was here—here and safe both. At least, her voice sounded fine.

"It's me, Kelly," I managed, forcing words out over a fist-sized, throat-closing knot that threatened to cut off all ability to speak or breathe. "It's your dad."

I don't know what I expected. Maybe I thought Kelly would come running up to me with her arms outstretched and her blond braids flying behind her the way they used to when she was little and we were all still living out at Lake Tapps. Instead, the tanned legs stopped moving altogether. She stayed where she was as if frozen, her face and most of her body concealed behind and beneath the spread of that mammoth umbrella.

"Daddy?" she returned uncertainly. "Is it really you? What are you doing here? How did you find me?"

I shot a triumphant glance in Mrs. Connors' direction. With her unblinking violet gaze piercing into me, I somehow caught myself and managed to remember Ralph Ames' cautioning words. Don't blow it, I told myself. Don't say something you'll regret.

With laudable self-restraint, I avoided blurting out the indignant, accusatory things I'd planned to say, such as—"I came to get you and send your ass back home." That would never do.

My problem with telling lies has always been that I'm incapable of carrying the process off with any kind of good grace. As soon as I try it, something in my facial expression gives me away. Generally speaking, that's probably a good thing. It keeps me out of poker games and politics.

This time, though, I did it. From somewhere inside me, I summoned up a set of more acceptable weasel words, ones that allowed both Kelly and me a little room to maneuver. "I came to see how you were," I returned carefully, "to see if you were all right, or if there was anything you needed."

The little girl, Amber, stopped pushing her bulldozer and sat gazing up at Kelly—a Kelly whose body and face were still obscured from view. When she didn't move, I did, starting to close the distance between us, but Marjorie Connors' surprisingly strong suntanned arm barred the way.

"Wait!" she commanded. "You wait right here."

I stopped as ordered. For the longest time, Kelly stayed where she was as well. Then, finally, she came shooting out from behind the umbrella, running toward me just like in the old days.

"Oh, Daddy!" Kelly cried, launching herself at me from four feet away and throwing her arms around my neck in a flying tackle that threatened to carry me over backward. She hugged me and kissed me at the same time. It was exactly like the old days—with two exceptions, one minor and one major. The minor one was easy. The blond braids were gone; Kelly wasn't my little girl anymore. I could live with that.

The major one, I wasn't so sure I could survive. As soon as she stepped out from behind the concealing umbrella, I could see that Kelly Louise Beaumont was pregnant.

Profoundly and undeniably pregnant. Damn!

I held her close, but all the while my mind was on fire. Where the hell is that lousy little son of a bitch of a singing actor now? I wondered. Just let me get my hands on that worthless fucker and . . .

What is it the Good Book says? Ask, and it shall be given unto you? Sure enough. Jeremy Todd Cartwright III—that no-good jerk who thought he was going to be my future son-in-law—chose that exact moment to make his grand entrance, driving into the yard in a worn old rattletrap Econoline van with three other people in it. He stopped directly beside us.

Kelly was standing on tiptoes with her arms wrapped around my neck, still laughing and crying, while tears ran down her face and dripped onto my shirt.

"Daddy," she said, taking me by the hand and leading me toward the van. "I'm so glad to see you. I wanted to call you and tell you, but I didn't know what to say, where to start. But come meet Jeremy. You're going to love him."

Sure I was! Like hell I was!

Unwillingly, I allowed myself to be led forward. We stopped by the driver's door of the beat-out van just as a long, tall kid in jeans and worn Birkenstocks clambered out. He was six-five if he was an inch, well-built, good looking, and impossibly clean-cut. The son of a bitch didn't have long hair. Or an earring.

He went around to the back of the van, opened the door, and then carefully handed out a series of loaded grocery bags to the other three passengers, who dutifully carried them into the house. Amber toddled up to one of the three—a woman whose hair color matched the child's—and followed her up onto the deck. Only then did Jeremy Todd Cartwright turn around and come back to Kelly and me.

He stopped directly in front of me and looked me in the eye. He didn't even have the good grace to look embarrassed.

"Jeremy," Kelly said breathlessly. "Look who's here. It's my dad."

She was holding me by the hand and blubbering joyfully, oblivious to everything around her, including the fact that it was all I could do to keep from reaching out and punching that goddamned upstart kid smack in the face.

"Jeremy, my father, J. P. Beaumont," Kelly continued. "Dad, Jeremy Cartwright. We're getting married Monday afternoon."

And Jeremy Todd Cartwright III, who couldn't have been a day over twenty-three, after one quick questioning look in Kelly's direction, turned back to me, nodded politely but warily, and extended his hand.

"Glad to meet you, Mr. Beaumont," he said.

His toothpaste smile pissed me off. I wanted nothing more than the chance to rearrange his mouthful of too-white, too-straight teeth. But Kelly is my daughter—my *only* daughter. She's had me wrapped around her little finger from very early on, from the first moment she realized she owned a finger. Jeremy Todd Cartwright put out his hand, and, so help me, I shook it.

What the hell else could I do?

3

After that initial meeting, I didn't hang around Live Oak Farm for very long. I didn't have a hell of a lot more to say. Not only that, it was close to six when I was supposed to meet Alexis and her friend. Besides, I didn't feel particularly welcome, especially since nobody bothered to invite me inside where dinner was about to be served to the motley group of boarders. I eventually grasped the none-too-subtle message that, without prior arrangement, food was not available for unexpected, drop-by guests. Not that I was particularly hungry. Finding out that your unmarried daughter is pregnant works as a natural and amazingly effective appetite suppressant.

I still didn't understand Marjorie Connors' place in the scheme of things, but she seemed to call the shots in addition to running a very tight ship as far as meals were concerned. Saying he was glad to meet me but that he had to get ready for the Green Show, Jeremy hurried into the house and left me alone with Kelly.

"Whatever that is," I muttered disagreeably behind him.

"The Green Show? It's sort of a pre-show entertainment," Kelly explained, "outside, in the courtyard. Jeremy's in both *Majestic* and *Shrew*, but he's also a very talented musician."

"Really. What does he play?"

"Lots of things," she answered proudly. "His specialty is the *krummhorn*."

The what? I had no idea what a krummhorn was, and I regretted asking. I didn't want to know. Why couldn't Jeremy be the kind of upright young man who slaved away over an IBM PC?

Kelly appeared embarrassed that I wasn't invited to dinner. She attempted to apologize. "If we had known earlier you would be here, Marjorie could have set an extra place."

Knowing Marjorie, that struck me as a narrow escape. "Don't worry about it," I said. "I'm meeting a friend for dinner, then we're seeing a play, *Romeo and Juliet*."

"You were lucky to get tickets this late," Kelly said. "How did you manage that?"

"My friend took care of it," I said.

"Who's your friend? Someone connected with the Festival?"

Which brought me right back to Alexis Downey and the problem I had been worrying about since before we left Seattle—what exactly should I tell Kelly about Alexis and vice versa? Admittedly, with Kelly standing there unmarried and more than slightly pregnant, the dynamics of the situation were much different from what I had anticipated. Still, I wasn't wild about telling my daughter that Alexis was this great gal and that we were down here in Ashland shacking up for the weekend at a local bed-and-breakfast.

Sexual revolution be damned, there are some things fathers don't say to their unmarried eighteen-year-old daughters, pregnant or not.

"Alex isn't directly connected with the Festival," I replied carefully, "although she knows plenty of people who are. I'll introduce you tomorrow morning. Can you come to breakfast?"

Kelly shook her head. "No, I work in the mornings, but I'm free in the afternoon. Tomorrow's *Shrew*, so I don't have to take care of Amber until tomorrow night." She snapped her finger. "Darn. I should have introduced you to Tanya."

"Who's she?"

"Tanya Dunseth, Amber's mother. You must have seen her when

the van pulled up. She's the one with all the red hair, just like Amber's. You'll see her tonight. She's Juliet at the Bowmer, and Kate in *Shrew*."

"I saw her go into the house," I said, "but don't worry about missing introductions. There'll be plenty of time to meet later on. Do you want us to come here and pick you up?"

"No. Jeremy works the backstage tour in the morning. We'll ride into town together. We can meet you outside the ticket office at noon. Do you know where that is?"

"No," I answered, "but I'm sure Alex does."

"Oh," Kelly said. "Well, I guess I'll go in to dinner."

She started away from me, moving slowly and ponderously up the stairs toward the back door. "What time is the wedding?" I asked. "Am I invited?"

Kelly stopped and stared down at her feet, although over that lump of belly I doubt she could see them. "Two-thirty," she answered quietly. "It has to be Monday. That's the only day the theaters are dark. Otherwise, our friends couldn't come. And yes, you're invited."

She had given me the smallest of openings. Naturally, I charged in with all cannons blazing.

"What about your mother?" I demanded hotly. "Don't you think she'd like to come, too? And what about Dave? What about your brother? Doesn't your family deserve the same kind of consideration as your friends from the theaters?"

Kelly's sorrowful gaze met mine while her eyes filled with tears. Without another word, she turned and fled up the steps, darting into the house. The screen door slammed shut behind her.

End of conversation. Just because she's always led me around by the nose doesn't mean we communicate. She bolted into the house in tears, while I marched back to my car. Marjorie Connors was lying in wait for me on the front porch.

"I said no bullying," Marjorie declared sternly.

"There wasn't any," I said, all the while wondering, What's with this broad? Who gave her the right to tell me how to treat my own daughter? "In case you didn't notice, Kelly was delighted to see me."

"That was before she came inside crying," Marjorie countered.

"Look, Mrs. Connors, I merely suggested that Kelly might want to consider inviting her own mother to this shotgun wedding of hers the day after tomorrow. That doesn't exactly constitute child abuse."

"It upset her."

"What are you, her self-appointed protector?"

The woman was annoying me, and I expect the feeling was mutual. Once more her violet eyes turned stormy gray.

"Don't come around here again, Mr. Beaumont. See Kelly in town if you have to. If I find you lurking on my property, I'll have you arrested for trespass."

I left without further comment. There wasn't any point. Marjorie Connors obviously had a huge attitude as far as men were concerned, although, oddly enough, Jeremy Cartwright seemed to get along with her just fine.

As I turned the Porsche around and headed into town, I realized some things in this world don't make any sense. The situation at Live Oak Farm definitely counted as one of life's imponderables.

Despite my previous misgivings, I had no trouble finding the Mark Anthony Hotel. It really was the tallest building in town. And it wasn't difficult finding Alex and her friend Denver, either. They were seated at a window table. Alex waved and smiled as I walked up. What I did have trouble with was turning left and going into the dining room when I really wanted to turn right and disappear into the bar.

For the first time in months, I wanted a drink. I wanted ten drinks.

"How are things?" Alex asked brightly.

"Fine," I returned with as much phony sincerity as I could muster. I must have pulled it off because Alex breezed ahead with introductions.

"Denver Holloway," she said, "this is the man I was telling you about, J. P. Beaumont. Everybody calls him Beau."

Denver put down her cigarette and held out a plump hand. She was a wide woman in her mid-to-late-forties. Her dark, wavy hair was worn in a short, neatly trimmed bob with a thick fringe of bangs. Enormous brown eyes peered out from behind huge tortoiseshell glasses.

"Dinky," she said with a self-deprecating smile. "I'm not, but that's what all my friends call me just the same."

I sat down.

"Dinky's directing the play we're seeing tonight," Alex continued enthusiastically. "*Romeo and Juliet* set in the Deep South in the sixties."

"In the South?" I asked. "As in southern United States?"

Dinky grinned and nodded. "Why not?"

"How can you do that?" I objected. "Doesn't it take place somewhere in Italy?"

"Where it was set when Shakespeare wrote it is immaterial," Dinky Holloway informed me. "It's a love story about two star-crossed young lovers caught in the middle of a blood feud. We don't change dialogue. Setting comes primarily through costumes and stage business. Have you ever seen *Romeo* produced before?"

I shook my head. "Not that I remember."

An effusively sweet young man sashayed up to our table and batted his eyes at me. He *did* wear an earring. "Care to start with a cocktail this evening?"

Most of the time, that's a fairly innocuous question, but not tonight, not when I was dealing with my own particular pair of star-crossed young lovers.

The waiter hovered expectantly. Dinky and Alex both ordered white wine. I gritted my teeth and ordered black coffee.

"Where's the telephone?" I asked.

I wanted to call Ralph and ask his advice. Since he has no children of his own, he is free to dispense the wisdom of Solomon when it comes to other people's kids.

The waiter smiled. "The pay phone at the top of the stairs is out of order, sir, but there's another in the bar."

The bar was the very last place I needed to go right then. A glance at the menu told me I wasn't the least bit hungry. "Order me a Caesar salad, would you please?" I said to Alex. "Excuse me, but I've got to use the phone."

She looked at me and frowned, then nodded. "Sure thing."

The bar was dark and smoky, full of laughter and the comforting clink of glassware. Walking into it felt safe and familiar, like coming home after a long, difficult absence. When I paused by a barstool, the bartender caught my eye. "What can I get you?"

It would be all too easy to perch on a stool and order a hit or so of my old pal, MacNaughton. Within minutes the welcome haze of warm oblivion would settle over me. Even one, I thought, would lessen the weight of my disappointment about Kelly.

"Mac and water," I said.

The bartender frowned. "What's that?"

"MacNaughton's and water," I answered loudly, turning up the volume as though the guy was partially deaf or maybe someone who didn't exactly speak English.

"That's Canadian, isn't it? We don't carry that brand, sir. Sorry. How about CC?"

It may have been nothing but a fluke of the international liquor-distribution system, but heavy drinkers are a superstitious lot. And J. P. Beaumont is no exception. I took their not carrying my brand as a sign from the Oracle.

"Forget it," I muttered irritably. "Where's the damn phone?"

The bartender shrugged and pointed. "Down the hall," he said.

We've come a long way from "Number please" days. The sound of a human voice—even a telephone operator's—would have been welcome right then, but no such luck. By the time I finished punching in Ames' number as well as the fourteen digits of my telephone calling card, my hand shook so badly I could barely hit the right buttons. On a Saturday night, naturally, Ralph was out. I didn't bother leaving a message on his voice mail.

I slammed down the receiver and grabbed for the slender Jackson County phone book. I thumbed through the pages, scanning down the column until I located a listing for the local office of Alcoholics Anonymous. A telephone volunteer directed me to the only meeting available that evening, an N.A. (Narcotics Anonymous) meeting that would start at seven in the basement of a downtown church. Any port in a storm. I took down the address.

Still strung too tight, I went back to the dining room and managed to limp my way through dinner with Alexis and her friend. Alex and Dinky, caught up in girl talk and in reminiscing about old times and acquaintances, never noticed anything wrong. At the end of the meal, I made arrangements to meet Alex outside the theater just before our eight-thirty curtain. Engrossed in their conversation, the two chatting women happily waved me on my way.

Twelve-step meetings frequently attract unusual people. The N.A. meeting in Ashland was more unusual than most. A lot of Oregon still lingers in the sixties. Parts of it never emerged from the fifties. The rural population contains a number of Cold War, bomb-shelter-type survivalists and more than a few renegade flower children. There are also increasing numbers of chronically under-and unemployed loggers and mill workers whose jobs have disappeared right along with spotted-owl habitats.

Enterprising folks from those diverse groups had countered bad times by turning to agriculture, producing Oregon's illicit but cash-rich crop of marijuana, which federal and state drug-enforcement agencies obligingly attempted to obliterate. Busted again, in more ways than one, and drowning in their troubles, these hard-luck Joes would appear in criminal courts where right-thinking judges ordered them into treatment.

Some of them turned up at the N.A. meeting in Ashland. They arrived in their heavy boots, flannel shirts, and bright red suspenders. Not necessarily remorseful but reasonably good-humored about it all, they joined in with the usual collection of housewives, waitresses, and professional men to form the nucleus of that particular Saturday night group. That nucleus also included several artsy-fartsy types, some of them no doubt connected to the Festival. The latter were generally better educated than the onetime loggers/hippies/survivalists turned ex-pot-growers; they weren't necessarily better dressed.

The rest of the people in attendance were like me—out-of-towners, tourists in Ashland for the plays. Even on vacation—maybe especially on vacation—a lot of us need extra help in holding our own peculiar demons at bay.

One good thing about N.A. or A.A. is that you can go to a meeting and take away only what you need at the time. No quizzes are administered, no grades issued.

That night what I needed to hear was the Serenity Prayer. Repeating it in unison, I heard myself say what I had come there to hear: "accept the things I cannot change." When those words penetrated my thought processes, I lost track of the world around me. I thought about what I could change and what I couldn't.

The baby, for example, was something I couldn't change, so I could just as well shape up and accept it. Now that I was calmer, I recalled how Jeremy had looked at Kelly just before he reached out to shake my hand. Glancing down at her, his eyes had glowed with concerned questioning and tenderness, too. He loved her, dammit. I probably shouldn't try to change that, either.

Halfway through the meeting, I noticed that the fellow across the table kept zeroing in on me. Late fifties and heavyset, he tried to be subtle about it, staring at me only when he thought I wouldn't notice. Once I became aware of him, he seemed vaguely familiar. At the beginning of the meeting, people had introduced themselves on a first-name basis, but I hadn't paid much attention. Since I had never before set foot in Ashland or southern Oregon, it seemed unlikely that I knew him. No doubt the portly gentleman resembled a double back home in Seattle.

When it came my turn to talk, I said something about how unfair it seemed that even after you quit using or boozing or whatever, your damn kids could still drive you crazy. That comment seemed to strike a raw nerve with almost everyone in the room. Drinking or not, being a parent is hell, almost as rewarding as trying to nail a scrambled egg to a tree.

The guy across the table picked right up on my comment, giving the problem his own personal spin. "It's not just kids, either," he said. "Take me, for instance. Ten years ago, I dumped my first wife. It didn't seem like that big a deal. She was a Lulu with a mean streak five miles wide, and we didn't have anything in common anyway. Besides I was trying to sober up, get my life in order. I figured I could do better. And I did. I figured—'What the hell? Better luck next time, right? I mean, what do drunks know about picking decent wives? Found me another wife, a real beauty, too, but now ..." He shook his head dolefully, as if searching for the courage to continue.

"I always thought booze was what made the first marriage go bad. Now I'm afraid I'm going to lose this one, too, that my wife will walk out on me. And I haven't had a drink in damn near ten years. I ask you, what kind of deal is that?"

Good question.

The meeting finished up promptly at eight because the people running it were well aware that most of the out-of-towners would be rushing off to an eight-thirty curtain in one of the town's live theaters, and theater is Ashland's bread and butter.

As I hiked back up the main drag toward the Festival, I came to an out-of-order stoplight where a shorts-clad uniformed police officer was directing traffic. I found myself caught in a crowd of theatergoers waiting to cross the street.

"Mr. Beaumont," a voice called from behind me.

Surprised to hear my name, I turned around. Red-faced and puffing with exertion, the man from the meeting came trotting after me, smiling and holding out his hand. Despite the early-evening heat, he was carrying a red down-filled jacket.

"Aren't you J. P. Beaumont from Seattle?" he rasped. "Guy Lewis, remember me?" Running to catch up had left him winded, so much so that I worried he'd die of a heart attack on the spot. "I'm the one who bought your Bentley at the auction, remember?"

Primed, I did remember. Guy Lewis looked familiar because he was, although four hundred miles from home my brain hadn't quite managed the critical connections.

Months earlier, under the helpful auspices of Ralph Ames, I had first met Alexis Downey, the director of development for the Seattle Rep. The two of them prevailed on me to convince the Belltown Terrace Syndicate to donate (read "unload") the building's cranky and mostly nonrunning Bentley to the theater's first-ever charity auction.

At the black-tie affair, Guy Lewis turned out to be the poor stupid jerk who had paid top dollar to cart away the Bentley, which I regarded as an incredibly expensive piece of junk. For all I knew, he had to have the damn thing towed. I remembered watching him and his much younger and very blond wife be congratulated by the enthusiastic auctioneer. At the time, I had suffered a sharp pang of conscience to which Alex had applied the soothing balm of reassurance. She swore the money had gone to a good cause, and that Guy Lewis, sole heir to his father's portable-chemical-toilet empire, wouldn't even miss it.

Encountering Guy Lewis on the street in Ashland, I wondered if that was true. Would he shake my hand or punch me out? Remembering the Bentley, I would have bet on the latter.

"I didn't know you were in the program," he said.

"I don't exactly go around advertising it."

He nodded. "Me, either. It helps to have a place to unload things." He sighed and shook his head as if warding off an errant thought. "Down here to see some plays, are you?"

I wasn't prepared to say the real reason behind my visit to Ashland, certainly not to him. "Yes," I answered.

"*Henry?*" he asked.

I had been in Ashland less than a day and had not yet adjusted to the way locals and visitors alike tend to shorten play titles to one-word monikers.

"Excuse me?"

Guy Lewis laughed. "Daphne and I are seeing one of the *Henrys* in the Elizabethan tonight. I forget which one. The Festival always seems to be doing at least one of those. They all tend to run together after a while. By the way, have you seen Alexis lately?"

My ears reddened. "Actually, Alex and I are here together."

Guy Lewis grinned and slapped me on the back. "Good for you," he said heartily. "Alex is quite a woman. Are you seeing *Henry*, too?"

I shook my head. "We're scheduled for *Romeo and Juliet*."

Guy Lewis nodded. "Oh yes," he said. "We saw that two days ago. It's excellent. Wait until you see the girl who plays Juliet," he added after a pause. "She's something else. By the way, there's a little backstage get-together at the Bowmer right after the play tonight. Just a few people mingling with the actors. I'm sure Alexis would enjoy it. Why don't you join us?"

"I'll check with Alex," I said.

By then we had crossed the street and walked far enough that we were approaching the brick courtyard located between the two theaters. The space between the outdoor Elizabethan and the indoor Bowmer was jammed with a happy, show-going crowd that was congregated around some central but as-yet-unseen point of interest. As we came closer, I heard the sound of music and laughter.

"That'll be the Green Show," Guy Lewis informed me. "Have you ever seen it before?"

I shook my head. "Looks like now's the time," I said.

I didn't tell him that I had any kind of personal interest in seeing this hitherto-unexperienced spectacle. Together we worked our way over to the edge of the packed throng until we could see the action.

On a small raised platform, a group of dancers costumed in Elizabethan attire was performing what was probably a distant precursor of today's square dancing. Behind them stood another costumed group of individuals, all of them playing strange-looking, mostly unfamiliar instruments. And in the middle of that group of musicians, tall and ramrod straight, stood Jeremy Todd Cartwright, honking away on a long, thin horn that might have been an old-time, fourth-grade Tonette after it overdosed on steroids. From the way his cheeks puffed, Jeremy was blowing his lungs out, but the resulting sound reminded me more than anything of a quacking duck. A tunefully quacking duck.

That's a *krummhorn*? I thought. He's going to support Kelly and a baby playing that thing? Give me a break!

The number ended. To a round of enthusiastic applause, the Green Show troupe gathered its instruments and started toward the entrance to the Elizabethan Theatre with most of the crowd moving along behind them. "Well," Guy Lewis was saying, "there's the wife. I'd best get cracking. Hope to see both you and Alex at the party after the show."

"By the way," I said, before he moved out of earshot. "How's that Bentley of yours running?"

"Great," he said. "Daphne found this terrific mechanic. He has it purring like a kitten."

With a casual wave, he blended into the crowd. A moment later, Alexis Downey appeared at my elbow. "Wasn't that Guy Lewis?" she demanded.

"As a matter of fact, it was."

"What's he doing down here?"

"Seeing some plays, I guess. By the way, Guy said there's a back-stage get-together at the Bowmer after the plays tonight. We're invited to come along. If you're up to it, that is."

"Damn!" I was surprised by the sudden angry vehemence in Alexis Downey's voice.

"Alex, what's the matter?"

"Dinky told me about that party," Alexis returned darkly. "It's a very intimate little affair designed to pull in some very major donors. I don't know who the hell they think they are, poaching on my fund-raising territory. All I can say is, it's a damn good thing we're here."

She flounced away from me toward the entrance to the Bowmer. "What do you mean?" I asked, trailing along after her.

"I have a verbal pledge from Guy Lewis that the Seattle Rep is a major beneficiary of his estate. If that bitch down here tries to change his mind, she has another think coming!"

My mother died years before I met Alex Downey, but right then the two of them sounded like soul mates. As a child, I spent years waiting for that "another think," expecting it to beam down from the sky like a righteous bolt of avenging lightning. Alex may have been upset, but it pleased me to hear that echo of my mother.

Also like Mom, Alex is slow to anger. Once riled, though, look out. As we took our seats, I counseled myself to hold my tongue.

Actually, keeping a low profile is good advice when it comes to dealing with any irate woman. It merits special mention in a chapter dealing with "Hell hath no fury . . ." and all that jazz.

I don't know that exact quote. I'm not literary enough to recall who said it, but avoiding scorned women is also sage advice.

Later on I would wonder if anybody ever bothered to pass along that judicious bit of folk wisdom to poor old Guy Lewis.

<u>4</u>

Married people do it all the time. They go to plays or parties or some other event so angry they barely speak to one another. I know I did it with Karen, but this was my first experience of that kind with a date. Even though she wasn't necessarily mad at me, Alexis Downey was so upset that she wasn't talking to anybody, me included.

As we waited for the play to start, I disregarded my own wise counsel and made a few feeble attempts at conversation. Alex rebuffed each one so totally that I gave up and kept quiet. When the play started, I watched. Alex continued to stew. I'm surprised the people seated behind us could see the stage with all the smoke that must have been roiling out her ears.

I guess I expected the words in a 1960s version of *Romeo* to be changed and updated, but as far as I could tell, the dialogue remained much as Shakespeare wrote it. The difference lay in the costuming and in what Dinky Holloway had referred to as "stage business"—the people and actions that come and go onstage around the principal actors, like background music in a movie.

Maybe everyone else found it perfectly delightful. Not me. I'm old-fashioned. If I'm going to endure Shakespeare, I want all the robes, capes, and costumes that make it *look* like Shakespeare. The priest who paraded around looking like a sanctimonious, Bible-toting Baptist minister didn't set well with me. The Capulet party that Romeo and his motor-cycle-riding buddies crashed turned out to be an old-fashioned ice-cream social. Those thuggish young men with packs of Camels rolled in their T-shirt sleeves and their slicked-back ducktails might have stepped right out of my Ballard High School yearbook.

Despite Guy Lewis' rave review, I didn't find Juliet all that terrific, but then I'm not partial to redheads. Right about then it stood to reason that a daughter who was headstrong and stubborn and who didn't listen to her daddy wouldn't rate high on my list of current favorites.

Of all the characters in the play, I sympathized most with old man Capulet, who, despite his white suit, straw hat, and good-old-boy mannerisms, was still, by God, a father trying to convince his strong-willed daughter to listen to reason. The Bard didn't name his creation *The Tragedy of Romeo and Juliet* because she shapes up and pays attention.

I don't believe it was an innocent fluke of casting that caused Dinky Holloway's Juliet, played by Tanya Dunseth, to be a red-haired beauty with translucently pale skin, while Romeo, played by a handsome young actor named James Renthrow, was exceedingly dark. I'd call James Renthrow an African-American, except the playbill says he's from Jamaica. In deference to fully accurate cultural diversity, I don't believe the term, "African-American" correctly applies to Jamaicans.

I will say that Dinky Holloway was doing her bit for the arts community in showcasing William Shakespeare's immortal story in a "context designed to challenge the sensibilities of the audience." That's also a quote from the playbill. It seemed to me that Romeo and Juliet had enough problems to begin with without adding race relations into the already explosive mix, but then maybe that's just the father in me talking.

During intermission, in an effort to pick up my end of the evening's flagging conversation, I unwisely asked Alex how Dinky would, in these politically correct times, stage something like *Othello*, for instance? The question provoked an immediate fire-fight between Alex and me, much to the amusement of people seated around us. Our neighbors may have enjoyed the fireworks, but I was more than happy when action resumed onstage. I spent the next act worried that we'd still be at each other's throats once the play was over.

I shouldn't have. Alex isn't one to pack grudges. Our intermission flare-up served to relieve the tension. By the final curtain, all was forgiven.

We left the theater in a throng of people. *Juliet* finished earlier than *Henry*. Outside, the noisy clang of staged swordplay told us the Elizabethan's production was still in full swing.

"What now?" I asked, shivering in the surprising cold. "Head home, or crash the party?"

"Are you kidding?" Alexis demanded. "I wouldn't miss it for the world. I want to know exactly what that woman is up to. The party won't start until after *Henry*. If you want to, we can go over to the Members' Lounge and warm up. Dinky gave us a pass."

Dinky again, but given the chill outdoor temperature, the option of waiting inside made sense. We dodged across the street through a flock of waiting tour buses and hotel shuttles. Alex led the way to the side, basement entrance of what looked like an old house. Inside, a vestibule opened into a furnished sitting room where a somewhat weary hostess presided over a small bar. She offered us our choice of beer, wine, coffee, or soft drinks. I took a soda. Alex chose wine.

"What time does *Henry* get out?" Alex asked.

She, too, had slipped into Ashland's contagious one-word-title syndrome. From reading the playbill, I knew the full title was actually *King Henry VI, Part Two*, but then, who's counting?

Glancing at her watch, the hostess shrugged. "Ten minutes or so," she said.

Alex and I retreated to a bench seat that occupied one whole wall beneath a row of old-fashioned double-hung windows. Setting aside her wine, she fixed her lipstick and dabbed powder on her nose. She reminded me of a soldier gearing up for battle.

"How did it go with Kelly?" Alex asked, snapping shut the lid of her compact.

That was one topic I didn't want to touch. "Can't we discuss something else?"

Alex retrieved her wine and eyed me shrewdly over the rim of it. "That well, huh?"

"Worse. I'd much rather make predictions about the party."

"In other words, focus on my problems instead of yours?"

"Right."

Alex gave me a quick smile that was more a reprieve than a pardon. She'd humor me and let me off the hook temporarily, but eventually I would owe her a full blow-by-blow account. I went for the deferment, thinking that later I'd be better able to talk about Kelly Beaumont and Jeremy Todd Cartwright III.

Leaning back against the window casing, Alex sipped her wine, studying faces as people began to filter into the Members' Lounge. "What do you want to know?" she asked.

"Who all is coming to the party besides Guy Lewis? Who's this mysterious 'she'? Whenever you mention her, sparks fly."

"Monica Davenport," Alex answered, lowering her voice. "She was my immediate predecessor as director of development at the Rep. Monica's down here now, working for the Festival in the same capacity. She and the T.W. were good pals back home in Seattle. In fact, I think Guy Lewis met Daphne at one of Monica's fundraisers."

"T.W?" I asked, not quite comprehending and thinking I must have missed something. "What's a T.W?"

Exasperated by my stupidity, Alex rolled her eyes. "Surely, you know about trophy wives," she answered. "I thought every middle-aged man in America wanted one."

"I don't speak initials," I returned. "Too subtle. Men are usually a little more explicit. Furthermore, I have it on good authority that T.W.s, as you call them, can be quite troublesome."

"Really." Alex grinned. "Well, Daphne Lewis fits the T.W. profile—twenty years younger than Guy if she's a day. According to my sources, she's a fast worker. The previous Mrs. Lewis moved out of the house one day, and Daphne moved in the next."

It felt weird. Hours earlier I had heard Guy Lewis' slightly different version of this same story. Unlike Alex, I knew life with the second Mrs. Lewis wasn't all sweetness and light.

"I never met Maggie Lewis," Alex continued. "I've heard she was tough as nails and put together like a Mack truck. You may have noticed, Daphne is definitely made of finer stuff."

"I noticed," I agreed, remembering how Daphne Lewis had looked the night of the charity auction. With her blond-bombshell hairdo and a beaded, split-up-the-side white satin dress, she had easily qualified as one of the most glamorous women in a roomful of top-drawer competition.

"I guess that's okay," Alex said. "Someone like Guy Lewis is rich enough to pay his money and take his choice. And he did pay. Through the nose. From what I heard, the divorce lawyers made out like bandits."

And would again, I thought, remembering Guy's comments at the meeting. Still, given the choice between a woman built like an eighteen-wheeler and someone like Daphne, most men would choose the latter. If they had the chance.

"You don't like Guy Lewis very much, do you?" I said.

Alex shrugged. "I don't have to like him," she replied, "but I have to get along with him, and with Daphne, too."

A new group of people came into the room. One of them, a well-dressed woman about Alex's age, breezed through, nodding and greeting people along the way. "Hi, Monica," someone said.

Like an interceptor missile breaking away from its host plane, Alexis Downey rose from where she sat and glided toward the newcomer with her hand outstretched and an amazingly cordial smile pasted on her lips. "Why, Monica Davenport," Alex gushed. "I was hoping I'd get a chance to see you while I'm here."

Monica smiled back, but I doubt she was thrilled. Outwardly,

Monica and Alex looked like long-lost chums, but I noted a razor-sharp undercurrent in their exchange of barbed pleasantries. Observing them at work was enough to convince me I'd never cut it in the theater-development game. I'm not that tough.

The next time the door opened, Romeo and Juliet strolled inside. Without makeup and out of costume, they were laughing and joking about something that had gone awry during the performance. I kept hoping Daddy Capulet would show up so he and I could exchange pointers on child-rearing practices. But while old man Capulet failed to put in an appearance, Juliet helped herself to a glass of sparkling cider and meandered over toward me, stopping in front of the seat Alex had just vacated.

Tanya Dunseth was wearing a purple loose-knit cardigan sweater over an electric-blue leotard. On her feet were a pair of bright pink Keds. At first glance, I would have thought she had come straight from a high school cheerleading session.

"Is this seat taken?" she asked.

"No, be my guest."

She smiled back, then joined me on the window seat, easing herself down and folding both legs gracefully under her, settling into one of those unnatural and highly suspect lotus positions. Just looking at her made my knees hurt.

For a moment, I was unsure what to do. Kelly had been most insistent about wanting to introduce the two of us, but that was before we had our little spat, before Kelly burst into tears. Still, though, Tanya was sitting there next to me. They were friends. My daughter cared for her daughter. It was dumb to sit side by side there and pretend ignorance.

"Miss Dunseth?" I said tentatively, unsure of her reaction.

Smiling and still wisecracking with Romeo across the roomful of people, she turned from him to me. "Yes?"

"You don't know me, but I'm J. P. Beaumont, Kelly's father."

Looking directly into her face, I could see that she was older than I'd thought. Somewhere in her mid-twenties, she had striking green eyes, high cheekbones, and a sprinkling of freckles that hadn't shown up under her stage makeup. As soon as she looked at me, her smile disappeared. An air of implacable seriousness settled over her fine features.

"I knew you stopped by today," she said. "I couldn't tell if Kelly was happy to see you or not."

So much for standing around exchanging inconsequential pleasantries. Tanya Dunseth believed in going for the gut.

"That's funny," I returned with a short laugh. "Neither could I."

She regarded me gravely. "Will you be staying for the wedding?"

"I don't know."

"Well, my daughter, Amber, is going to be both flower girl and ring bearer. It'll be a fairly nontraditional ceremony."

"I'm sure," I said.

"Did you meet Jeremy? He's really crazy about Kelly. They're both very lucky."

Almost unconsciously, I found myself glancing at Tanya's left hand, where there was no wedding ring and no visible indication of one, either. I didn't know I was being so painfully obvious until she called me on it.

"Don't bother looking for a ring," she said curtly. "I was married once, but not now. It didn't work out. That's why I *know* they're lucky."

More people crowded into the room, laughing and talking. The newcomers came straight from the Elizabethan still wearing their warm coats and jackets, some of them carrying blankets. As they edged toward the bar, Monica held up her hand for attention.

"I know it's crowded in here," she said, "so don't get too comfortable." In a room too packed for any semblance of comfort, her announcement was greeted with general laughter.

"We'll be here only a few minutes longer, just enough to give the cast time to change out of their costumes and put away props. I'm so glad you were all able to be here tonight, and I'm looking forward to giving you a behind-the-scenes look at your arts contributions in action."

She continued with a canned speech, reeling off numbers about goals set and achieved. While she droned on, the outside door opened again. This time only two people came in—Guy and

Daphne Lewis, Guy wearing his red down jacket and Daphne in one of those lush Icelandic wool sweaters. Faced with the jam of people inside the room, they paused in the doorway.

Monica finally shut up, and the din of conversation returned to normal just as Guy caught sight of me and waved. He leaned down and whispered something in Daphne's ear, motioning with his head in Tanya's and my direction.

Daphne smiled while her eyes strayed across the room, searching the sea of faces. Just as her eyes seemed to settle on me, the smile fled her face, only to be replaced by a petulant scowl, like that of someone remembering some unpleasantness. Beside me, I heard Tanya Dunseth's sharp intake of breath.

Concerned, I glanced toward her in time to see her mouth drop open. A tremor like an electrical charge seemed to shoot through her body. She stared toward the couple in the doorway in what seemed like stricken amazement, while the cider from her glass spilled, unnoticed, into her lap.

And that was it. Nothing more. The incident happened so quickly that I didn't even question it until much later. Daphne and Guy started what turned out to be a slow progress across the room, nodding, chatting, and schmoozing as they came. Meanwhile, Tanya grabbed up her sweater, abandoned her empty glass, and melted into the crowd. At first I thought she was going for a refill, but she never returned to the window seat. I didn't see her again for the remainder of the night.

Eventually, Guy and Daphne fought their way through the crush of people. He approached with a broad grin on his face and with Daphne safely in tow. "I didn't mean to chase away your pretty friend," he apologized. "I wanted you to meet my wife. Daphne, this is the man I was telling you about, J. P. Beaumont."

Daphne's scowl had disappeared. She looked me up and down in a frankly assessing manner that exuded sex appeal. She tossed her blond mane, then extended a perfectly manicured and much bejeweled hand. "Why, Mr. Beaumont, I'm so pleased to meet you. I understand you're the one who donated that perfectly wonderful Bentley so Guy here could buy it for me."

The last thing I wanted to talk about right then was the stupid Bentley, but before I had an opportunity to hem and haw very much, Alex showed up at my elbow.

"Why, Guy, Daphne!" Alex said easily, casually insinuating herself between Daphne Lewis and me. "What a pleasant surprise to see you. I didn't know you'd be down here this weekend."

Daphne smiled. "We didn't either, did we, Guy? Monica invited us. So nice of her, don't you think? We were just talking about the Bentley Guy picked up at the Rep auction. You know all about that, of course. I certainly hope folks at Belltown Terrace aren't grieving too much over losing it."

"They're pretty well recovered." I smiled back.

I could have counted on one hand the number of condo residents who actually missed that damn Bentley. Almost everyone in the building had been stranded somewhere or other due to the machine's infernal "intermittent ignition problem," which none of our so-called handpicked mechanics had been able to fix.

"So you're able to get along without it?"

"We're managing," I said. "I understand from your husband that it's running perfectly."

Daphne Lewis nodded, then frowned. "I didn't know you and Guy actually knew each other. He never mentioned you to me."

"Come now, Daphne," Alex teased. "All men need a few little secrets now and then. Otherwise they start feeling insecure."

Someone else showed up, shook Guy's hand, and effectively moved him out of the conversation. I felt as though I owed the women some kind of explanation about how Guy and I knew each other, but I didn't want to bring up the meeting. Anonymous twelve-step programs don't work that way.

"We ran into one another in the courtyard during the Green Show," I stammered, trying to sound casual. "We both thought it was strange, running into someone we knew this far from home."

"It's not unusual at all," Alex said. "You'd be surprised at the number of people who come down from Seattle every year."

Just then Monica Davenport raised her hand again. This time, instead of a long-winded speech, she settled for a mercifully brief announcement, saying it was time to head back across the street.

The two large theaters in Ashland, the Elizabethan and the Bowmer, share a common courtyard and also a common backstage area. The catered party was being held backstage. While Alex busied herself politicking, I wandered off by myself through a maze of dressing rooms and folded scenery.

It interested me to see the props laid out on tables. During a performance, when stagehands are working backstage in the dark with cues coming hard and fast, I'm sure every second counts. Each item needed onstage must be in its assigned place in order to be readily available at the exact moment it's needed. To facilitate that, an outline of each prop was painted on table surfaces in orange, glow-in-the-dark paint.

On one table, I recognized several of the props from the evening's performance of *Romeo and Juliet*. One outline was empty, indicating that something was missing—something roughly the shape of a knife. Glancing around, I suspected it was the old-fashioned kitchen knife Juliet had called her "happy dagger" just before using it to do herself in.

I noticed the knife was missing from its appointed place, but I didn't worry about it. What the stagehands did with their props was none of my concern. I was an uninvited guest who had been allowed to crash the party.

For a time, I cruised the buffet table. Since I knew only a total of three or four people from the entire gathering, there wasn't much else to do but eat and/or drink. Luckily, my earlier urge for MacNaughton's had passed, and I was safe on the other side of it. For that moment, anyway, I no longer wanted a drink, but watching strangers waste themselves at the hosted bar wasn't exactly my idea of a good time. Alexis was too busy mingling to pay any attention to me. Finally, bored and overheated, I stepped outside.

The outside courtyard was blessedly cool and quiet. I stood there breathing in the still night air and looking up at the dark but starlit canopy of sky overhead. I was so far lost in thought that I almost missed the first warning sounds of squealing brakes and skidding tires. What did penetrate was a heavy sickening thud, followed by the grinding crunch of metal on metal and the tinkling shatter of glass.

If you've ever heard an automobile smash into flesh, it's a sound that welds itself to your memory no matter how much you want to forget. Years of training drill cops to respond automatically when faced with such an emergency. It's not so much a matter of conscious decision as it is reflex. I ran toward the sound of the accident long before the last of the glass finished falling.

"Help me!" a woman shouted. "There's been an accident. Somebody please help."

Racing toward the sound, I came to a Y in the courtyard. Turning right, I charged down a darkened staircase between two buildings to where I saw headlights and milling figures in the street below.

It was past midnight, an hour when most small towns would have closed up shop, but this was Ashland on opening weekend. Lots of people were still up and about. Already a small crowd had gathered in the street. I had to push my way through to see what had happened.

A once-perfect '76 Plymouth Duster with its engine still running sat in a still-swirling cloud of dust. The twisted front bumper and mangled hood were buried deep in the shattered plate-glass window of a vacant storefront. As I neared the car, some quick-thinking passerby reached in and switched off the engine.

Nearby the woman continued to sob hysterically. Fearing the worst, I checked the interior of the Duster but found no passengers. Off to the side, I saw a man crouching on the curb of the sidewalk. He held his face in his hands, and I thought he was hurt.

I hurried over to him. "Are you all right?"

The man, a kid of eighteen or nineteen, looked up at me and nodded mutely, but I saw he wasn't nearly all right. His face was awash in a mixture of tears and blood. He was bleeding profusely from a deep gash over his left eyebrow.

"I didn't see him, honest," the kid whimpered brokenly. "I swear to God, I didn't see him at all."

"Was there anyone else in there with you?" I asked.

He stared up at me blankly. "Just me," he mumbled as if in a daze. "Nobody but me." Shaking his head, he attempted to mop the blood away from his eye with his shirtsleeve.

"I don't know where he came from. One second he wasn't there, and then he was. He just stumbled out in front of me. Stepped right in front of the car. I never had a chance to stop."

In the background, the woman was still sobbing, with people trying to comfort her. She was saying pretty much the same thing the boy did, that whoever it had been had come flying toward her vehicle out of nowhere.

"Is he dead?" she asked. "Somebody please tell me."

When he heard those words, the boy closed his eyes and sagged heavily against me. I eased him down onto the sidewalk, resting him on his back. Convulsive shivering indicated he might be going into shock. I slipped out of my jacket and draped it over him, then I handed him my handkerchief.

"Hang on, buddy," I told him when his eyes blinked open. "Hold this against that cut of yours. Put some pressure on it so it doesn't bleed so much. I'll be right back."

With that, even as I heard the sound of sirens in the distance, I went looking for the pedestrian who'd been hit. He wasn't hard to find. I'd heard the sound of the impact, and I knew what to expect. At least I thought I did.

The victim lay on the hood of a second vehicle—the woman's older-model Oldsmobile. One foot and arm had smashed through the shattered windshield. I hurried over to him and felt for a pulse. Finding none in his limp wrist, I thought I'd check his carotid artery just to be sure. As I reached across his chest, however, a sharp pain bit into my own arm. I looked down at my wrist and found, to my surprise, that I was bleeding. Thinking I must have cut myself on a piece of broken glass, I tried moving the man's sports jacket aside.

That's when I saw the knife. The blade protruded stiffly from his chest like an evil shark's fin. The force of his landing on the hood of the Cutless must have driven the knife handle well into his back and pushed the blade up through his rib cage. From the position in his chest, I was sure the blade had gone directly through his heart, killing him instantly.

"Step aside," someone was saying urgently. "Coming through. Coming through."

A young uniformed cop appeared at my elbow and bodily shoved me aside. "Is he dead?" the cop asked as he, too, began searching for a pulse.

"I think so," I told him. "But be careful of the knife. It's sharp as hell. I already cut myself on it."

"What knife?" the young officer demanded shortly. "I thought this was ..." And then he saw it, too. "I'll be damned!" he exclaimed. "There is a knife here."

Gingerly, avoiding the blade, the cop checked the man's throat and shook his head. "He's a goner all right," he said. "Hell of a way to go!" Then he added, more to himself than to me, "but what did it, the knife or the car?"

That was the $64,000 question. I didn't answer because it wasn't my place to. After all, I was on vacation. It seemed like a good idea for me to find myself an EMT and see if my wrist needed stitches. I started to walk away, but the young officer stopped me.

"Wait a minute, sir," he said. "Maybe you'd better tell me exactly how it is that your arm got cut like that."

Vacation or not, I knew it was the beginning of another long, long night.

5

No doubt things would have gone more smoothly if the dead man hadn't turned out to be someone else I knew from Seattle. It seemed as though the whole goddamned city had jumped in their cars and followed me down I-5 to Ashland. I half expected my old hometown nemesis, Maxwell Cole—the intrepid, walrus-mustached columnist from the *Seattle Post-Intelligencer*—to turn up any minute for an impromptu interview. I was surprised he didn't.

An hour and a half later, after the emergency-room doctor finished stitching my wrist back together, I found myself closeted in a small conference room in Ashland's Community Hospital while Gordon Fraymore, Ashland's sole police detective, swallowed Tums by the fistful and gave me a going-over.

Fraymore was older than I by a good five years, which meant he had been a cop that much longer as well. Since we were both long-term police officers, it seems reasonable that we would see eye to eye. We didn't. Not at all. He took an instant dislike to me. Just because cops are sworn to uphold the peace doesn't mean some of them won't be assholes. That's how Gordon Fraymore struck me—a born asshole.

"Tell me again how it is you happen to know this Martin Shore character," Fraymore said, drumming his fingertips impatiently on the smooth Formica tabletop.

The murder victim's identification had been accomplished through picture I.D. discovered on the body. As soon as Detective Fraymore mentioned Martin Shore's name aloud, I realized I knew him.

"I already told you."

"Tell me again."

"Shore had his own private-investigation firm up in Seattle. Specialized in criminal-defense-type work and some insurance claims. We ran into each other now and again, usually at the courthouse. I knew him, but just in passing. We weren't friends by any means."

I neglected to mention the degree to which Martin Shore and I weren't friends. His offices were in a run-down part of Georgetown, a neighborhood in Seattle's South End. Scuttlebutt had it that Shore was an ex-cop who had been drummed off the force in Yakima, Washington, where he was alleged to have been moonlighting as a porno distributer. He weaseled out of the charges without even having to cop a plea. Given that kind of history, I don't know how he managed to come up with a P.I. license, but then, I don't work for the Department of Licensing.

I'm not fond of private investigators, so Martin Shore started out with one strike against him. In my book, porn dealers are the scum of the earth. Strike two. Since this was a murder investigation, it seemed best to keep those very personal opinions well under wraps. Rat or not, Martin Shore was dead, and Gordon Fraymore was the detective charged with finding his killer. Fraymore was casting his net in every direction, and I didn't want to wind up in it. Actually, Fraymore already had himself one convenient scapegoat—Derek Chambers, the unfortunate driver of the Duster, who was still waiting and agonizing somewhere in the hospital.

From a few things he said, I suspected Fraymore was somewhat confused, that he had inadvertently mixed up exactly who had been driving what. He was off on a wild tangent, thinking the woman had been driving the Duster and Derek Chambers the

Buick. And while Fraymore blundered around in total ignorance, Derek and his worried parents were isolated in a hospital room down the hallway with a uniformed cop standing guard outside the door.

I wish I could say those kinds of mistakes never happen. I can't. I've made a few of them myself. In the heat of a new investigation, when a cop is working under incredible pressure, one piece of a puzzle unaccountably gets shifted to the wrong side of the board. With any kind of luck, the detective realizes where he went wrong and corrects his mistake, straightening out both his mind and his paper before any harm is done.

As an impartial observer of events in Ashland, I found it easy to see what was happening. I wondered how long it would take for Gordon Fraymore to wise up. It sure as hell wasn't my job to point out the error of his ways. Cop or not, Fraymore struck me as a heavy-handed jerk. The longer the mix-up was allowed to continue, the more harm it would do to Derek Chambers and the more embarrassing it would be for Detective Fraymore. In fact, if it hadn't been for what Fraymore's stupidity was doing to Derek and his anguished parents, I could have cared less.

"Let me ask you this," Fraymore was saying. "Did you have any idea Martin Shore was going to be in Ashland this weekend?"

"None whatsoever. As a matter of fact, I didn't know *I* would be until just yesterday morning."

Fraymore frowned. "I thought you said your daughter was getting married, that you came here for a wedding."

"I didn't know about the wedding until yesterday, either," I snapped. Gordon Fraymore could go ahead and draw his own conclusions on that score. "I may have been late getting my invitation," I added, "but the wedding is scheduled for two-thirty Monday afternoon, if you want to check it out."

"Oh, I'll do that," Gordon Fraymore assured me. "Most definitely. I'll be checking everything. Twice if necessary. Tell me again what you were doing just prior to your being found at the crime scene?"

I took a deep breath and told him again. "I left the donor party in the Bowmer. I told Alex I wanted to get some air."

"I take it Alex is Alexis Downey, the lady waiting for you out in the lobby?"

I nodded.

"She your wife?"

"We're just good friends," I answered.

"I see. Where exactly did you go when you went out to get some air?"

"Out into that little brick courtyard between the theaters and the ticket office. I was standing near the telephone booths looking up at the stars when I first heard the crash. As soon as I heard it, I knew what it was. I ran down the stairs between the buildings to see if I could help."

"Commendable," Gordon Fraymore said. "Did you see anybody else on the stairs or in the courtyard?"

"No."

"Hear anything?"

"Other than the crash and breaking glass? No."

"I understand you work Homicide in Seattle?"

I didn't remember telling him that. "That's right."

"You're sure there isn't a chance that Martin Shore screwed up one of your cases and you decided to get even?"

"There's no chance." It was time for a little cop-to-cop courtesy. "Look, I'm tired. My arm hurts. Can't we finish this tomorrow?"

"Where are you staying?"

"One of the B and B's. Oak something."

"Oak Hill?"

"Probably. Sounds like it, but I don't remember for sure."

"Both you and Miss Downey are staying there?"

"Ms. Downey," I corrected. If I couldn't get away with calling Alexis "Miss," then neither could Gordon Fraymore. "That's right. We're both staying there."

"Why not with your daughter?" he asked pointedly. "Didn't Marjorie Connors offer to put you up?"

I wasn't in the mood to discuss my daughter or Marjorie Connors' singular style of nonhospitality, and where Alex and I stayed was none of Gordon Fraymore's damn business.

"Live Oak Farm doesn't have enough room," I answered. "Can I go now?"

He studied me for a long moment. "I suppose," he said deliberately. "Just don't head back for Seattle without letting me know."

"Right."

I got up and walked as far as the doorway, but by then Fraymore had pushed once too often. I couldn't resist a parting shot. "What about Derek Chambers?" I asked.

Fraymore had picked up a nail clipper and was digging something out from under his fingernails. "What about him?"

"When are you going to tell him what really happened?"

Fraymore looked up and glowered at me. "About the knife, you mean? When I get damned good and ready. With smart-assed kids like that, it doesn't hurt to let 'em squirm awhile. That's what we do in small towns, Mr. Beaumont. We scare the shit out of kids in order to get them to straighten up and fly right."

The Constitution notwithstanding.

I said, "That kid deserves better than sitting out there thinking he's killed a man. So do his parents."

"What makes you think he didn't kill him?" Fraymore countered. "Maybe the knife wound wouldn't have been fatal if he hadn't been hit by the kid's car first."

"You'd better check the investigating officer's paper, Detective Fraymore. Derek Chambers' car may have hit Martin Shore first, but it was landing on the hood of the Cutlass that rammed the knife through his heart. Derek was in the Duster."

For a long, tense moment, Detective Fraymore and I stared at each other, then he shuffled through the stack of papers piled on the conference room table in front of him. Pointing with one thick finger, he scanned down one of the sheets. Eventually, his finger stopped moving, and his ears reddened. By the time he raised his eyes from the paper, his face was glowing deep purple.

I knew just from looking at him that both Fraymore and I would have been better off if he had uncovered the error himself.

"You can go now," he said coldly.

And I did. As the door to the conference room closed behind me, I realized I was in almost as much trouble with Detective Gordon Fraymore as Monica Davenport was with Alexis Downey.

When she saw me, Alex hurried to my side and gave me a quick, anxious hug. She carried my bloodstained jacket. "Are you all right?" she asked.

"Pretty much. Let's get out of here."

Alex had found me at the scene of the accident, and she had driven me to the hospital in the Porsche. Now, though, as we left the hospital, she handed me the keys. I gave them right back.

"You drive," I told her. "I'm worn out."

The Oak Hill Bed-and-Breakfast was a mile or so south of the theaters on Siskiyou Boulevard. Without knowing it, I had driven past it several times earlier in the afternoon while searching Ashland for Live Oak Lane. The big old two-story house was quiet and dark when we arrived, but Alexis had a key. She let us in through the front door, then led the way through the living room and up a creaking set of stairs.

"This is it," she whispered, opening a door at the top of the stairs. "It's a blue room, so they call it Iris."

While I was at the hospital having my wrist sewn up, Alex had moved our luggage in from the car and had carried it upstairs. All we had to do was undress and fall into bed. My wrist hurt like hell. To keep it from throbbing, I lay with it propped up on an extra pillow next to my head. Alex snuggled up close to my left side and put her head on my chest.

"You should have seen that boy's parents when they showed up at the hospital. The mother was crying. The father didn't say much, but I could tell he was frantic. I felt terrible for all three of them."

"Great minds think alike," I told her.

Alex continued, "It made me glad I don't have kids. I kept trying to put myself in their place. How do parents cope with something like that? The man is dead. Nothing's going to fix that. I mean, Mom and Dad can't kiss it and make it better."

She paused. For several minutes, we lay in silence while an

occasional car drove past on the street outside. There are lots of things in life parents can't fix. I didn't speak because I couldn't, not with the huge lump back in my throat.

"You're so quiet. Are you asleep?" Alex asked.

"No."

She turned toward me, snuggling her head under my chin. "What about you, Beau? What would you do if something like that happened to Kelly or Scott? How would you handle it?"

Alex was only making conversation, but this was the worst-possible time for her to ask that particular question.

"Kelly's pregnant," I answered. That response was both unforgivably abrupt and totally indirect, but it covered the bases. Alex propped herself up on my chest and stared thoughtfully into my face, her concerned frown visible in the pale moonlight.

"Oh," she said. "So that's it. I'm so sorry."

"Me, too," I mumbled. "Kelly doesn't seem to be, though. She's happy as a clam, and so's that damn fiancé of hers. The wedding's set for Monday afternoon at two-thirty. Since I'm invited, I suppose you are, too, if you want to go, that is."

I made no effort to disguise the hard edge of bitterness in my voice. Why should I? My eighteen-year-old daughter was pregnant and throwing her life away for some jerk of a two-bit actor.

Wordlessly, Alex lay back down and once more snuggled her head under my chin. The soft heat of her breath warmed my skin. My nostrils inhaled the clean, fresh scent of her hair. As gentle fingers began stroking my breastbone, some of the aching tension drained out of my body.

"What about your ex-wife?" Alex asked softly much later when I was almost asleep. "Is she coming?"

"I don't know for sure, but I doubt it. Karen doesn't know about this, and I don't think it's my place to tell her."

"Oh," Alex said, and that was all.

I had meant to ask Alexis Downey about the denouement of the donor party and exactly how things were going in the theater-development wars. I meant to ask her if she had been able to keep

Monica Davenport's grubby little paws out of Guy Lewis' wallet, but before I had a chance, the comforting touch of her caressing fingers lulled me to sleep.

It wasn't at all how I had imagined spending the first night of our romantic weekend away from the man-hating Hector and Alex's damnable futon, but in lots of ways it was much nicer.

And it was probably far better than I deserved.

When I woke up, brilliant rays of warm morning sunlight streamed in through the window. Alex—wide awake, showered, and wearing a terry-cloth robe—was curled up in a rocking chair by the window. She sat with a pair of reading glasses perched on her nose and with a thick, leather-bound volume tucked under her face.

"What are you reading?" I asked.

"Shakespeare," she replied. "The complete works. We're scheduled to see *Shrew* tonight. The dialogue's great. I wanted to review it for myself. By the way," she added, "breakfast is in fifteen minutes. You'd better get a move on."

Sniffing the air, I savored the mouth-watering aromas that drifted upstairs from the kitchen. "I think that's what woke me up," I said, crawling out of bed and heading for the bathroom.

"Hope you don't mind baths," Alex cautioned. "Showers are out. Oak Hill was the only place in town with a last-minute cancellation, and this was the last available room. Consider yourself lucky."

As soon as I walked into the bathroom, I understood what Alex meant. Space for this recently added bathroom had been carved from an attic area directly under the slope of the eaves. The tub-enclosure alcove wasn't tall enough to accommodate a shower stall. In fact, I couldn't even stand up in it without bumping my head on the ceiling. With my arm bandaged, though, showers would have been out of the question anyway.

I missed my morning shower, but breakfast more than made up for it. Alex and I arrived in the huge dining-room and took the last two places at the far end of a spacious dining-room table that comfortably seated twelve. By the time we appeared, the room was abuzz with lively chatter. Talk ceased long enough for a round of introductions. Guests came from as far south as San Diego and from as far north as Alex's digs on Queen Ann Hill.

The Oak Hill's owner—a retired schoolteacher named Florence who functioned as hostess, chief cook, waitress, busser, manager, and concierge—passed platters heaped high with French toast, delectable sausages, and sliced fresh fruit. She plied us with pitchers of juice and hot coffee and kept conversation flowing. Table talk focused mostly on who had seen which plays yesterday, what they thought of same, and who would see what today.

Toward the end of the meal, someone asked about the bandage on my arm. With little encouragement, Alex told a rapt audience about the previous night's activities. There's nothing like murder and mayhem to liven up a waning mealtime discussion.

Once the topic of murder came up, I figured I was in for it. Being identified as a police officer—especially a homicide detective—in a group of civilians is no favor. The cop immediately becomes the focus of all kinds of public pet peeves concerning the judicial system—from police brutality to overly enthusiastic traffic enforcement. With a brand-new local murder under discussion, I figured I was in for a real grilling.

And that would have happened most places. Ashland was different. To my surprise, that highly literate group of breakfast conversationalists quickly veered away from the specifics of Martin Shore's murder into a hotly contested philosophical discussion on the ethics of the death penalty. It's no news that I was the only person unconditionally in favor of capital punishment, but everyone else turned out to be just as opinionated as I was.

All in all, it was a delicious, interesting, and altogether enjoyable meal. It put me totally at ease, lulled me into a false sense of security and lighthearted fun. As a consequence, when Alexis and I walked back up to our room afterward, I was shocked when we ran into Kelly coming down the stairway. She was headed for the laundry on the other side of the kitchen, her arms laden with a huge bundle of dirty sheets and wet towels.

"Kelly!" I exclaimed in dismay. "What are you doing here?"

She glanced first at Alexis and then at me. "Hello, Dad," she said. "I work here mornings. I thought you knew that. I saw your car outside and thought that's why you stayed here."

"I had no idea!"

Alexis stepped forward with a ready smile. "Hi, Kelly. I'm Alexis Downey. Alex for short. I'm so glad to meet you."

Now it was Kelly and Alexis who stood looking at each other and sizing one another up in the same way Jeremy Todd Cartwright and I had surveyed one another the evening before. At last Kelly smiled. "I'm happy to meet you, too, Alex," she said. The dignity of her response belied both her age and the dirty linen.

"Right now I have to start the wash, or it'll never get dry. We'll talk later—at lunch. I'm off around eleven-thirty." With that, she continued down the staircase and disappeared.

I watched her go with a very real sense of wonder. I was so amazed that for the time being I forgot to be embarrassed about her seeing Alex and me together. "She's all grown up, Alexis. How did that happen? Where have I been?"

Alex grinned. "Daddies are always the last to know."

We proceeded up the stairs and into our room, where the bed had been neatly made. Two sets of clean towels and washcloths hung on the bars in the bathroom. I was astonished to think that Kelly—my very own messy Kelly—had carefully placed them there and that she had actually made a bed. With her own hands. That was so out of character, I would have been less surprised if someone had told me she was an alien being from another planet.

"If you had known her when she was little. . . ."

Alex turned to me. "How long have you been divorced?"

"Six years, going on seven. Why?"

"When you don't see someone on a daily basis, especially little kids, they tend to stay frozen in your mind at the age they were when you knew them best. For years my grandmother sent me three pairs of panties on my birthday. Every year I had to exchange them because every year they were too small.

"Kelly's all grown up now, Beau. She's not eleven or twelve anymore. It looks to me as though she's behaving in a very responsible fashion."

I thought about that. "In other words, butt out and mind my own business?"

Alex shrugged. "Maybe that's a little stronger than I would have said it myself, but yes, that's pretty much what I mean."

Alex left me standing in the middle of the room, walked over to the door, and clicked home the security lock. When she came back, she kissed me full on the lips.

"Hey, big guy," she murmured. "How about a quick roll in the hay? This is supposed to be our romantic getaway, remember? So far you haven't laid a glove on me."

God knows I wanted her, but my ears reddened at the very suggestion. "With Kelly right downstairs?" I croaked.

Alex laughed. "Why not? She's doing laundry, remember? She won't even notice."

"But what if the bed squeaks? What if the floor does?"

"What if?"

Taking me by the hand, Alex led me over to the bed. I sat down on it tentatively and bounced once or twice, testing the springs. I couldn't hear any telltale squeaks, but without being downstairs to listen, how could I be sure? Meantime, Alex slipped out of her shorts and panties and peeled her T-shirt off over her head. Seconds after the T-shirt hit the carpeted floor, so did her lacy white bra.

Alex walked over to me and pulled me against her bare skin with fierce, hungry urgency. Grasping my head, she buried my face in the soft, fragrant swell of her breasts.

"Please," she whispered. "Kelly will never know. Even if she did, she won't mind. I think she knows where babies come from."

"But . . ."

"Kelly isn't a virgin anymore. She doesn't expect you to be one, either."

Put that way, with Alex's suddenly taut nipples grazing against my skin and lips, I could hardly turn her down. No right-thinking

male would have, not unless he was totally crazy—and, most as-
suredly, I am not crazy.

Eventually, with some careful urging on her part, I did manage
to rise to the occasion. But given the choice between making love
while my daughter was downstairs washing clothes or doing it
with Alex's crazy cat lying there eyeing us malevolently from the
opposite pillow, I confess I'd choose Hector every single time.

6

We fell asleep. Considering the lateness of the hour when we'd arrived home from the emergency room, that was hardly surprising. Alex woke me just in time for us to go to lunch with Jeremy and Kelly. Before we left the room, I personally made sure the bed was perfectly straight.

Jeremy showed up wearing his Birkenstocks and driving the Live Oak Farm van. Once we were all together, he recommended we go directly to a restaurant called Geppetto's in hopes of beating the noontime crowd. I soon saw the wisdom in that advice. Within minutes of our being shown to a table, twenty people stood waiting in line for seating as matinee theatergoers came out in droves, prowling the area for pre-play sustenance.

Ashland, like an army, travels on its stomach. Each day the town fills up with hundreds of out-of-town visitors who expect to be fed regular meals before, after, or between performances. The fact that nobody goes hungry is one of the logistical miracles of unrepentant capitalism.

When the harried waiter arrived to take our order, all three of them—Jeremy, Kelly, and Alex—ordered the eggplant hamburger.

Eggplant, for God's sake! It reminded me of Ron Peters, my long-time friend and ex-partner, in his old beansprout days. I fumed and ordered a real hamburger.

Kelly shook her head in disapproval. "Daddy," she chided, "how can you eat all that red meat?"

"Easy," I returned. "Years of practice."

My comment provoked the slightest hint of a smile in the corners of Jeremy Cartwright's otherwise strained mouth. I wondered if he was nervous about having lunch with me. I certainly hoped so. I remembered being scared witless the first time I had dinner with Karen's folks.

"I have tickets for *Majestic* this afternoon, if you'd like to go," he offered.

"Oh, Jeremy. How awesome!" Kelly exclaimed, sounding every bit the eighteen-year-old she was. "How did you manage that?"

Jeremy shrugged modestly. "Just lucky," he said.

Alexis Downey beamed. "*Majestic*'s a terrific show. One of my favorites. I understand you play the Laredo Kid?"

"Yeah," he said. "I only auditioned for the part on a dare. I never thought I'd actually get it."

The in-crowd theater talk left me in the dark. "What's it about?" I asked.

"About this old-time movie character—that's me," Jeremy answered. "I appear like a vision to this other guy who grew up going to movies and watching those real old western serials."

Watch it, Buster, I thought. I used to love those "real old" western serials.

"Now he's out West working on an Indian reservation," Jeremy continued. "My character is stuck in the past with all these old scripts and stereotypes of what women should and shouldn't do. He can't adjust to this new kind of modern woman who can go to school, cook gourmet meals, fix her own car, and save her boyfriend every time he gets into hot water."

"Sounds fascinating," I said.

Alex kicked me in the shins. "It is," she said. "And we'll be delighted to go, Jeremy. It'll be a good counterpoint to *Shrew* tonight."

If I personally had any objections, they'd been summarily over-ruled. The waiter brought our orders. Even he looked somewhat disgusted as he slapped the loaded real meat hamburger platter on the table in front of me.

With the arrival of food, conversation ground to a halt. Uncom-fortable silence expanded until it seemed to stretch to the far corners of the universe. Each bite of hamburger turned to dry sawdust in my mouth, although everyone else at the table wolfed his or her food with obvious relish. I could just as well have ordered the eggplant.

"Is your mother coming to the wedding?" Alex asked, innocently lobbing a live hand grenade onto the table. Fortunately, I had just swallowed a mouthful of burger; otherwise I would have required an on-the-spot Heimlich maneuver. Kelly's gaze faltered, and her hands dropped nervously to her lap while a vivid flush spread up her neck and cheeks.

"Mom doesn't know about it," she responded. "Coming to the wedding would just upset her."

"Upset" didn't quite cover it. I doubt that's the word Dave Living-ston would have used, either.

The expression on Alex's face remained utterly composed. "If I were your mother," she said with an impassive smile, "I'm afraid I'd be terribly hurt if I wasn't invited."

"Even if you thought your daughter was making a horrible mis-take?" Jeremy chimed in.

I did choke at that one, couldn't help it. At least the kid was smart enough to recognize the lay of the land.

Alex nodded. "Even if," she replied.

That was followed by another period of dead silence. "We'll think about it," Kelly said finally, but Alex wasn't finished.

"If the wedding's tomorrow," she pressed, "there isn't much time for your mother to make arrangements. She's in California, isn't she?" Kelly nodded. "She'll have to make plane reservations, and all that."

"I'll try to decide today," Kelly agreed.

It was a major concession, and I wasn't entirely sure how it had happened. I smiled at Alex, grateful for the miracle, while Kelly changed the subject. "How was the backstage tour this morning, Jeremy?" she asked.

"Everybody's upset," he said, "because of the knife and all."

Knife? It was as if someone had twanged a gigantic rubber band in the middle of my forehead. "What knife?" I asked.

"The Henckels—the twelve-inch slicer—we use for *Romeo*. When the stage manager realized it was missing from the prop table this morning, he spent an hour looking before he had Dinky Holloway report it to Detective Fraymore. You know, because of what happened last night. Nobody knows when it disappeared. . . ."

"I do," I interjected.

"You do?" Three pairs of eyes searched my face.

"It was missing when I looked at the props during the donor party," I said. "I remember seeing the empty orange outline on the table. At least it was something shaped like a knife. I didn't worry about it, though. It wasn't my problem."

"It's somebody's problem now. Dinky came back to the theater practically tearing her hair out. Fraymore was going out to the farm to take Tanya's fingerprints."

"Tanya's!" Kelly exclaimed. "Why would he do that?"

"Don't worry," I assured them. "It's just routine. If it is the knife from the show, both Juliet's and Romeo's prints may be on it. So a print technician will take both Tanya's and James Renthrow's prints as well as any stagehands who may have handled the knife. Once they catalog the *known* prints that should be there, then they can sort out the *unknown* ones that shouldn't."

"I see," Jeremy said. "So it's a process of elimination?"

"Right," I answered. "It's called disqualifying prints."

Jeremy breathed a sigh of relief. "I'm glad to hear that. I was afraid it meant she was really in trouble."

"Any reason why she should be?"

"Daddy," Kelly complained. "Stop being a detective."

"I can't help it. Curiosity becomes a way of life."

Iced tea and eggplant had evidently propped up Jeremy's confidence. He was feeling expansive. "It's just that Tanya's had so much bad luck," he said. "First her parents died in that fire when she was twelve. Then she got in a beef with her guardian and ended up on her own by the time she was fourteen. She's been self-supporting ever since. In all that time, she never lost track of her goal."

"Which was?"

"To be an actress. And look at her. She is. For someone her age, she's accomplished a lot. Especially when you consider she's raising Amber all by herself."

"What happened to her husband?"

"Oh him." Kelly sniffed disapprovingly. "I guess Bob couldn't stand the competition. He was ten years older than Tanya. When she landed better parts than he did, he took off."

"How old was Amber when he left?" I asked.

Kelly and Jeremy exchanged veiled glances before Kelly answered. "Tanya told me he left the day he found out she was pregnant."

Oops. One more time, open mouth and insert foot. Once again Alex came to my rescue. "How old is Amber?"

"Two and a half."

"I know what actors make around here," Alex continued. "It isn't much. How has Tanya managed?"

"She couldn't have if it hadn't been for Marjorie," Kelly explained. "That's Marjorie Connors," she added for Alex's benefit. "Our landlady. She runs Live Oak Farm, where we all live. Tanya couldn't afford an apartment by herself. She was about to be thrown into the street when Marjorie invited them to come stay with her."

Jeremy nodded. "Marjorie's great. That's the kind of thing she does. She was volunteering at the theaters when she heard about what was going on with Tanya and Amber. She knew Tanya was broke, so they worked out a way Tanya could help around the farm in exchange for the rent. That's what we all do, more or less."

"Is that how you ended up there, too?" Alex spoke with her eyes focused on Kelly's face. If I had asked the question, Kelly probably would have thrown the remainder of her eggplant burger in my face, told me it was none of my business, and stomped off in a huff. Since Alex asked, though, it was okay.

"Pretty much," Kelly answered.

"Sounds like a nice lady," Alex went on. "I'd like to meet her sometime. Maybe at the wedding."

Jeremy shook his head. "I doubt that. Marjorie doesn't like weddings. She says marriage is a barbaric holdover from the Middle Ages that turns women into slaves and men into tyrants." Jeremy delivered that last sentence in a brusque voice that mimicked Marjorie Connors' clipped delivery perfectly. Both Kelly and I laughed. Maybe Jeremy was an actor after all.

For a change, since Alex alone of the three of us had never met Marjorie Connors, she was the one left out of the joke.

Jeremy glanced down at his watch. "Sorry to rush. I've got a cast call pretty soon. If we don't leave now, I won't have time to take Kelly home and bring the others into town."

"I take it you operate the Live Oak Taxi?" I asked.

He grinned. "Like Kelly said, it helps pay the rent." He started to fumble gamely for his billfold, but I told him to forget it, that I was buying. They left a few minutes later, even though it was just barely twelve-thirty. Alex and I lingered at the table. It was hot in the restaurant, and I switched from coffee to iced tea.

"What do you think?" I asked.

"Of them?" Alex shrugged. "They're sweet. And very much in love."

She sat there stirring sugar into her iced tea in an artless, casual gesture. Watching her, I was surprised by how much I liked it; by how much I liked her. It was as if she had somehow tiptoed around the defenses and crept into my heart through a back entrance I didn't know existed.

"Could I ask you a personal question, Ms. Downey?" I asked.

"Shoot," she said.

"Let me lay it out for you this way, ma'am. Here we are having lunch with my daughter and the young twerp who is all set to marry her without so much as a by-your-leave. In the middle of this highly pressurized lunch, you come right out and ask if they've invited Karen to the wedding. Don't get me wrong; I'm not complaining, but would you mind telling me why you did that?"

She looked up at me and smiled, her deep blue eyes flashing in merriment. "You really don't know?"

"Haven't a clue."

"Karen's Kelly's mother, right?"

"Right."

"She's also your ex-wife. Divorces notwithstanding, mothers expect to go to their daughters' weddings. Period."

"So?"

"So, in case you haven't noticed, I'm not interested in a one-night stand or even a several-month stand with you, Mr. J. P. Beaumont. I'm not that kind of girl. I like you a lot, but if there's ever going to be anything permanent between us, then we'd better make damn sure that if we're invited to Kelly and Jeremy's wedding, Karen and Dave Livingston are, too."

Just like that, I got the picture. Talk about a slow learner! So when we went to see *The Majestic Kid* that afternoon, I sat up and paid attention, and not just because my future son-in-law was playing a lead role. I figured since this was a play about a girl who kept bailing her boyfriend out of the drink, then I needed to take lessons.

During intermission, Alex excused herself. I thought she was going to the rest room. Instead, she must have used a phone. When she sat back down beside me, she squeezed my arm.

"It worked," she said. "I checked with Kelly. She and Jeremy talked it over on the way home. Karen and Dave are invited to the wedding after all."

"Hot damn!" I breathed. By then I understood Karen's presence at the wedding was in my own best interest.

"Well," she hedged. "It's not all smooth sailing."

"Why not? What do you mean?"

"They want you to make the phone call."

"Me!" I choked. "I have to do all the dirty work?"

Alex smiled and nodded. "I told Kelly you wouldn't mind at all.

That's what fathers are for. We'll call Karen as soon as the play is over and before we meet Dinky for dinner."

I watched the second act of *The Majestic Kid*, but I can't say I enjoyed it very much. Alex, of course, savored every minute of it. Why wouldn't she? She didn't know Karen Moffit Beaumont Livingston. I did.

Expecting the immediate outbreak of World War III, I wasn't willing to use a public pay phone to call Rancho Cucamonga. After the play, we took the Porsche, drove to a shady parking place near a park, and called on my cellular phone. I did try Dave's number at work but ended up with voice mail. Taking a deep breath, I dialed the Livingstons' home number.

I hoped Dave would answer, but of course he didn't. "Hello, Karen," I said. "It's Beau."

Her guard came up just like that. "What do you want?"

Karen didn't used to be that defensive, and I don't blame her, not anymore. It's a perfectly understandable device to keep from being hurt again. Since she wasn't that way back in the old days when we were first married, I have to accept some of the responsibility for how she is now. Being married to an alcoholic isn't a bed of roses, so I'm willing to shoulder some of the blame. Some, but not all.

"I've found Kelly," I heard myself blabbing into the phone. "She's in Ashland, Oregon, and she's okay. . . . No, she's fine, really. Karen, listen to me. No, I'm telling you, she's all right."

Karen was crying into the receiver so hard I wasn't sure if she heard a word I said. I looked over at Alex for help and encouragement. She nodded, urging me forward, but she didn't offer any other help. In this deal, I was strictly on my own.

I forged ahead. "Karen," I said reasonably, "calm down and listen. This is important. Kelly is getting married on Monday. Tomorrow. I'm calling to see if there's any way you and Dave and Scott can make it up here on such short notice."

The words had the same effect as a bucket of cold water. "Married?" Karen sputtered. "She can't do that."

"Yes, she can."

"Who's she marrying?"

"A boy named Jeremy Cartwright."

"When?"

"I already told you. The wedding's set for two-thirty tomorrow afternoon here in Ashland, Oregon." I paused and took a deep breath before I said the rest. "Kelly's pregnant, Karen."

I held the phone away from my ear during the angry tirade that followed, but sooner than I would have expected, Karen grew oddly silent.

"Look," I said. "I know this hurts like hell, but you'll have to decide whether or not you want to be part of it."

Seven hundred and fifty miles away, the telephone receiver clattered noisily onto a tabletop in Rancho Cucamonga. That in itself was a pretty definitive answer. I figured it was a final one, but a moment later Dave Livingston came on the phone.

"Thanks for saving my ass and not letting her know I called you," he said. "I'll handle things on this end. Where can I call you once she comes around?"

"You think she will?"

"Yeah," Dave said. "I'm sure of it."

I looked down at the phone in my hand. There really wasn't any place for him to return a call. Alex and I had play tickets for the Elizabethan. I had no intention of spending the remainder of the afternoon and evening in the car waiting for the telephone to ring.

"Call my home number in Seattle," I said. "Leave a message for Ralph Ames."

"Who's he?"

"My attorney. If you have trouble with airline connections or anything like that, call Ralph and let him go to work on it. He'll sort it out."

"You have an attorney who handles airline arrangements?" Dave asked. "It must be nice."

"He's a friend," I explained. "Call him if you need help."

I hung up and looked at Alex. "Way to go," she said.

Then I dialed my home number in Seattle. Ralph still wasn't

there, but he would be soon. He'd pitch in and do whatever needed doing. I left a message. Maybe voice mail isn't all bad. After that, I put down the phone and turned to Alex. "Okay. I've done my duty. Now what?"

She glanced at her watch. "We've just got time to meet Dinky for dinner."

"Where?"

"It's a surprise."

"Great. I love surprises." I turned the key. "Which way?"

"Back through town then north past the light. Stop at the phone booth."

"Stop at a phone booth? Are you putting me on?"

"That's what the directions say," Alex said. "I've got them written down right here. It says there's no sign outside, just a three-by-five card on the door. Dinky says it's an old gas station, but the food's great."

"Sure it is," I said, unconvinced. "Every old gas station serves great food. They've all turned into AM/PM Minimarts. What are we having? Ho-Ho's?"

"Beau," Alex declared firmly, "Dinky would never steer us wrong."

At the intersection, I turned left on Siskiyou Boulevard. "Wanna bet?" I said.

Fortunately, we didn't bet. The food at Cowboy Sam's New Bistro probably would have been excellent, if we had actually stayed around long enough to eat any of it. We drove to an ancient, porticoed gas station north of town. The only distinguishing feature visible from the road really *was* a phone booth, but the inside of the building had been remodeled into a series of small, intimate lace-curtained dining rooms. The several glossily enameled wooden tables—I counted only eight—were already filling up.

The proprietor, who must have been Cowboy Sam himself, led us to a table where Dinky Holloway was already seated and waiting. Even to someone who had only seen her once, she didn't look quite right. To Alex it must have been even more apparent that something was dreadfully wrong.

"Dinky, what's going on? You look terrible."

Dinky gave Alex a wan smile. We started to sit down. The way the table was arranged, I headed for the chair that was next to the wall, but this was a very old gas station. The low, sloping ceiling was too short for me to stand upright next to the wall. There seemed to be a lot of that going around in Ashland: first the sloping bathroom ceiling at the Oak Hill B & B; now the same kind of construction at a converted gasoline station. I was beginning to think Ashland was built by and for midgets.

Alex and I quickly traded seats while Denver Holloway studied me with a frankly assessing look. "Are you really as trustworthy as Alex says?" she asked.

I glanced at Alex. "I'd like to think so, why?"

Dinky reached into a cavernous purse and extracted a semi-clear plastic container, the kind you get from video stores.

"What's that?" I asked.

She put it down on the table and then pushed it to the center as though she didn't want it too near her.

"Just what it looks like," she answered. "A videotape. It showed up in my inter-office mail this afternoon."

Since Denver Holloway was regarding the container with the kind of guarded wariness most people reserve for a coiled rattlesnake, it seemed possible she was leaving something unsaid.

"What kind of videotape?" I asked.

"Filth."

"Filth?" I repeated, not sure I had heard her correctly. "As in porno flick?"

She nodded grimly. "It came today along with this." She pushed a piece of paper across the table. Typed on it was the following: *Dinky, Someone like this is a liability to the Festival and will drive away donors. Get rid of her as soon as possible. Monica.*

"As soon as I read it, I went storming down to Monica's office and bitched her out. I'm a director with some artistic integrity. I'll be damned if I'll be threatened by some hotshot golden girl pulling the purse strings."

Alex looked at me and rolled her eyes. "That's one meeting I'm glad I missed. What happened?"

"Monica denied it," Dinky continued. "Said she'd never seen any videotape, and that she hadn't sent the note, either."

"What happened then?"

"I went back to my office to play the tape."

"And?"

Dinky's face crumpled. "It's awful. I've never seen anything like it. When I realized what it was, I turned it off."

Whatever Denver Holloway had seen, it had rocked her to the very core. There are only a few things guaranteed to produce that kind of appalled reaction in decent, law-abiding folks.

"Snuff film or kiddie porn?" I asked.

Dinky swallowed hard. "I couldn't believe what I was seeing, and she wasn't even that old. It's monstrous." She paused before continuing in a small, constrained voice. "Ever since, all I've been able to think about is what'll happen to her now, and what about the baby?"

Alex reached out and put a comforting hand on Denver Holloway's wrist. "The girl in the video is someone you know?"

Dinky nodded, her face a pasty white. Two gigantic tears spilled from her highly magnified eyes and dribbled slowly down her pale cheeks. "It's Tanya," she whispered miserably. "Tanya Dunseth— my Juliet. She must have been only eleven or twelve, but I recognized her instantly. I'd know that profile anywhere. What's going to happen to her?"

Full of brisk reassurance, Alex patted the back of Dinky's hand. "Nothing's going to happen to Tanya, and no one's going to hold it against her. She's the one who's been victimized. After something like that, it's even more of a wonder that's she's been able to do what she's done. What a remarkable young woman!"

"But you don't understand," Dinky added shakily. "I recognized the man, too. The one in the videotape. He's younger than his picture in the paper today, but I never forget a face. It's him all right."

Suddenly, it all came together for me. "Martin Shore?" I asked in astonishment. "Martin Shore is the one on the tape?"

Dinky nodded.

"The dead man," Alex said, shaking her head. "I can't believe it."

"It's true," Dinky replied, her face suffused with grief. "I don't know what to do."

"This is important," I said at once. "We have to take the tape to Detective Fraymore, no question."

Dinky shook her head. "I was afraid that's what you'd say. Why?"

"Because it's against the law to conceal evidence in a homicide investigation, that's why. We're talking motive and opportunity here. I, for one, don't want to be charged with being an accomplice after the fact, and neither do you."

By now the restaurant had filled up. During our low-voiced, highly charged discussion, I had twice waved off the proprietor of Cowboy Sam's New Bistro. Now he approached us more determinedly. "Would anyone here care to see the wine list?" he asked.

I took several twenties out of my billfold and fanned them out on the table. Then, using a cloth napkin to protect any possible fingerprints, I picked up the box containing the videotape.

"The lady isn't feeling well," I said to Cowboy Sam, nodding in Dinky's direction at the same time. For her part, Denver Holloway did indeed look violently ill. "I'm afraid we won't be able to stay for dinner. Not tonight."

7

Other people went to see *Shrew* in the Elizabethan that night. Alex and I didn't. Instead, we accompanied Dinky Holloway and spent most of the early evening closeted in Ashland's surprisingly modern city hall along with Detective Gordon Fraymore. He listened to what Dinky had to say in total silence. When she finished, he used a handkerchief to preserve fingerprints when he picked up the tape.

"Right back," he said. "I'm going to take this down the hall and have a look-see." He was gone a long time—half an hour or more. Back in the office again, he placed the tape in the middle of his cluttered desk.

"Looks like Shore all right," he muttered. "I thought there might be somebody else in the film as well, maybe another male we might have seen before or possibly even another kid. They sometimes do that—use more than one, but not this time."

"You watched the whole thing, didn't you?" Dinky said accusingly. "That's disgusting." Alex nodded in grim agreement, her lips pursed into a thin line of protest.

The expressions on both their faces said neither one of the

women was buying Fraymore's excuse for watching the movie. I think they thought he was down the hall getting his rocks off. I wasn't fond of Gordon Fraymore, but I knew what he was up to. I didn't fault him for watching whatever was in that video because, unlike Dinky and Alex, I knew why he was doing it—because it was his job.

I think the general public has come to accept the idea that objects equal evidence. The video case, the letter, the envelope, all might possibly contain trace evidence or latent prints that could prove valuable. What is less apparent is the importance of the tape itself and what information might possibly be gleaned from it.

It's a lesson I learned the hard way back in the mid-seventies when I was a new guy to Homicide and there was no such thing as videotape. Vice brought in an especially ugly 16-mm snuff film that featured a twelve-year-old Seattle girl who had disappeared on her way home from school. I barfed my guts out the first time I saw it. My partner, a world-weary old guy named Bert Claggerhorn, sat us down in the film room, and we watched that damn movie over and over, hour after hour.

Finally, I raised hell and said I'd be damned if I'd watch it one more time, and I didn't. But Bert went right on ahead without me. The amateurs who specialize in pornographic films are just exactly that—amateurs. They're not overly concerned about production values. After watching the film enough times, Bert finally noticed that an overlooked television set was playing in the background. Either the cameraman forgot to turn it off, or, more likely, he was using the volume to help mask the sounds of what he and his pal were doing.

After spotting that one telling detail, Bert ordered blowups made, one from every foot or so of film. When the blowups came back, some of them showed soaps and afternoon game shows that can be seen on television sets anywhere in the country. But filming must have run long, with occasional pauses in the action. Toward the end, the programming carried on over into the evening news, and that's how Bert nailed those bastards.

Studying the blowups, he was able to identify several newscasters and a weatherman who appeared only on the local Bellingham station. Armed with that knowledge, we zeroed in on the Bellingham area. Once we narrowed down the locale and trained the full focus of our investigation there, it didn't take long to flush out our two "movie-mogul" creeps. A bloodstained mattress, the same torn one that was clearly visible in Bert's blowups, was still on the bed. Eventually, those bloodstains were traced to the victim. Thanks to Bert's detailed study of that film, the killers were found and put away for good.

Fraymore seemed bemused by the intensity of Dinky's reaction. "I'm conducting an investigation here, Ms. Holloway," he said. "I understand your abhorrence toward this particular film, but we have to be thorough. That movie gives us something we didn't have before—motive."

In view of the first skirmish in Fraymore's and my little turf war, I should have kept my mouth shut altogether, but keeping my mouth shut has never been one of my strong suits.

"What are you going to do about Tanya Dunseth?" I asked the question straight out, recognizing my blunder as soon as Fraymore turned his narrowed gaze in my direction.

"What business is that of yours?" he demanded.

With Alex looking on, I didn't want to back down. I shrugged noncommittally. "I just want to know, that's all."

Fraymore's thick neck bulged over his eighteen-inch collar. "Did I miss something here?" he asked. "Did I turn my back and all of a sudden you hired on as an investigator with the Ashland Police Department?"

The sarcasm wasn't lost on me. There was no humor in his delivery. Fraymore was the local chief dog, and I was a mangy, out-of-town cur encroaching on previously marked territory.

"I don't believe I have to remind you that you have no legal standing whatsoever in this jurisdiction, *Mister* Beaumont," Gordon Fraymore continued. "The City of Ashland has no letter of mutual aid on file with the City of Seattle. In other words, butt out. That badge of yours is no good here. Furthermore, I don't appreciate interference from visiting firemen. You just go on about your business—see some plays, get your daughter married off, do whatever it is you want to do while you're down here, but leave the law enforcement end of things to me."

I may be slow, but I got the picture. "Right."

Fraymore's and my verbal scuffle went right over Dinky Holloway's head. "You wouldn't really arrest Tanya, would you?" Dinky asked, as though it were only a remote possibility, if that.

Listening with a cop's ear, I knew better. It wasn't just what Fraymore said, it was also how he said it. Tanya Dunseth was in deep trouble. Dinky might have regarded Tanya as a talented young actress and fine mother, as a valued cast member and fellow employee. Gordon Fraymore saw her as a suspected killer, plain and simple. In the world of homicide investigators, suspected killers become convicted ones. And that seemed the most likely outcome in this case.

Presumably, Gordon Fraymore could have sidestepped Dinky's question the same way he had avoided mine, but he didn't. Denver Holloway represented the Festival, the business entity in Ashland that, more than any other, made the detective's regular municipal paychecks possible. Having a suspected murderer onstage at the Oregon Shakespeare Festival wouldn't be good for the Festival or for Ashland.

Fraymore was smart enough to realize that if he was going to have to arrest one of the Festival's star players, if he was going to bite the hand that fed him, he had best handle everyone else from there with kid gloves—starting with Dinky Holloway.

"I might have to," he conceded uneasily, popping Tums as if they were candy. I wondered what was causing Gordon Fraymore's severe indigestion—bad food, general overeating, or Martin Shore's murder.

"How many plays is Tanya Dunseth in?" he asked.

"Three," Dinky answered. "*Romeo, Shrew,* and *The Real Thing.*" "Big roles?"

Dinky nodded. "Important ones. Substantial ones."

In the silence that followed, Gordon Fraymore gave his sprouting five o'clock shadow a thoughtful rub. "It's like this, Ms. Holloway.

If I were you, I'd be out there right now preparing people to take over Tanya's parts. That is confidential information. If word about it leaks out, she'll know we're onto her and take off like a shot."

Dinky bit her lip and nodded. "I understand," she said.

By the time we finally left Fraymore's office, it was 8:20. Ashland is a small town. It would have been easy for us to drive to the theater district, park, and make it to our seats in the Elizabethan in plenty of time for an eight-thirty curtain. But somehow our hearts weren't up to seeing *Taming of the Shrew*. Alex and I opted for something to eat. We invited Dinky to join us, but she begged off.

"I've got to go somewhere and think," she said. She started away, then came back. "He is going to arrest her, isn't he?"

"It looks that way," I agreed. "You heard what he said."

"It'll be terrible for the Festival. Nothing like this has ever happened before. Tanya's an important part of the season. She's a great Juliet, an outstanding Kate. The understudies aren't nearly as good. How long do I have?"

"I don't know. Several days maybe. Possibly as long as several weeks, but I doubt it. Fraymore is under tremendous pressure to get this case solved in a timely manner. He's going to give it everything he's got. If things don't happen fast enough to suit him, he'll make them happen."

Dinky opened her purse and groped for a pack of cigarettes. "Do you think Tanya actually did it?" she asked. Her hands trembled as she attempted to light her cigarette. I finally lit it for her.

"You know Tanya better than I do. You tell me."

Dinky shook her head mournfully. "I don't know what to think. All I know is, I never should have told anyone about the tape. I should have just kept quiet."

"You're not the only one who knew about the tape," I reminded her. "Whoever sent it to you knew about it. Besides, the tape alone won't convict her. There's lots more to it than that. Fraymore's right. The tape does provide motive, but he has to look at opportunity, physical evidence, the availability of the weapon. Tanya certainly had access to that."

"So did lots of other people," Dinky countered, "that is, if you believe Gordon Fraymore's damn Henckels slicer is *our* Henckels slicer. They're not all that uncommon, you know. And ours is a prop. Killing someone with a prop knife is about like shooting someone with a cap pistol. Impossible."

I remembered the way the stage lights had glinted off the metal blade as Juliet had plunged it home. "It looked lethal enough to me," I said.

"That's the whole point," Dinky returned. "Looks are everything. From a distance, prop knives are supposed to *look* dangerous, but they're dull. Deliberately dull. We keep them that way so no one gets hurt."

It felt pretty damn sharp when it sliced into me, I thought. And my wrist wasn't sporting make-believe stitches, either. The coincidence of *two* identical Henckels slicers was more than any self-respecting homicide cop could accept. That went for me as well as Gordon Fraymore.

"But couldn't someone have sharpened it?" Alex asked. "All it takes is one of those little rocks. . . . What are they called?"

"Whetstones," I supplied. "You're right. With a whetstone and ten minutes, a dull knife can be as good as new. A grinding wheel would take about thirty seconds. I'm sure the scenery shop has one of those."

"Oh," Dinky muttered, crushing out her cigarette stub on the sidewalk. Without another word, she stalked off toward her ancient Datsun wagon.

Alex and I drove back downtown and lucked into a parking place. As we set off walking down a virtually empty main street, a trumpet blared a brief, shrill flourish, announcing curtain time at the Elizabethan. It seemed likely that the people watching *Shrew* that night would be seeing one of Tanya Dunseth's last public performances.

We turned away from the theaters and walked in the opposite direction. It was Sunday evening. Most of the gift shops, stores, and businesses were locked up for the night. The restaurants were still moderately busy as locals, finished for the day and the week in their own shops, ventured out for an evening meal now that most of the out-of-town visitors were otherwise engaged.

Toward the end of June, sunset doesn't arrive in southern Oregon until well after eight-thirty. In the gathering dusk, Alex and I wandered the deserted streets. Holding hands and not talking much, we window-shopped for a good half hour before stopping at an old-fashioned ice-cream parlor complete with a genuine soda fountain. There, over root-beer floats, we finally allowed ourselves to discuss what was going on.

I knew that Alex was upset. Even though she had never met Tanya Dunseth, she was convinced that Tanya was the real victim of the piece, that as someone who had suffered appalling abuse at Martin Shore's hands, Tanya had the God-given right to dish out whatever revenge she could manage. In fact, Alex held that a quick death was far too good for him. That was a surprising statement from an authentic card-carrying liberal.

"I think we should warn her," Alex declared as she hit the bottom of her glass and noisily sucked up the dregs of her float.

"Warn her?" I repeated. "Are you crazy?"

"Don't you think we should?"

"Absolutely not," I said, shaking my head.

"Why?"

"Didn't you hear what Detective Fraymore said? Warning her is the last thing we should do."

"She should have a chance to make some kind of care arrangements for Amber," Alex declared.

I tried to be patient. "You're not listening, Alex. This is a murder investigation. Homicide. Cops don't call up their top suspects in advance and say, 'By the way, maybe you'd like to hire a baby-sitter before we come drag your butt off to jail.' And they don't like it if other people do, either."

"She wouldn't really run away."

"What makes you think she wouldn't? And if she did and Fraymore found out about it, the two of us would end up in deep ca-ca, to quote the Laredo Kid."

Despite the seriousness of our discussion, Alex smiled at my reference to the afternoon's play. "At least you were paying attention to the dialogue," she said.

For a minute, I thought she might drop the subject. No such luck. The lady had a one-track mind. "If Tanya goes to prison—for years, let's say—what happens to Amber then?"

I shrugged. "The state appoints a guardian, most likely a relative."

"What if there aren't any? Didn't Kelly and Jeremy say something about her folks dying in a house fire when she was little? That's how she ended up with a guardian."

"There's always Amber's father."

"Right," Alex replied caustically. "If he walked out the day Tanya found out she was pregnant, I'm sure he's great fatherhood material. There has to be something we can do."

"Alex, listen to me. There's not one thing you and I can do. It's out of our hands. It never was *in* our hands."

She looked at me reproachfully. "I suppose you're right," she said at last. "It's just so awful. I mean, it's bad enough that she was forced to be in that terrible movie in the first place. . . ."

"Hold it," I said. "You're jumping to conclusions. What makes you so certain she was forced? She may have been a willing participant. Not legally, of course. But Kelly and Jeremy said she was out on her own. She probably made good money."

"At twelve?" Alex demanded. "Are you kidding? Kids that age don't make informed choices."

"Willing or not, here it is all these years later. She thinks she's put that part of her life totally behind her. Then, out of the blue, Martin Shore turns up and threatens to blow her nice, respectable new life right out of the water. I think he tried to blackmail her. When she didn't come across right away, he sent the tape to Dinky."

"How could it be blackmail?" Alex returned. "Tanya Dunseth doesn't have a dime. The actors down here aren't in it for the money. If she weren't poor as a church mouse, she wouldn't be living at Live Oak Farm."

"Maybe he wanted something besides money," I said.

"What?"

"Maybe he wanted her to work for him again, make another movie. In fact, since the tape showed up in Dinky's inter-office mail, maybe someone inside the Festival was working as Shore's accomplice. Anyway you slice it, a porno flick featuring a rising young legitimate actress would be a hot property."

"I don't like the way you're talking about this," Alex said levelly.

"How do you want me to talk? It's only a theory."

"Whatever's in that video was bad enough to make Denver Holloway physically ill. Here you are talking about it as though it's the latest money-making sitcom some network is getting ready to put into syndication."

"Porn's big business," I told her. "We're talking millions of dollars."

"I refuse to think about it that way," Alex returned. "I absolutely refuse." She didn't raise her voice, but the way she said the words should have warned me. I trudged right on.

"I'm a cop, Alex. I have to think that way. It's part of who I am. I've been working the streets for a long time now. Over the years, I've seen plenty of twelve-year-old hookers, little girls—and little boys, too, for that matter. Kids who would do anything for a price, including turn an unsuspecting John into a stiff. Once you've seen that a time or two, it's hard to regain your belief in absolute innocence."

What followed was a long silence. As the gulf between us grew wider, I felt a dull ache in my gut. Alexis Downey and I were having our first major disagreement—one that couldn't be walked around or ignored or swept under a rug. It wasn't over something inconsequential like lumpy futons or man-hating cats. We were staring into the fundamental differences between us, grappling with disparities that arose out of who we were, what we did, and what we believed.

I was seven years older than Alex. I had been a cop for almost twenty years, more than half her lifetime. Cops see too damn much.

"Well," she said finally, shaking her head and steadfastly pulling us back from the edge of the cliff. "I still think for blackmail to work, Tanya would have to have money."

The thought came to me then—a sudden, clear inkling of what else Martin Shore might have wanted from Tanya Dunseth. Just thinking about it made me feel incredibly old. And dirty. And right back on the edge of the precipice.

"Not necessarily," I said. "Maybe he wanted something else."

"What?"

Alex still didn't understand, and I didn't want to tell her, didn't want her to have to know some of the things I know—the ugly things all cops learn sooner or later because they have to. Because they don't have a choice. Alex sat there, her eyes holding mine, waiting for me to say something.

"The streets aren't the only things that have deteriorated over the last few years," I said. "Other things have gotten worse as well."

She frowned. "What's that supposed to mean?"

Choosing my words carefully, I tried my best to explain it without having to come right out and draw Alexis a picture.

"Years ago, eleven-or twelve-year-olds were young enough for this kind of filth. Not anymore. In terms of perpetrators getting away with it, the best candidates for sexual abuse and exploitation are still female children under the age of three. They can't testify, can't say who did it or what they did."

As she grasped what I was saying, Alex's eyes widened in horror. She studied me searchingly for some time after I finally shut up. "You mean Shore would try to blackmail Tanya to let him use her baby the same way? To make a movie?"

"It happens," I answered miserably. "I swear to God, Alex, this kind of crap goes on all the time. You have no idea."

"You're right," she spat back at me, suddenly furious. "I guess I haven't! And I don't think I want to, either!"

Without another word, she stormed out of the shop. I made no attempt to stop her. She needed to be alone for a while. So did I. It's no wonder so many disillusioned cops end up divorced and living alone. Who can live with them? According to the suicide statistics, they can barely stand to live with themselves.

I don't know how long I sat there. Eventually, one of the kids waiting tables came over and took away the remains of both root-beer floats. When he asked me if I wanted anything else, I looked up at him stupidly. The second time around I finally managed to order coffee. He must have thought I'd gone crazy.

Beating yourself up is simple, especially when you've had as much practice at it as I have. In retrospect, I could see exactly what I'd done wrong. Of course I should have kept quiet about my suspicions. Of course I shouldn't have brought up any of it. I was a dumb-ass bum for even mentioning such a thing. But I had, and now I couldn't take it back. The damage was done, and I couldn't see any way in hell to make it better.

Unless, I thought, brightening suddenly at the prospect—unless I could somehow come up with some other theory and prove myself wrong. For people who are expert self-castigators, it's easy to recognize how being totally wrong can turn into a walk-away victory. And if, in order to prove myself sufficiently wrong, I had to bend a few rules, so what? It wouldn't be the first time.

And that's how I really ended up getting involved in Gordon Fraymore's case. Personally involved, I mean. Not because I particularly wanted to, and not, God help me, because I wanted to make his life miserable. Not at all. What I really wanted was to find some way to redeem myself in Alexis Downey's eyes.

I had trotted out only one of my pet theories. I had plenty more where that came from. The first one had been ugly enough to drive Alex away from me and out into the night. There were no guarantees that the real answer, whatever that might be, wouldn't be even worse. But if it meant not losing Alex permanently, I had to make the effort.

So I sat there all by myself and drank cup after cup of coffee. I tried to think my way into Gordon Fraymore's case the same way I'd be trying to think myself into one of my own if I were back home in Seattle and officially assigned to a new homicide investigation. Only here there was an added dimension. My only access to the killer was through what I had learned or could learn from Detective Gordon Fraymore.

At the start of a case, I usually try to do a mental sort, drawing a picture of who all the players are and trying to see how they're interconnected. Because most people are killed by someone they know, that process often leads directly to the killer or to people who know the killer.

To that end, I grabbed a folded napkin out of the holder and began drawing little *X*'s and *O*'s all over it. At the center of the diagram were Tanya and Amber Dunseth. In a circle around them were Martin Shore, Jeremy, Kelly, Monica Davenport, Dinky Holloway, and me. I was about to quit when I realized there were two other people I needed to add, equal *O*'s on the same line—Daphne and Guy Lewis.

I closed my eyes and tried to remember exactly how it had been when Daphne and Guy had stepped inside the Members' Lounge prior to the donors' party. There had been no mistaking Tanya Dunseth's intense reaction. My only problem was figuring out which of the two she'd been reacting to—Gordon or Daphne.

And then something clicked in my mind and gave me my first little glimmer of hope. Guy Lewis. Here was a man who'd already discarded one wife and was having trouble hanging on to number two. Was it possible he was in the market for yet another trophy wife, or maybe just a trophy plaything? I had thought his wave was intended for me, but I wondered now if perhaps it had been intended for Tanya. Maybe he knew more about Tanya Dunseth than just her roles on stage.

Filled with purpose now, I shoved my coffee cup aside, stuffed the napkin into my pocket, and headed for the Mark Anthony. Alex had told me the Lewises were staying there. This time I had no trouble ignoring the smoke, laughter, and pulsing music from the bar. I hurried to the nearest house phone.

"Guy Lewis, please."

"Is he a registered guest?"

"Yes."

There was a long pause. "I'm sorry, Mr. Lewis checked out this morning."

I put down the phone. Disappointed, I was conscious of the smoke and the sounds in a different way now, but I hurried back out into the street before they had a chance to ensnare me. Outside, I was momentarily undecided.

The first few playgoers were just now trickling down the hill from the theaters. Soon it would be a river of people. Seeing them, I decided to go back to Oak Hill. Alex and I had only one house key between us, and Alex had taken that one with her. If I went home now, maybe one of the other guests would take pity and let me inside the house as they returned from the plays. Maybe I could ask Florence for a duplicate. Otherwise, I'd have to go looking for someplace else to stay.

I found the Porsche where we'd left it parked. Seeing it, I was awash with guilt at the idea of Alex walking all the way home in the dark by herself. That night I was a living, breathing guilt magnet.

I drove back to the B & B. Except for a night-light burning in the living room, the place was dark, including the windows in the Iris Room up under the eaves. Either Alex was asleep or she hadn't come home. No other cars were parked beside the house. That meant I was the first one home.

Discouraged, I got out of the car. The weight of the world bore down on my shoulders as I walked up the steps.

"Beau? Are you all right?"

Alex spoke to me out of a gloom of shadows. I walked toward the sound of her voice. She was seated on a swing at the far end of the porch, wrapped snugly in one of the blankets from our bed.

"I waited up to let you in," she said. "I knew you didn't have a key."

"Thanks." I sat down gingerly on the far end of the swing. "I'm sorry about tonight. I never should have . . ."

"Don't apologize," she said. "I was shocked by what you said, but maybe you're right. Maybe Amber is what Martin Shore wanted."

That sounded very much like forgiveness. I gave myself permission to hope.

Alex continued, "So I thought to myself, if that's the case, she probably did kill him, and she's going to need a good lawyer, so I went ahead and called Ralph."

"You called Ralph Ames?"

"Who else? I hope you're not mad at me. He was the first lawyer I thought of, and I know he's good. And I happened to know where to reach him after hours."

"Oh, he's good all right," I agreed. "What did he say?"

"He said he'd be here tomorrow for the wedding, and we could talk about it then. If he can't handle it himself, I'm sure he'll recommend someone. He says he'll fly into Medford first thing. He'll be here around nine."

It was a done deal. Further comment seemed unnecessary.

"And he said for you not to worry about Karen and Dave. That's all handled. They're meeting Scott and should be getting into Medford shortly after Ralph does. They'll rent their own car. They should be here by noon."

The first of the other playgoers' cars turned into the driveway. In the sudden wash of headlights, Alex leaned over and kissed me on the side of my neck.

"What do you think?" she asked. "Is that okay? I worried I was overstepping the bounds."

"You didn't overstep anything," I answered. "And I think it's more than okay. I think it's great."

And right that minute, so was I.

8

I'm not one to spend time worrying about the future. When some people learn they're about to become parents, they peer down a long time tunnel and see everything from front teeth falling out to learner's permits, from Tee-ball games to high school graduations.

My mother always told me that living in the future was borrowing trouble, and I believed her. Consequently, I never gave much thought to my daughter's wedding day; never imagined how it might be with Kelly garbed all in white, in a church festooned with flowers, and all that. Karen had, so the way it turned out was a whole lot harder on her than it was on me.

It didn't start out all that badly. Ralph breezed into town and stopped at the Oak Hill Bed-and-Breakfast at five after ten the next morning. He dragged a loaded suitcase into the living room and set it down.

"What's that?" I asked.

"I wasn't sure you packed any suitable father-of-the-bride attire," he said. "I brought some along just in case."

As a matter of fact, once I knew Dave Livingston and Karen would be in attendance, I had been concerned about clothes. For one thing, Dave Livingston is a natty dresser—he had turned up in Wickenburg, Arizona, wearing a three-piece suit, for God's sake. I was sure he would show me up. Alex had taken me to task, telling me it was Kelly's day, and it wasn't a competition, but it had bugged me all the same.

By the time I woke up that morning and thought about calling Ralph to have him bring along some other clothes, it was too late. He was already on his way. But that's the kind of guy Ralph is— the kind of friend. He had figured it out and acted on his own without needing any coaching from me.

After I carted the suitcase up to Alex's and my room, we took Ralph, some mugs, and an extra pot of coffee and adjourned to the lawn chairs on Oak Hill's secluded backyard deck.

"So tell me about this friend of Kelly's who's in so much hot water," Ralph said. "You all must have had an exceptionally busy time of it down here."

And so we told him. Ralph Ames listened patiently while Alex and I took turns recounting the various pieces of Tanya's story— telling him about Martin Shore's death and about the pornographic-film connection between Shore and the Festival's rising young actress. We told him about the Henckels slicer that had disappeared from a Festival prop table only to show up later as a murder weapon. We did a joint rendition of what we could remember of Tanya Dunseth's background, repeating as close to verbatim as possible what Kelly and Jeremy had told us. We were just in the process of recounting her economic rescue by Marjorie Connors when Florence, the retired schoolteacher/owner of Oak Hill B & B, came rushing out onto the deck.

By then Florence had been informed of the father/daughter connection between her part-time maid, Kelly Beaumont, and me. Florence seemed somewhat flustered.

"Sorry to interrupt, Mr. Beaumont," she said, "but someone named Karen is at the front door. She wants to speak to you. She looks a lot like your daughter. Could it be Kelly's mother?"

It certainly could. Nodding and prepared for some unpleasantness, I got up and headed inside. As I walked past, Alex reached out and gave my leg an encouraging pat. "Want me to go along?" she asked.

"No, I'm a big boy. I think I can manage." All the same, I wasn't looking forward to the coming encounter.

I found Dave Livingston and Karen seated on the now-sunny porch swing where I'd discovered Alex concealed in shadows the night before. Karen is an attractive woman—always has been. She seemed to have lost weight since I last saw her, and that was fine. She had regained some of her girlish figure, but her face looked haggard. Her eyes were red and puffy, as though she'd spent most of the previous night crying. The skin on her cheeks seemed drawn too thin over her jawline, and dark smudges encircled her eyes. Standing next to her, Dave Livingston didn't look so hot, either. They were both worn-out.

I glanced around, searching for my son, Scott. I caught sight of him—rangy, well-built, and full grown—still out in the driveway, lounging casually against a rented Lincoln Town Car with his hands shoved deep in his pants pockets. He nodded in my direction, but he made no move toward the porch. Smart boy, I thought. It was wise to stay out of range until it became clear whether or not pyroclastic blasts would be the order of the day.

Before I stepped out the door, I pasted what was supposed to be a sincerely welcoming grin on my face, although I probably succeeded only in looking idiotic. "Hello, Karen," I said.

Secretly, I hoped she'd be impressed by the fact that I'd beaten the odds and stayed sober far longer than she or anyone else had expected. If she cared or even noticed, she didn't say.

Dave got up and ambled over to shake my hand. For some reason, he seemed genuinely happy to see me. Karen didn't. She sat in the swing staring up at my face.

"Hello yourself," she said woodenly.

It's sad to realize how people change; hard to believe that a man and woman who once meant the world to one another can drift apart completely until they're reduced to being virtual strangers; all but impossible to acknowledge that they can evolve so far from what they once were—lovers, sharing their innermost thoughts, dreams, and secrets—to alien beings with less than nothing to say to each other.

"Great day for a wedding, don't you think?" I asked, wanting to lighten things up and hoping no one would notice the sudden catch in my throat. Instant tears brimmed in Karen's eyes just as they had in Kelly's when we'd exchanged words on the farmhouse steps at Live Oak Farm two days earlier. Like mother, like daughter, I thought. I've always been a sucker for tears.

"I wanted her to have a perfect wedding," Karen choked. "I never wanted it to be like . . . like this!"

Dave hurried back to Karen's side. He sat down next to her and placed a comforting hand on her knee. "It'll be all right, Karen. You'll see."

"Well," I said awkwardly, "I'm glad you came."

Karen swallowed hard. "I didn't want to," she retorted with some of her customary bite. "And I wouldn't have, either, if Dave hadn't insisted. He said if we didn't make the effort now, we might lose Kelly for good."

Dave glanced up at me in a frank but silent appeal for help. His look touched me. For the first time, I realized that having spent years living with the same woman, the two of us had something in common, a bond. So do veterans of foreign wars.

"That's probably true," I said. "About losing Kelly, I mean. I'm sure she'll be delighted to see you."

After that, I floundered around some more, desperately searching for something sensible to say, something relatively noncontroversial. My mother always insisted weather was a safe topic, no matter what. Squinting up at the sun, I gave that a try. "I imagine you've heard that the ceremony's going to be outdoors, at a place called Lithia Park," I said. "It's a good thing the weather's so nice today."

"We haven't heard a thing," Karen responded icily, her voice taking on a sharp and all-too-familiar edge. "I suppose you're paying for all this?"

Allegedly, it takes two to make a quarrel. I'm not so sure. I was doing my best not to fight, but Karen's baiting made it tough to keep from lashing out in return. It seemed to me she had a hell of a lot of nerve acting so pissed. What had I done?

To be honest, probably a lot. I've never claimed to be the best of all possible husbands and fathers. When Karen left me to marry Dave—which she did with unseemly haste, I might add—she wiped me out financially. Took my money and ran, as the saying goes. I know from the kids that Dave makes good money and that he and Karen are pretty well off.

When Anne Corley died much later, leaving me as the astonished sole beneficiary of her estate, I made no secret of my changed and much improved circumstances, and I wasn't chintzy about sharing that money with the kids. Unlike some divorced dads, I never ducked my child support. So why was Karen so mad at me?

At the time, I decided she was simply furious with the world in general, and I was the most likely target. Whatever the cause, over the years I've read all those sad letters in Ann Landers' column, the ones about feuding former spouses routinely spoiling their children's weddings. I was determined not to let that happen here. This particular wedding already had far too many strikes against it.

"I'm not paying for a thing," I answered, keeping my hackles down and my tone civil. "Kelly and Jeremy haven't asked me to. They're doing it all themselves."

"Jeremy!" Karen scoffed. "Who is he, anyway? Where does he come from? What does his father do? Are his parents here? And how pregnant is she?"

In order of importance, I believe Karen saved her top-priority question for last. I realized that once she and Dave saw Kelly, the question of how far along Kelly was would no longer be an issue.

"More than slightly," I said.

"Too late to do something about it?"

Which told me the real bottom line. Like me, Karen had come hightailing it to Ashland thinking she could somehow convince Kelly to call off the wedding. No doubt she hoped to persuade her daughter to give up the baby or to have an abortion and get her life back on track.

One of the differences between us was that I'd had the benefit of an extra day, a critical twenty-four hours of adjustment time that had allowed me to make an uneasy peace with the changed order of things. During that time, I had caught a glimpse of Kelly and Jeremy both. I had seen them struggling together to do whatever kinds of work were necessary for them to live independently, away from all parental influence.

If they were making their own way in the world and not asking for any help, it seemed to me that we, as parents, no longer had a right to tell them what to do. If we ever had that right in the first place.

"It's too late to put the toothpaste back in the tube," I said as kindly as I could. "If we're smart, we won't even try."

"You're saying I'm supposed to come all the way up here, go to the damn wedding, and that's it?"

"Actually," I said with one of Ralph Ames' cheerful, looking-on-the-bright-side smiles, "you get to do one more thing."

"What's that?"

"You get to keep your mouth shut. We all do."

Dave Livingston was suddenly overcome by a paroxysm of coughing that may have disguised a chuckle. When I looked over at him to see if he was all right, he winked at me and nodded.

"That's what I've been trying to tell her ever since we left home," he managed.

Karen turned her scathing glance on him. "Don't *you* start," she raged.

Dave stifled. Meantime, Scott realized it was safe and gradually edged his way onto the porch. When he got within reach, I grabbed his shoulders and hugged him, holding him close.

"Hiya, Pop," he said with an easy, affable grin. "I hear you're going to be a grandfather."

It wasn't until Scott said the words aloud that it finally hit home—the grandfather part, I mean. Until then, the idea of grandfatherhood had somehow gotten lost in the shuffle of all the other wedding details and logistics. Like I said before, I'm not the kind of guy who puts a lot of focus on the future.

Behind me the front door opened, and Alexis Downey stepped

out onto the porch, joining the rest of us as easily as if she were already an official part of this somewhat prickly extended family. She offered her hand to Scott and then waited to be introduced.

At Alex's and my advanced respective ages, the words "boy-friend" and "girlfriend" somehow stick in my craw. I'm never quite sure how to go about explaining our relationship.

"Scott," I said, "this is my friend Alexis Downey, Alex for short. Alex, this is my son, Scott."

Alex looked up at him. Scott's a good-looking kid if I do say so myself. "I'd recognize you anywhere," she said with a cordial smile. "You look just like your dad."

I introduced her to Karen and Dave as well. "I didn't know you had friends in Ashland," Karen said stiffly, taking in everything about Alexis Downey in one long, critical inspection.

"Oh, I'm from Seattle," Alex returned. "Beau and I drove down to Ashland together on Saturday."

With those two sentences, the formal lines of battle were irrevo-cably drawn, at least on Karen's side, although I couldn't for the life of me figure out why. I thought Karen was done with me. Our divorce had been final for more than six years. She had even been kind to me, years before, when Anne Corley died, so why was she angry or jealous now? None of it made sense. Maybe to someone else, but not to me.

"Kelly just called," Alex continued lightly. "She says the people out at the farm have put together an informal buffet brunch in honor of the bride and groom. We're all invited to stop by before we get dressed to go to the park."

"What farm?" Karen asked. "Kelly lives on a farm?"

"It's a boardinghouse kind of arrangement," I explained. "The landlady lets her tenants work off part of the rent so it doesn't cost so much for them to live there."

"I'll bet it's filthy," Karen said. "The landlady's probably some kind of kook."

It was weird to find me, of all people, defending Marjorie Con-nors, but in hopes of maintaining the peace, I did.

"No," I said, "you're wrong. I've met the lady in question. She's definitely no kook. Far too severe for that. Jeremy told us that Marjorie is altogether opposed to marriage. I'm surprised she's even allowing a brunch, but let's not disappoint them. Live Oak Farm isn't far, but we'll all need to take cars. Alex and I will lead the way."

We sorted up into a three-vehicle minicaravan, with Ralph Ames and Scott in Ralph's rental Lincoln bringing up the rear. I wondered how many more Lincolns there could possibly be at the Medford airport, but it was a relief for Alex and me to be alone together in the Porsche—and in relative peace and quiet.

"You're doing fine," she assured me. "Just maintain your cool and keep clam."

I smiled at that. "Keep clam" is a Seattle insiders' joke, attributable to Ivar Haglund, one of the Emerald City's best-loved and now-deceased seafood restaurateurs.

"Karen's really on a tear today," I said, shaking my head. "I don't think I've ever seen her quite this way before."

"Probably just the shock of it all," Alex suggested. "She's upset and taking it out on whoever's within range." Alex stopped for a moment as if considering. "Karen wasn't always like this?"

"No," I answered. "Not at all. One of the things I always liked best about her was her sense of humor, her ability to find the bright side in even the direst circumstances. She had her moments, of course, like we all do, and then she was hell on wheels, but most of the time, she was fine."

"People change," Alex said with a shrug. "That's life."

I was glad Karen was riding with Dave as we threaded our way through the abandoned automobiles and past the remains of the demolished barn. We stopped in the yard near where skeletal but unusable steps led up to the front porch where ancient Sunshine still ruled supreme. The dog hobbled over to the edge of the decking, barking feebly. No one seemed to pay any attention.

"How do we get past that dog?" Karen demanded.

"We go around back," I said, leading the way.

Halfway around the house, Kelly met us. When she and Karen saw each other, they both stopped and stared. Someone had pinned

Kelly's long blond hair up in an elegant French twist on the back of her head. The hairdo made her look far older, more sophisticated. She wore a one-piece tent-dress-type smock in navy blue with white collar and cuffs. She looked glowingly happy and healthy, the way pregnant women often do. Her smile was as radiant as any self-respecting bride's.

"Hello, Mom," Kelly said softly. "How are you?"

And then they were in each other's arms, both of them laughing and crying and talking at once.

Alex leaned over to me. "See there?" she whispered. "That wasn't so bad, now was it?"

Dave had dropped back and was walking with Scott and Ralph. He caught up with us just in time to see Karen and Kelly embrace. His jawline tightened.

"I forgot something back in the car," he muttered. Turning around, he hurried back the way we'd come. Dave's a fairly tall man, but he walked with his shoulders hunched forward. As he went, he swiped impatiently at his face with his sleeve. He was crying, and I wondered what about.

God, I'm stupid sometimes!

Live Oak Farm's brunch was held in the great outdoors. There were far more people than I had expected, twenty-five or thirty in all, not counting family, including several cast members I recognized from the two shows we had managed to see. Tanya was there, laughing and talking, most of the time with Amber balanced handily on one outthrust hip. I watched her with some interest, wondering not only whether or not Gordon Fraymore had spoken to her, but also if he was right.

Cop instinct said that Fraymore would have made a move prior to this. For a murder suspect, Tanya Dunseth put on a hell of a show. To a casual observer, she might have seemed at ease, totally in control, but I am first and foremost a detective. My life and the lives of my fellow officers often depend on how good I am at reading people, at deciphering their actions and motives, at predicting behavior. Beneath Tanya's animated facade of forced gaiety, I sensed a brittleness that hadn't been there Saturday night in the Members' Lounge. Fraymore had talked to her, all right, and Tanya Dunseth was scared to death.

As I stood back and observed her, it was strange to compare her smooth portrayal of the doomed Juliet to this other role, a real-life one that didn't suit her nearly as well. I don't suppose that's surprising. After all, a play's just that—a play. Romeo and Juliet, the actors, had laughed and joked with one another within minutes of the final curtain. Martin Shore's murder had occurred in real life; Gordon Fraymore's hulking presence was no laughing matter.

Questions of guilt or innocence aside, I had to salute Tanya for her valiant effort at not letting her personal problems interfere with Kelly and Jeremy's prenuptial celebration. She wasn't big, and she didn't appear to be particularly strong, but Tanya Dunseth was one tough cookie.

Gradually, I was drawn away from observing her and back into the ebb and flow of the party. With all the laughter and easy conversation, it seemed more like a post-wedding reception than a pre ceremony buffet. Since I wasn't paying for any of it, I kept quiet, opening my mouth only when spoken to or to chow down on the plentiful food.

Heavily laden tables decorated with red-checkered tablecloths dotted the entire back deck. Someone had spread garlands of flowers along the tops of the deck's newly framed handrails. Jeremy had warned us that Marjorie Connors didn't approve of weddings and wouldn't be a part of this one, but I wondered about that. Although she wasn't physically present, I felt Marjorie's handiwork—and her capable touch—everywhere.

The food was festive and delicious—cold fried chicken, various kinds of pasta, Jell-O and potato salads, sliced cheeses, baked beans, fresh fruit pies, and hunks of still-warm, freshly made, round-shaped bread that Ralph insisted had to have come from a DAK automatic bread-maker, whatever that was. The bread looked funny, but dabbed with sweet butter, it tasted fine.

Jeremy showed up wearing a pair of neat new chinos, a clean white shirt, and regular shoes. I was relieved to see he had ditched the Birkenstocks in honor of the occasion. He seemed appropriately nervous as he was introduced to Dave and Karen, then he backed off, leaving them to visit with Kelly. When it came time to eat, he ended up sitting with Alex and me at one of the smaller tables.

"You're probably wondering about all this," he said, glancing around at the milling people while I worried about whether or not he was somehow able to read my mind.

"Since we only have the one night for our honeymoon, we don't want to stay at the reception very long, but two-thirty was the earliest we could have the park. After the ceremony, we'll head over to Salishan, on the coast, just as soon as we can get away. This gives us a chance to visit with some of our friends. And relatives," he added lamely after a pause.

Damn. I was starting to like the kid in spite of myself.

It must have been about one or so when the party started to break up. For one thing, we all had to go somewhere else and change into our wedding clothes. Everyone was busy—clearing away dishes, taking care of food, folding up tables and chairs. And with the adults all occupied, Amber Dunseth managed to slip away.

Losing a child is every parent's worst nightmare, but little kids get lost all the time. One second they're where they're supposed to be. The next minute they're gone completely. Tanya was first to raise the alarm. Before long all the partygoers were drafted into the search. We spread out in every direction, beating the bushes, looking, and calling.

Thinking Amber might have toddled off down the road, I went that way, and I was the one who happened to luck out and find her. She had somehow made her way out to that battered hulk of a wrecked Chrysler and had climbed up on the moldering old bench seat. I found her there, sound asleep in the warm sun. Careful not to frighten her, I woke her gently and was carrying her back to the house when Scott came racing down the road toward us, yelling.

"Dad! Dad, come quick!"

I had heard that terrible note of panic in Scott's voice only once before in his whole life. He had been teaching Kelly to ride his bike, even though we'd warned him repeatedly that she was too little and couldn't handle a two-wheeler. When the bike wrecked, she'd gone ass-over-teakettle on a patch of newly graveled pavement. She was lying in the road scraped and bleeding when Scott came running to me for help.

"What is it?" I called back, quickening my pace. "What's wrong?"

"It's Kelly," he managed. "She fell."

I ran then. When we met, I thrust Amber at him like a quarterback handing off a football. "Where?" I demanded.

"Around the side of the house. There's a door with steps leading down to the basement. I think it's real bad," he added. "Go quick."

After that I ran, as fast as I ever remember running in my life. I had to push my way through a milling knot of people clustered around the basement door. A slash of dust-filled sunlight glinted down into semidarkness, lighting a set of heavy plank stairs. At the bottom, another clutch of people crouched on their knees in a tight circle.

"Is she all right?" I heard myself asking as I scrambled down the stairs. "Is she okay? Somebody tell me what happened."

Kelly lay in a rag-doll heap at the bottom of the stairs, her feet still on the next-to-last step. The force of her fall had knocked the pins loose from the French twist, letting her blond hair spill around her head like pooling water on the hard, packed-dirt floor. Dave Livingston knelt beside her while a stricken Jeremy stood over them, staring off into the middle distance with his hands dangling uselessly at his sides.

"What happened, for God's sake?" I repeated when nobody answered me. "Did she faint or what?"

"At least she's breathing," Dave said. "Pulse is rapid but weak. Where's that blanket? Dammit, I told somebody to get me a blanket."

"Here!" I looked up in time to see a white-faced Karen thrust a blanket in my direction. I handed it down to Dave, and the two of us struggled clumsily in our hurry to cover Kelly's appallingly still body.

"Did someone call nine-one-one?" I asked.

"Alex said she would," Dave answered grimly. "I hope to God they hurry."

Behind me on the stairs I heard the unmistakable sound of someone starting to retch. Jesus Christ! Was somebody going to throw up? Why the hell didn't he just go back outside and stay out of the way?

I looked up then, hoping to dodge out of the path of flying puke, and that's when I saw the spectral figure that held Jeremy Todd Cartwright's eyes captive.

In the far corner of the room, a human form dangled heavily at the end of a rope. I was still squinting through the semidarkness and trying to make out exactly who and what it was when someone switched on the light.

There, caught in the frail yellow glow of a single bulb, was Daphne Lewis, still wearing the Icelandic sweater she had worn in the Members' Lounge. The farmhouse was old-fashioned post-and-beam construction. In the course of refurbishing the place, new lumber had been sistered onto old to provide bracing for some of the sagging originals holding up the floor joists. The rope, complete with a professional-looking hangman's noose, had been strung through the intersection of two of those braces.

As soon as I saw the deadly hangman's noose, I knew it was something I had seen before—onstage at the Black Swan Theater. It was one of the props from *The Majestic Kid.*

There was no point in running over to Daphne. Obviously dead, she was far beyond help. Kelly was the one who needed all our attention.

I clung to the stubborn hope that she wouldn't die. And that the baby wouldn't, either.

9

Tires crunched in the gravel beside me, jarring me out of my torpor and back into the present, back to an awareness of the world around me. I had no idea how long I'd been walking, nor did I care. Since I'd left Ashland Community Hospital, time had ceased to exist.

"Get in, Mr. Beaumont. I'll take you back to the hospital." Gordon Fraymore reached across the front seat of his Chevrolet Lumina and opened the door.

"I'd rather walk."

"Don't be stubborn. Do you want to see your granddaughter or not?"

Granddaughter. Granddaughter? It took a moment to assimilate the word. "Kelly's baby? A girl. She's all right then?"

"The baby's fine."

Without another word, I climbed in the car. "And Kelly?" I asked, buckling my seat belt. "My daughter. How's she?"

Fraymore shrugged and shook his head while he wrenched the car into a sharp U-turn and accelerated in the opposite direction.

"Couldn't say. All I know is, they said the baby's fine and asked me to find you and bring you back."

"Thanks," I said.

"Nothing to it. After you see the baby, we have to talk."

"Sure, sure. No problem."

Eager to be back at the hospital, I was surprised to see how far I'd walked and how long it took to drive there. I had covered a distance of several miles without even noticing. Given the kind of mindless daze I was in, it's a wonder a car hadn't hit me.

We drove for some time in silence. Finally, Fraymore cleared his throat. "The way I figure it, your daughter must have fainted when she saw the body there in the basement."

"Must have," I agreed.

"You knew her, didn't you?"

"Knew who?"

"The dead woman."

"Daphne Lewis? Yes. Vaguely."

"You're a regular walking, talking crime wave all by your little lonesome, aren't you, Detective Beaumont? Seems like everyone you know who's here in Ashland is either getting hurt or murdered or both."

Most police officers would have taken the situation with Kelly into consideration and cut me a little slack. Not Gordon Fraymore. His capacity for civility seemed remarkably limited, even for a cop. A few grunted sentences had totally depleted his supply of congeniality.

With my impaired mental faculties, we pulled into the hospital parking lot before I could phrase an appropriately malicious response. Indignant, I hopped from the car and marched off toward the building. When my feet touched the ground, I bit back a yelp of torment. I had been in the car for only a few minutes. As soon as I put weight on my feet, a spike of pain from my bone spurs shot up both legs from heel to hip. So much for signing up for one of those Volkswalks.

Limping toward the door as best I could, I was met by a somber

Alexis Downey, who hurried outside to greet me. "How's Kelly?" I asked.

Alex shook her head. "Still touch and go. The doctors are doing a craniotomy to relieve the pressure."

Her words struck terror in my soul. With Kelly suffering a concussion, a fractured skull, and possible swelling on the brain, the options for prognosis included everything from total recovery to permanent brain damage. Informed by a lifetime of having seen too much, I prepared myself for the worst.

"They're afraid Kelly's going to die, aren't they?" I said. "That's why they went ahead and took the baby."

"No, that's not it at all," Alex replied. "She went into premature labor. With her unconscious, a C-section was the only thing they could do."

"How's Jeremy holding up?"

"Not very well. He's been down by the nursery staring in the window ever since they brought the baby up from the operating room. I feel sorry for him. He doesn't have anyone."

"Is that a hint?" Alex said nothing, but I got the message.

Inside the waiting room, I was faced with two distinct types of emotional quicksand. I could venture into the emotion-charged mire with Karen, Dave, and Scott, who were seated on a couch and love seat and huddled in hushed conversation, or I could go talk to Jeremy. He was visible in the hallway outside the nursery window, leaning forlornly against the glass. I chose Jeremy.

He barely glanced up when I stopped behind him. "How's it going?" I asked.

He shook his head and didn't answer. Then, after a deep breath, he said, "Karen's fine."

"Well, of course she is," I returned impatiently. What kind of goofball comment was that? I wondered.

"Why wouldn't she be? She's right out there in the lobby. I saw her just a minute ago."

I looked over his shoulder and peered into the nursery window. Inside, only one baby—a tiny, red-faced, pink-swathed gnome—

lay on her back in a movable incubator. Her face was screwed up in a full-volume screech that sliced through the intervening window. A handwritten three-by-five card attached to the incubator's plastic hood read, KAREN LOUISE BEAUMONT.

So that's who Jeremy meant. *This* Karen was indeed all right. Pissed off, same as her grandmother, but all right just the same.

"It was the tetracycline," Jeremy said despairingly while I gazed with rapt attention at the squalling infant.

"I beg your pardon?"

"The tetracycline," he repeated. "Kelly was taking it for a strep throat. Nobody told her the medication would neutralize her birth-control pills. Believe me, Mr. Beaumont, we didn't want it to be this way. We both wanted a big church wedding with all the trimmings, but . . ."

He broke off, sobbing and disconsolate, and slumped against the gray wall. I wanted to hold him, to offer him comfort, but my feet were welded to the floor, my hands Superglued to my hips. I didn't know what to do or say.

"I love her," Jeremy went on hopelessly. "What'll I do if she dies? Oh God, what'll Karen and I do then?"

It was a despairing, gut-wrenching plea for help, for answers. I wanted to say, "Snap out of it, Jeremy. Pull yourself together. Don't even *think* such a thing." I'm superstitious enough to believe that giving way to such thoughts can open the door for potential disaster.

At last my hands moved, almost of their own volition. I reached out and put one arm across Jeremy Todd Cartwright's quaking shoulder. "You make do," I said slowly. "You take it one day at a time and do the very best you can for you and for your child."

Jeremy shuddered in a herculean effort to pull himself together. "Is that what you did after your second wife died?"

So Kelly had told him about Anne Corley, about what had happened between us. Anne wasn't exactly a deep-dark family secret, but it startled me to hear Jeremy mention her. It felt strange to be discussing her with a young man I hardly knew, but then I realized that the pain of what had happened to me then uniquely qualified me to help Jeremy now.

"Pretty much," I said.

He was silent for a time. "Do you think she'll die?"

"I don't know. What do the doctors say?"

"The doctors don't talk to me," he snorted bitterly. "They talk to your wife—excuse me, to your ex-wife, to Kelly's mother, but not to me. I'm only the father here, not the husband."

Once more he dissolved in anguished tears. Jeremy Cartwright was a boy in man's clothing. My heart went out to him. This time, I wrapped both arms around his broad shoulders and held him close. He clung to me desperately, like a small frightened child, even though he stood a good two inches taller than I am. Hot tears coursed down the back of my shirt, leaking under my collar and trickling in tiny rivulets between my shoulder blades. At last he quieted and pulled away.

"Come on," I said, taking his arm. "Let's go outside."

"I can't leave," he objected. "She's still in the O.R."

"Just outside to get some air," I told him. "It'll do you good. Someone will come find you if you're needed."

I led him out to the same concrete bench where I had sat some hours earlier. The sun had moved far to the west and was headed down behind the line of encircling hills. Despite sitting in the hot afternoon air where the temperature still hovered in the high 90s, Jeremy shivered uncontrollably.

"Cold?" I asked.

He nodded. "How can that be?" He stared down at the film of gooseflesh covering his arms.

"A kind of delayed shock, maybe," I suggested.

He balled his hands into fists, watching them open and close with puzzled interest, as though they were unfamiliar appendages attached to some alien body.

"I called the hotel and canceled our reservation," he said huskily. "Since we can't use the room, I didn't want to pay for it. We can't afford it. I don't know how we're going to pay the hospital bill. We had budgeted enough for the baby, but this . . ." He broke off, shaking his head.

"You don't have hospitalization?"

"For me," he answered, "but not for Kelly and the baby. I couldn't add dependent coverage because we weren't married."

"It'll be all right," I said. "Don't worry about that."

Gordon Fraymore came out through the hospital doors just then, looked around, spotted us, and then started in our direction. "They want you inside," he said when he reached us.

"Both of us?" I asked.

"No, him." Fraymore nodded curtly toward Jeremy, who rose at once and rabbited away. Uninvited, the detective took Jeremy's vacated spot on the bench. First he popped a Tums, then he lit a cigarette.

"I'm pissed at you, Beaumont," he said evenly enough. "So's the county sheriff, for that matter. I just thought you should know."

The word "mister" had evidently disappeared from Gordon Fraymore's lexicon.

"The sheriff? How come he's mad at me? I don't even know him."

"Believe me, he knows you," Fraymore said. "I gave him the full scoop. Live Oak Farm's in the county, so Daphne Lewis is theirs same as Martin Shore is mine. We figure the two homicides are related, so we're conducting a joint operation."

Great. Complete stranger or not, whoever the sheriff of Jackson County was, he already hated my guts. Gordon Fraymore had seen to it.

"So why are you bent out of shape?"

"Because you held out on me, for one thing. Why didn't you tell me Tanya Dunseth had some kind of beef going with Daphne Lewis?"

"Because I didn't know."

"Like hell you didn't!" Fraymore returned more forcefully. "We've talked to several people who were in the Members' Lounge the other night. They all tell me the same thing—that Tanya Dunseth fell all apart as soon as Daphne Lewis walked into the room. You were there. You must have seen it."

He had me dead to rights. I nodded. "There was a reaction, but I couldn't tell for sure if it was because of Daphne or because of Guy," I returned. "They came in together. For all I know, it could have been either one of them or both."

"You should have told me about it," Fraymore insisted.

"You're talking twenty-twenty hindsight," I said. "At the time it happened, nobody was dead yet. Later, after Martin Shore died, there was no way to tie those two incidents together. Besides, it didn't seem like that big a deal. I still don't see any connection."

"The connection is none of your business, but it is a big deal," Fraymore countered. "A woman's dead, dammit. I'm tempted to file obstruction charges against you."

"Give me a break. You know as well as I do that if I had volunteered any information, you would have climbed my frame for violating your turf."

Fraymore frowned and seemed to consider. Finally, he said, "I'll think about giving you that break. In the meantime, you'd better tell me everything you know."

"Like what?"

"Like what the hell happened at that party—and I *do* mean *everything*."

"We were still in the Members' Lounge waiting for *Henry* to get out when Tanya came in with that young actor who plays Romeo. She happened to sit down next to me. We started visiting."

"Another coincidence, I suppose?" Fraymore ventured dryly.

"Hardly. She and my daughter are friends. Kelly takes care of Amber, Tanya's daughter. We were still chatting when the Lewises came in. When Tanya saw Daphne and Guy, she looked like she'd seen a ghost. She was so startled she spilled her drink."

"Did she say anything to you about them?"

"No."

"Did she talk to them?"

"No, not at all. As soon as she saw them, she took off. I thought she was going to the bar to refill her drink, but she left the party completely."

"And didn't come back?"

"No."

"Did she show up later at the Bowmer?"

"She might have, but I didn't see her there."

"Let's go back to the Lewises. Did they speak to you?"

"Briefly. We exchanged a few words."

"What about?"

"Mostly about cars, as I recall."

"Cars? Did they say anything to you about Tanya?"

"Not really. Guy mentioned that he had seen her play Juliet and thought she was very good."

"He didn't hint around that something might be going on between either himself and Tanya or Daphne and Tanya?"

"No, not at all. Why don't you ask Guy Lewis about it?" I asked. "Maybe he knows."

"Guy Lewis left town."

"Oh," I said. It didn't seem wise to mention to Gordon Fraymore that I already had spoken to the desk clerk at the Mark Anthony and had learned that very thing. If the detective discovered I'd been nosing around on Guy Lewis' tail, my already shaky situation would deteriorate immeasurably.

"So tell me how it is that you, a lowly Seattle homicide dick, happen to know people like Guy and Daphne Lewis in the first place."

"From the Seattle Rep," I said.

"What's that?"

"The Seattle Repertory Theatre. We're all donors," I explained. "We met through Alex—Alexis Downey, the Rep's director of development. She organized a benefit auction a few months back. My partners and I donated a car to the auction, and the Lewises bought it."

"What kind of car was this?" Fraymore asked. "I've seen that hot little number you're driving around down here. Or does that 928 belong to your girlfriend?"

"Why don't you run a check on it and find out?"

"Why don't you save us both time and effort and tell me?"

"The Porsche is mine. The Lewises bought a Bentley."

"My, my. Porsches. Bentleys. For a city cop, you do run with a rich crowd."

"Who I run with doesn't concern you," I snapped. "What does this have to do with who killed Daphne Lewis or Martin Shore?"

"Just trying to sort out the players, Beaumont. You know how it is. We've gone eight whole years without having a murder here in Ashland. Longer in the county. This is usually a pretty peaceful and quiet community. Then you appear on the scene. All of a sudden, we're the murder capital of southern Oregon, with two vicious homicides in as many days. You can see how a poor small-town cop might wonder about a high-living Seattle police detective who happens to turn up in the same general vicinity of both crime scenes."

He ground out his cigarette. "Tell me, Beaumont, if you were me, what would you make of someone like you? Seems like a hell of a coincidence that I keep tripping over you wherever I turn, especially since I have a funny feeling you're still not telling me everything you know."

"But I have," I said. Well, almost everything.

"Tell me about Guy Lewis."

"What about him?"

"Did you know he was going to be in Ashland this weekend, or is it the same story you gave me about Martin Shore, another one of those odd flukes that you just happened to land here at the same time."

"You got it."

"The first you saw him was at the donors' party after the play?"

I didn't want to mention the N.A. meeting, because I knew that would send Fraymore off on another wild-goose chase. People who aren't in the program don't often understand people who are.

"No," I said. "We ran into each other during the Green Show before the play—another fluke."

The corners of Gordon Fraymore's mouth twitched ever so

slightly, warning me of trouble. "Don't screw with me, Beaumont. I don't believe in flukes, especially not when I know damn good and well it's a lie."

"How so?"

"I may be small potatoes in your book, but I'm nobody's dummy. While you've been out walking the streets the last few hours, I've been doing my job. I spent some time talking to one of our officers who was out directing traffic Saturday night. We were having trouble with the stoplight going up to the Festival. Remember?"

Now that he mentioned it, I did remember waiting to cross the street.

"Jack's a good cop," Fraymore continued. "Young, but very observant. He remembers you and Lewis walking across the street together. Jack says Guy Lewis was huffing and puffing and all out of breath. He says Lewis was packing a red down jacket."

"All right. So we ran into each other on the street before the Green Show. What difference does that make?"

"A hell of a big difference," Fraymore answered. "You know it as well as I do."

Actually, I did. As a homicide cop, I knew exactly how Gordon Fraymore's mind worked. For one thing, even under the best of conditions, cops hate coincidences with an abiding passion. Right that minute Gordon Fraymore's conditions sucked. He was under tremendous pressure. Here it was, opening weekend of the summer season in Ashland—the biggest weekend of the entire year—and Fraymore had his hands full, with not one but two separate homicides. Everyone in town, from the president of the board of directors of the Oregon Shakespeare Festival down to the lowliest busboy in the least expensive restaurant, had a vested interest in Gordon Fraymore's solving those two crimes. Unsolved multiple murders are real bad for tourism.

In order to fix the problem, Fraymore was doing what any right-thinking cop in the world would do—looking for someone connected to the murders whose story contained some small discrepancies. We both knew my story about meeting Guy Lewis at the

Green Show was shot full of holes, which meant I was hiding something. Worse, in both murders, I happened to be the only common denominator. Well, not the only one. There were actually two. The other was Tanya Dunseth.

"So you've decided I'm your man?"

"Not entirely. I still haven't figured out what your connection is to all this," he said, "but you can rest assured I will. Since you're a fellow cop, I was more than half inclined to give you the benefit of the doubt. Right up until you lied to me. Now all bets are off."

"Is that a threat?" I asked.

"More like a promise. Take it however you like. All I'm telling you is, if I were you, I wouldn't leave town. You stay right here in Ashland until I say you can go, got it?"

"Come on, Fraymore. Don't go dishing out orders. Remember me? I'm the one who brought you that videotape the minute I saw it. If I weren't on the up-and-up, why would I do that?"

"You tell me. To throw me offtrack maybe? What I can't figure out for the life of me is why a man in your position would get involved with that little two-bit piece of baggage in the first place. Seems to me as though someone with Bentleys and Porsches out the kazoo wouldn't bother with someone like her."

So that was it. He thought I was messing around with Tanya Dunseth. "I already told you. Tanya's my daughter's friend."

Fraymore smiled a mirthless, chilly smile. "Tell your daughter from me that she should choose her friends a little more wisely next time. And so should you. I don't know who Tanya Dunseth is, but I can sure as hell tell you who she isn't. I've been checking into the bio information she gave the Festival. None of it adds up."

My mind zipped back to the lunch at Geppetto's with Jeremy and Kelly talking about Tanya Dunseth's blighted childhood. "You're saying none of it checks out? Her parents didn't die in a house fire when she was a little kid?"

"That's exactly what I mean. The parents Tanya Dunseth listed on her job application aren't just deceased. They never existed in the first place. And, according to the hospital in Goldendale, neither does she. Not only that, I have physical evidence linking her to both victims."

"What kind of evidence?"

"Now, now, that would be telling, wouldn't it. So take this as a warning, Detective Beaumont. If you're somehow in on all this, I'm going to find out and nail your ass to the ground. And if you're not, then stay the hell out of it!"

I could feel the circle of proof tightening around Tanya Dunseth's neck. I couldn't tell for sure if Fraymore actually believed I was in on it, or if he was using me to carry a message to Tanya, hoping to provoke her into doing something stupid.

"Are you going to arrest her?" I asked.

"You just don't understand, do you, fella? You just don't *comprende* the words MIND YOUR OWN BUSINESS. Let me put it another way. Stay the hell out! I may not arrest Tanya Dunseth today or tomorrow or even next week—but I will eventually. In the meantime, I'll be watching her very closely. I wouldn't want Little Miss Porno Flick to slip away.

"I'm not booking her today, and not because I think she's innocent, either. I'm what you might call a fiscally responsible cop. I don't want the city of Ashland to have to pay room and board on her until it's time—until I've built an airtight case. When I do get around to arresting her—and you can count on it that I will—then you can bet I'll make it stick. Watch yourself, Beaumont, or some of her crap will land on you."

"Wait just a minute. What if Daphne Lewis and Martin Shore were in on something together? What if they were trying to blackmail or discredit Tanya Dunseth?" I asked. "Why else would that video show up here after all this time?"

"So what if they were?" Fraymore agreed. "Blackmail's no reason to rub people out. That's not the way it works. Maybe you should take Tanya Dunseth aside and explain the facts of life. That's why we have courts of law in this country, so people don't have to go around killing other people just because they've got their noses out of joint."

"Is there a connection between Shore and Daphne?"

Fraymore shrugged. "You tell me. I'm looking. I haven't found one yet, but I will. I'm that kind of guy."

The hospital door opened, and Ralph Ames emerged. He's from sunny Arizona. Unlike the rest of us, he keeps a pair of sunglasses in his pocket at all times. He slapped them on his face before taking two steps into the glaring sunlight.

"I understand that guy's your attorney," Fraymore growled, watching a tanned and fit Ralph Ames stride confidently toward us across an expanse of grassy lawn. "What's he doing here?"

"He came for the wedding."

"Not because you had some idea you might need him?"

"No, because he's a friend of the family," I replied.

Nodding sagely, Fraymore stood up. "Sure he is, and I'm a god-damn monkey's uncle. Do me a favor. Tell this 'friend of the family' that he should stick around for a day or two. If I get lucky, he may wind up doing some legal work after all."

Fraymore walked away then, leaving me alone. The emotional turmoil of the past few days had taken its toll, but I wasn't in such a fog that I didn't recognize a barefaced threat when I heard it. The oversized detective crammed his bulk into the Lumina and slammed the door, speeding away in a spray of gravel.

As I watched him go, a very real sense of apprehension settled over me. I didn't worry that he'd find any evidence linking me to Tanya Dunseth. There wasn't any. Not yet. But, given sufficient imagination and vindictiveness, damning evidence could easily be manufactured. From the way he acted, the things he said, I knew for sure that Gordon Fraymore was a vindictive man—vindictive and probably jealous as well.

He was a moderately successful detective on a tiny police force. In terms of official rank, we were on much the same level. But there are hazards connected with being a big fish in a very small pool.

Not only that, the guy drove a damn Chevy. It's both laughable and sad, but the American male has not yet escaped the mental trap of believing you are what you drive. A Lumina doesn't stack up very well against a Porsche 928. I had given away a Bentley for the hell of it as well as for a sizable tax deduction, while Gordon Fraymore would most likely never even touch one.

With someone like him, an old-fashioned, piss-in-your-soup-type threat can be ignored only at your own peril.

Sure as hell, Tanya Dunseth wasn't the only one in what the Laredo Kid would have called deep ca-ca. So was J. P. Beaumont.

10

Ames joined me on the concrete bench, nodding in greeting. "What was that about?" he asked. "Your friend Fraymore looked distinctly unhappy when he rumbled out of here."

"He's no friend of mine, and don't let appearances fool you. He's happy as can be. He just threatened to throw me in jail."

"Well," Ames returned mildly, "in that case, it's a good thing I'm here."

I scowled. "Funny, those were his very words. You two must be on the same wavelength."

Ralph grinned. "How come he wants you behind bars?"

"For interfering in his investigation."

"Oh," Ralph said. "Too bad, but that being the case, I could just as well go tell Alex it's no deal." He got up and started away. I couldn't figure out what was going on.

"Wait a minute," I said. "What's no deal? What are you talking about?"

Ralph stopped in midstride and turned back. "I've decided to look into Tanya Dunseth's situation. Alex thought maybe you wouldn't mind riding along out to the farm to make introductions.

But it's not necessary, certainly not with Fraymore on your tail. It isn't worth it."

"Hold on. Are you saying you intend to drop everything and hang around here to personally handle whatever criminal charges Fraymore may lodge against Tanya Dunseth?"

Ames nodded. "If there are criminal charges, yes."

"You'd do that for someone who A: You don't know and B: Is probably guilty as sin?"

"That's pretty much the size of it," he replied cheerfully.

I decided the man had gone off his rocker. "How can you, when you don't even know what the charges are?"

"No problem," Ralph smiled. "Fraymore will tell me eventually. He has to, you know."

Usually, I appreciate Ralph Ames' droll sense of humor. Sometimes I even *enjoy* it. This was not one of those times.

"But, Ralph . . ."

"Don't 'But, Ralph' me," he interrupted. "I'm a member-in-good-standing of the Oregon State Bar. After years of practicing glorified accounting, of doing nothing but reading and analyzing corporate balance sheets and annual reports, I'm ready for a change of pace. It'll be fun to try my hand at criminal law. I was damn good at it once upon a time, and I believe I still am. Actually, I'm looking forward to it."

Dumbstruck at the whole cockamamie idea, I tried to dissuade him. "Listen, Fraymore as good as told me it's only a matter of time before he places Tanya under arrest. He claims he has physical evidence linking her to both murders. He told me all that minutes ago."

Ralph remained adamant. "So what? She's still entitled to the best possible defense. That's exactly what I intend to provide."

I tried hitting him in the pocketbook. "Come on now, Ralph," I reasoned. "I happen to know your services don't come cheap. I may be able to pay, but Tanya Dunseth is a twenty-something single mother who can't even afford her own apartment. Defending her is going to require a hell of a lot of time, effort, energy, and money. How is she going to pay you?"

"She isn't," Ralph replied. "Nobody's asking her to. I wouldn't take money from her even if she had it. I haven't done *pro bono* work for a long time—years, in fact. I meant to all along, but I'm always so busy that I never quite get around to it. I've made up my mind. This time I am."

The voice of sweet reason wasn't going to convince him otherwise. Ames may have decided, but I suspected Alex Downey of behind-the-scenes manipulation. "How'd she do it?" I demanded.

Ames frowned in assumed innocence. "How did who do what?"

"How did Alex flimflam you into this?"

Caught in a classic case of gotcha, Ralph Ames was sheepish but not the least remorseful. "Never mind," he said. "Since you're not going to be involved, it doesn't matter."

"It does, too. Let me guess. Alex has spent the entire afternoon playing amateur detective. With her vast background of police-work experience, she's convinced Tanya Dunseth is an innocent victim who's being railroaded by the justice system. Somehow or other, she's suckered you into believing it, too. Don't feel like the Lone Ranger, Ralph. For a while, back when Martin Shore was the only victim, Alex almost had me believing it, too. Now I've changed my mind. Fraymore brought me to my senses."

"You maybe, not me," Ralph asserted with a dangerously quiet but determined edge to his voice. His tone more than anything should have alerted me, but I kept after him.

"How'd she do it, Ralph? Hold a gun to your head? What kind of weapon does it take to convince an otherwise intelligent, usually reasonable man to run around tilting at windmills?"

Ames came back and sank down heavily onto the bench beside me. "The woman's a born salesman," he answered forlornly. "Alexis Downey doesn't have a qualm in the world about going straight for the jugular. She used the only argument that was guaranteed to work."

In a pathetic way, he was still trying to joke around about it, but something about his dejected appearance betrayed the fact that he was genuinely disturbed. What was going on?

"Such as?" I pressed. "Tell me. I want to know."

Ralph shook his head. "Forget it. You're not involved. Can't be—not with Fraymore breathing down your neck. It was wrong of me to even bring it up."

And that's when I knew exactly how Alex had done it—as soon as Ralph refused to tell me. The look on his face gave him away.

"Anne Corley?" I asked. "Is that it?" Several years later, my heart still stumbles at the sound of her name. "Alex hit you with Anne?"

Ralph nodded. "She said, 'You would have defended Anne Corley if they'd arrested her, wouldn't you?' And it's true. I would have. In a minute. You and I both know Anne was guilty. On the face of it, Tanya Dunseth's case is almost the same thing. I'd be a complete hypocrite if I didn't do everything in my power to help. I owe Anne Corley that much."

Ralph didn't add the words "We both do" to the end of his sentence. It wasn't necessary. I supplied them myself. With unerring instinct, Alex had hit on the one sensitive issue guaranteed to grab both Ralph Ames and J. P. Beaumont by the short hairs and haul them into line. Neither one of us had been able to save Anne Corley. I wondered if Ralph really believed he could salvage Tanya Dunseth.

That's when I realized Ralph didn't actually believe Tanya Dunseth was innocent, either. "What do you go for, temporary insanity?"

Ralph frowned. "That might work for Martin Shore because of the movie connection. I'm not so sure about Daphne Lewis. That's one reason I need to talk to Tanya."

We sat without speaking for several long minutes. The door to the hospital lobby opened, and a family of visitors emerged. There was an elderly woman—a grandmother, I suppose—a middle-aged couple, and two adolescent children. They came out wearing the saddened faces and speaking the subdued talk of people who have not received good news. Seeing them reminded me of why I was there.

"What's going on inside?" I asked. "Any word?"

The change of subject helped a little, and Ralph smiled slightly when he answered. "I thought we were going to see some real fireworks."

"Fireworks? Why? What happened?"

"Alex and Karen almost got into it."

"How come?"

"The doctor came out and said that *one* person could go into the recovery room and sit with Kelly, to be there with her when she started coming out of the anesthetic. Karen got up to go, but Alex suggested maybe Jeremy should. And he did."

I shook my head in disbelief. "You mean Karen actually backed down?"

"That's right," Ralph answered.

I was thankful not to have been caught in the cross fire of that particular skirmish. Sitting on the bench and talking with Gordon Fraymore was grueling enough and not anywhere near my idea of a good time, but being sucked into the brewing power play between Alexis Downey and Karen Beaumont Livingston would have been far worse. For me, anyway.

"Has anyone actually talked to the doctor?"

"He ventured into the waiting room far enough to deliver a prepared-speech-type update to the entire assembly. He seemed aware of the fact that Kelly's visitors come from two entirely separate camps. He talked about a depressed skull fracture and said things were 'hopeful.' That's a direct quote."

" 'Hopeful' doesn't sound all that good to me," I said gloomily.

"Don't complain," Ralph responded. "It's a whole lot better than 'hopeless.' "

Point taken and noted. "Hopeless" was a hell of a lot worse, as anyone but a complete jackass would realize.

"Thanks for reminding me," I said. And meant it.

We stayed on the bench a while longer. I didn't say what I was thinking, but Ralph had left me enough room to make up my own mind. Finally, I stood up and started toward the car. Ralph got up to follow. "Where are you going?" he asked.

"I thought you wanted to drive out to Live Oak Farm and see

your client," I told him. "If she's home, you'll be better off seeing her there *before* Gordon Fraymore locks her up in jail."

We reached the Porsche together, but on opposite sides of the vehicle. Ralph caught my eye across the sunroof.

"Thanks for not hassling me about all this," he said. "It doesn't make much sense, but this is something I have to do."

"Don't worry," I said. "I understand."

And I did. Of course the idea of dropping everything to defend Tanya Dunseth was crazy as hell, but Anne Corley still haunted Ralph Ames almost as much as she did me, so I, of all people, was in no position to argue. My mother always warned me about stones and glass houses.

With that we both climbed into the car and slammed our respective doors. Only when we were well down Siskiyou Boulevard did we speak again. "When Fraymore finds out what we're up to, he's going to shit a brick. I probably will end up in jail."

Ralph grinned. "Don't worry," he said, laying on his best lawyerly charm. "If that happens, I'll make you the same deal I'm giving Tanya. Strictly *pro bono*. I won't charge a dime to bail you out."

"Gee, thanks, Ralph," I told him. "I knew I could count on you." And then we both laughed.

The tension in the car dissipated a little, but not very much, and not for very long. By the time we reached Live Oak Farm, it was back, as strong or stronger than before.

In the first cooling of evening, we stopped beside the uncompleted front steps leading up to the farmhouse. A pair of worn sawhorses stood nearby. An array of power tools lay scattered on the porch. Someone had spent the afternoon actively working on the reconstruction project, although now it was apparently break time. Several new eight-by-twelve support posts were visible underneath the flooring, but the jack still stood in place; the steps remained an unusable skeleton.

Although I could detect no distinct cooking aromas, dining-room-type noises emanated from the open windows as soon as I turned off the car engine. Ralph and I piled out of the Porsche and walked up to the edge of the front porch. Sunshine heaved herself to her feet and walked over to examine us through cloudy, cataract-obscured eyes. From the looks and sound of her, I figured Sunshine wasn't long for this world. The old dog managed only one croaking, halfhearted bark before Marjorie Connors stepped outside.

"Hello, Mr. Beaumont," Marjorie Connors said quite civilly for her. "How's Kelly?"

The woman didn't act as though all was forgiven, but at least she didn't threaten to call the sheriff. That was some small progress.

"Better," I said. "She's out of surgery."

Marjorie nodded. "Good. What can I do for you?"

"We'd like to see Tanya Dunseth, if you don't mind."

Marjorie raised one questioning eyebrow, but she voiced no objections. "We're just now picking up after dinner," she said. "It's cooler out on the back deck. Why don't you wait there? I'll send Tanya out as soon as we finish."

Halfway around the house, we walked past the entrance to that fateful basement. The wooden door was padlocked shut and sealed with strips of yellow crime-scene tape. I kept my eyes straight ahead.

On the back deck, all evidence of the late-morning buffet had been totally erased. Some more or less permanent deck furniture remained, but most of the tables and chairs and all the food, table-cloths, and garlands had disappeared from the face of the earth. It was as though everyone at Live Oak Farm wanted to forget we were all supposed to be down in Lithia Park celebrating a wedding.

I didn't blame anyone for wanting to forget. I did, too.

On the lowest level of the deck stood a redwood picnic table with two splintery benches. We both sat. While we waited for Tanya to appear, I studied Ralph Ames. Not particularly tall or powerfully built, he was an unlikely-looking candidate for the role of knight in shining armor. I knew a daily regimen of swimming laps in his Scottsdale pool kept his body in fighting-trim condition. He was dressed casually that day, which, for Ralph, meant a Polo golf shirt, impeccably creased Ralph Lauren trousers, and blemish-free Johnston & Murphy loafers. Wing tips. With tassels.

"What will you do if Tanya turns you down?" I asked somberly.

"She won't." Ralph's reply was brisk and confident. "I'm prepared to play hardball."

Tanya, her hair pulled back in an unruly ponytail and wearing shorts and a tank top, emerged from the house a few minutes later. She was drying her hands on the back of her shorts, while Amber trailed behind, dragging along an assortment of toys. We both rose to meet them.

"Sorry it took so long, Mr. Beaumont," Tanya apologized. "House rules say we all have to clean up together after mealtimes."

Plainly, Tanya Dunseth was not at all herself. Her skin seemed exceptionally pale. Ralph and I sat back down, but she didn't.

"How's Kelly?" Tanya asked anxiously. "Is she all right?"

"I hope so," I told her. "According to the doctor, it's still too soon to tell."

"And the baby?"

"Karen's fine," I said. "A few weeks early, but fine."

Tanya breathed a relieved sigh. "I was so worried. It's bad enough that Kelly's hurt. I don't know what I would have done if something happened to her baby. I know it's all my fault. None of this would have happened if Kelly hadn't been helping look for Amber."

"Don't blame yourself. Kelly was doing what anyone would do. But that's not why we're here. Right now I'd like you to meet a good friend of mine, Ralph Ames. He's an attorney."

At the word "attorney," an expression of guarded wariness crossed Tanya's face. She didn't actually move away from us, but there was a perceptible drawing back—a distancing.

"He's is a personal friend of mine," I continued reassuringly. "I guess you two weren't introduced at the brunch." Tanya shook her head.

Ralph smiled and reached across me to her, holding out his hand. "The name's Ralph," he said.

They shook hands, but Tanya's heart wasn't in it. She stood there facing us like a watchful bird poised for flight. At the slightest provocation, I was afraid she would scoop Amber into her arms and disappear. If she did that, Gordon Fraymore would be pissed off at everybody, including Ralph Ames, self-appointed attorney for the defense.

"I asked Beau here to bring me out so I could meet you," Ralph said, speaking calmly, addressing himself directly to Tanya. "I wanted to talk to you in private."

She examined his face with a puzzled frown. "How come?"

"I believe you may need our help," he answered quietly.

Tanya's mouth tightened. She folded her arms in front of her. "Why would I?"

With a glance at me, Ralph said, "I presume Detective Fraymore has been by to talk to you?"

Her eyes flitted apprehensively from Ralph's face to mine. "Several times so far, but I don't see how that's any concern of yours."

"Do you mind my asking what he said?"

"Yes, I mind," Tanya replied with a flash of anger. "I mind a lot."

She vacillated between being frightened and argumentative. Didn't she understand what was at stake here? Surely, she realized Gordon Fraymore meant to arrest her. Or did she? I couldn't tell.

Meanwhile, Ralph was growing frustrated. He's used to having his polite, understated manner achieve the instant results, but this time that tried-and-true technique wasn't working. He must have drawn much the same conclusion, because his next depth-charged statement jarred me, and it shocked hell out of Tanya Dunseth.

"Beau here and I haven't actually seen the videotape of you and Martin Shore, but we know all about it," Ralph said quietly.

He might as well have dropped a bomb onto the middle of the wooden deck. Tanya's body stiffened. She glared at Ralph from flat, angry eyes. "I didn't kill him," she declared. "I didn't kill either one of them."

"Did Detective Fraymore ask you about them?"

Tanya ignored Ralph's question. "Are you really an attorney?" she demanded. "I'll bet you're from the Festival. Did they send you out here to make me quit?"

"Please, Miss Dunseth. I'm not with the Festival. We're here to do nothing of the kind."

"Then how do you know about the tape? Who told you? Fray-more?" Her eyes darted furiously from Ralph's face to mine.

"Actually," Ralph said, "Mr. Beaumont is the one who first brought the tape to Gordon Fraymore's attention."

She turned on me. "Thanks a lot," she jeered. "Nice guy. Remind me to return the favor sometime."

"You don't understand," Ralph interjected quickly in my defense. "He had no choice in the matter. As soon as he realized both you and Martin Shore were in the film together, he was legally constrained to turn it over to the investigating officer. That's the law, Tanya. It's the way things work."

"Not if I didn't kill him," she retorted.

"And you didn't?"

"No."

"But you did know him."

"Of course I knew him. I was on the tape with him. You said so yourself. I just want to know one thing. That tape was made years ago. Where did it come from after all this time? Did they find it on Martin Shore's body? In his room?"

"Fraymore didn't tell you?" Tanya shook her head.

"It came from Denver Holloway."

Tanya's eyes widened in alarm. "Dinky? The director?"

Ralph nodded. "She received it in her mail yesterday, along with a note from Monica Davenport asking if she knew anything about your previous acting experience."

The shock of that news wiped out Tanya's last reserves of strength. Her knees wobbled under her. She grabbed the edge of the table for support and eased herself down onto the bench while Ralph leaped to assist her. Amber had been playing contentedly near her mother's feet. Now, instinctively knowing something was wrong, the child clambered onto her mother's lap. Tanya gripped the child tightly as though drawing some of the child's natural resilience into her own grown-up body.

"So the Festival knows about that, too," Tanya breathed.

Ralph nodded. "I'm afraid so," he said.

Tanya shook her head despairingly. "I haven't done anything

wrong, but that's the end of it. The Festival won't keep me on, not with all the adverse publicity."

"Don't you see? That's why we came," Ralph said. "I'd like to be your attorney."

"Do I need an attorney?"

"Did Gordon Fraymore tell you you were a suspect?"

"No, but . . ."

"You are," Ralph asserted. "In not one but two cases, and unless someone helps you, you're going to jail. Now tell me, was Martin Shore blackmailing you?"

Staring blankly at Ralph's face, Tanya shook her head. "No. Why would he?"

"To get something you had that he wanted."

"What would that be? I don't have any money."

"Maybe he found out you were becoming an established actress, and he wanted you to make another movie for him."

"No," Tanya said, shaking her head. "I'm too old for what he does."

I had stayed quiet because Ralph was doing an admirable job without any help from me. In that kind of situation, it's best not to interrupt. Now, though, I couldn't help asking a question of my own. It was, after all, the question that had dragged me into this fracas to begin with.

"What about Amber?" I asked. "Is it possible that he wanted to use Amber instead?"

An almost visible jolt shot through Tanya Dunseth's body, a tremor just like the one I had seen two nights earlier in the Members' Lounge. Tanya hugged a now sleeping Amber tightly to her breast, but the gaze she turned on me was filled with murderous intensity.

"Is that why he came to town?" she asked in a hoarse whisper.

"We don't know," Ralph answered for both of us. "That's what we're trying to find out."

"It wouldn't surprise me," Tanya hissed. "If they had tried that, I would have killed them myself. In fact, just thinking about it makes me wish I had."

"But you didn't?" Ralph asked.

"No. So help me God, I didn't."

Ralph is good, but he missed the most important part of what Tanya Dunseth had said. My homicide-trained ear zeroed in on it.

"You said 'they,'" I pointed out quietly. "They who?"

Tanya looked over at me, her eyes suddenly steady and solemn. "Martin Shore and Daphne Lewis," she said. "Who else did you think I meant?"

Ralph and I exchanged startled glances. "You knew them both?" I asked.

Tanya shook her head. "Go away," she said. "I don't want to talk about it anymore."

"But you're saying Martin Shore and Daphne Lewis were connected? That they knew each other?"

"I've said too much already. Leave me alone." Her eyes filled with tears.

Gordon Fraymore had told me he was looking for a connection between Daphne Lewis and Martin Shore. He claimed that if one existed, he hadn't found it yet. Either he had lied to me—a distinct possibility—or Tanya hadn't told him what she'd just told us. Which was it?

"When Fraymore was here, did you tell him about that?"

Tanya shook her head. "He's getting paid to find things out. Why should I tell him anything? Why make it easy? Like you said, he already thinks I killed them, and he's going to arrest me."

She stood up suddenly. "Where are you going?" I asked.

"To put Amber in her crib. She's too heavy to hold like this. I'll be right back." With that, Tanya Dunseth hurried into the house, leaving Ralph and me sitting on the picnic benches and stewing in our own juices.

"Will she come back out?" Ralph asked.

"Beats me," I said. "That's anyone's guess, but I don't think we'd better go in after her. We weren't invited."

Where Marjorie Connors was concerned, I wasn't about to take any chances.

11

We were ready to give up and leave when Tanya returned to the deck. Her eyes were red; she'd been crying. She had changed out of her shorts into a denim skirt. In the soft evening light, she seemed both insubstantial and defeated. This time she sat down on the bench next to Ralph. She folded her hands together on the table and sat staring at them.

"I wouldn't want what happened to me to happen to anyone else, but I'm not ashamed of what I did," she said thoughtfully. "Even though I was very young, I'm willing to accept full responsibility for all of it. No matter what anybody says, where I ended up was way better than where I started. But now it's not just me anymore, either. There's Amber to worry about. I've spent all afternoon trying to decide what to do. It's hard to know where to turn, who to trust."

"You have to start somewhere," Ralph replied.

She looked over at him through lashes still veiled in tears. "You want me to talk about it?"

"If you want us to try to help you, yes."

"But it's so hard. I've spent years trying to forget it—to block it out of my memory, to make myself believe that it never happened. Or, if it did, that it happened to someone else."

Ralph reached over and gently placed one hand over Tanya's. "Please tell us, Tanya," he urged quietly. "It's the only way."

When Tanya spoke again, her voice was a hushed whisper. "I thought I had forgotten about it, but then, as soon as I saw Elise, it came back. All of it."

"Elise?" I asked. "Who's she?"

"Elise was what she called herself years ago when I first knew her. Detective Fraymore told me her name was Daphne Lewis."

"This was when you saw her in the Members' Lounge?" Tanya nodded. "What came back?" Ralph prodded.

His insistence propelled Tanya up off the bench, away from the table and us. She paced over to the handrail where she stood facing off the deck, gripping the railing with thin, white-knuckled fingers. For several long minutes, she didn't speak.

"Tanya," I said finally. "Were Shore and Daphne in the movie business together?"

"Yes."

"I can see why it's difficult for you to talk about it, but you have to understand that the people who make kiddie porn are animals, the very worst kind of vermin. Whatever Martin Shore did to hurt you . . ."

Tanya Dunseth spun around and faced me, her face distorted into an ugly mask by a burst of derisive, caustic laughter. "Martin Shore? He never hurt me, not once. Oh, he tried, but he wasn't any good at it. What Jacques liked—that was his name back then, Jacques—was that I was still so flat-chested and young-looking. He thought that meant I was a virgin. The idea of cracking a virgin on film was a real turn-on for him."

She paused. "I wasn't, though," she continued. "Hadn't been for years, but I let Jacques think I was. I always wanted to be an actress, and I told myself it was my first real acting job. When he came into the room to get me, I knew he wanted me to be scared, so I acted scared. When he wanted to hurt me, I screamed and cried and

pretended like it hurt. And when he wanted me to like it? Well—
I knew how to do that, too."

Her voice drifted away and disappeared, the way a dying breeze
leaves behind an unexpected silence. I felt as though her story had
taken an unforeseen detour, wandered off the beaten path and left
me flailing around an unfamiliar crossroads in the dark. Tanya was
telling us a story I hadn't expected to hear.

"You say Martin Shore never hurt you?"

"Never. Sometimes I had to fight to keep from laughing. Nothing
poor old Jacques ever did to me for the camera was any worse
than what my own father had done to me a hundred times before.
Nothing that happened to me later was worse than that."

Her father? Stunned by Tanya's words, I glanced at Ralph Ames.
His face was ashen, his jawline set. The horrific similarity to Anne
Corley's own story was far closer than either one of us could
possibly have imagined. Or wanted to.

"That's my first conscious memory," she added quietly, "my
father coming into my room at night. His shadow would fall across
my bed, and then he'd be standing in front of the window, blocking
out the moon. For years the memories ended there."

I found myself cursed with sudden, unwanted insight. "Is that
what you meant when you said seeing Daphne brought it back?
You remembered?"

"Yes," she said.

No wonder she had spilled her drink in the Members' Lounge.

When Tanya continued, her eyes gazed off into space, her voice
distant, remote. "I remember the terrible weight of him on my
body, so heavy I could barely breathe, the ugly noises he made,
and the pain, the terrible pain. And I remember going to the
bathroom in the dark to clean myself up. Afterward, I cried myself
to sleep. Why didn't my mother ever come to me or hold me? Why
did she let it happen?

Finally, Tanya fell silent, and a long, involuntary sob shook her
body. I wanted to go to her and do for her what her mother never
had, put an arm around her and offer some word of comfort, but
I didn't dare. For one thing, I didn't know what Tanya's reaction

would be. For another, I didn't trust myself to talk. No words are enough to counter that kind of parental betrayal.

Even Ralph was stunned beyond his depth. We both sat there like lumps and waited for the wild onslaught of tears to subside.

"Is that how you ended up with Shore and Daphne?" he asked at last. "To get away from your father?"

Tanya nodded. "Like I said, Daphne wasn't her name then, not when I first met her in Walla Walla. She called herself Elise—Elise Morgan. She was only a few years older than I was, but she claimed to be a well-known New York model. She and Jacques went to small-town schools all over Washington and Oregon running seminars that told star-struck kids like me to forget about investing in modeling school. Not to bother. All they needed to break into modeling was a great portfolio."

"Ah," Ralph said in sudden comprehension. "The old modeling-portfolio scam. Were they really selling portfolios?"

"Some of the time," Tanya replied.

"Martin Shore was the photographer?"

"Sort of," Tanya answered. "I mean, he took the pictures, and they did sell some, but mostly they claimed to be running a contest. An all-expense-paid modeling shoot in Mexico was the grand prize. To me, that looked like the perfect way out of the trap. I couldn't wait to sign up. As soon as I filled out the entry form, I knew I was on my way to stardom."

"How exactly does it work?" I asked.

Ralph explained. "These guys go around the country, usually to small towns, and offer to turn ordinary kids into overnight modeling successes. All they have to do is pose for and buy this outrageously expensive portfolio of modeling photographs. Taken by none other than the world-famous Jacques himself. Right?"

Tanya nodded.

"Did Jacques have a last name?" I asked, trying to put together a starting place for unraveling this part of the story.

Tanya shook her head, but Ralph Ames answered for her. "You don't understand, Beau. Topflight fashion photographers don't bother with last names, do they, Tanya?"

She allowed him a wan smile. "I didn't find out the truth until after I won the contest." Leaving the handrail, Tanya came back over to the table and sat down on the opposite bench.

"It turned out there was no contest. It had been a model search, and I was exactly what they were looking for; I fit the profile. They wanted a scared, desperate kid, reasonably good-looking, who would do almost anything to get away from home. It didn't take long for them to figure out that my parents wouldn't bat an eye if their underage daughter suddenly disappeared without a trace. And they wanted someone whose parents wouldn't be above taking a bribe to keep quiet about what happened."

"Your father did that?" I asked. "He actually sold you to them for money?"

Tanya looked me in the eye when she answered. "Why not? It meant one less mouth to feed, and it gave him a bundle of money my mother knew nothing about, money he used to play the ponies."

I've been in Homicide forever, seen things that would turn most people's stomachs. I thought I had lost my ability to be shocked, but it turned out I hadn't. Tanya's story appalled me, shook me in a way that seeing a mere dead body never could. It almost made me ashamed to call myself a man.

Maybe I was more susceptible right then because of what was happening with Kelly, but I couldn't abide the idea that Tanya Dunseth's own father had committed such unspeakable crimes against her; that he had sold her to the likes of Martin Shore and Daphne Lewis to do with as they wished. Although considering what he himself had been doing to her, even selling her into bondage to a kiddie-porn czar had been a favor, an inarguable improvement.

I lost track of the conversation for a time, stopped listening because I was too outraged to hear more. I wanted to hop in the Porsche, drive straight to Walla Walla, and slam a balled fist into somebody's sick, sallow face. How could a man do such a thing to his own child? How could anyone?

When I came back to the conversation, Ralph Ames was still patiently asking questions. The process seemed even more difficult for him than it was for her. From time to time, his voice cracked under the strain of it, while Tanya continued to answer his questions in a quiet, steady voice barren of any emotion.

It struck me as odd that Tanya's disclosures seemed to have a far greater impact on her two male listeners than they had on her. It was as though in revisiting those scenes from her horrific childhood, she somehow conquered the demons that lived there. She emerged from the battle with a kind of newly minted poise that was more than slightly unnerving.

"When did you meet up with Jacques and Elise?" Ralph asked.

"I was around fifteen, a sophomore in high school."

Ralph frowned and looked at me. "Didn't Denver Holloway say the girl in the film was younger than that?"

"It was me, all right," Tanya said. "I'm sure of it. I started taking birth-control pills when I was only eight. My father brought them to me. I don't know if the pills fouled up my natural development or if I was just a late bloomer. I didn't have my first period until I was fourteen. My second came a year later. My lack of boobs drove my father crazy. He was always pinching me there to see if I was growing. He kept telling me he wanted me to be a 'real' woman. I hoped I never would be."

"Birth-control pills for an eight-year-old?" I demanded. "How the hell did he get away with that? Where did he get them? Didn't your mother notice?"

"If she noticed, she didn't care," Tanya replied. "Besides, my father was a sneak. Each month, he'd give me the new package. I had to take all the pills out of their little foil wrappers and put them in a vitamin bottle. He told me that I had to take a pill every day or I'd end up with a baby that would be blind and deformed. He said he'd have to drown it in the pond the way he did kittens whenever our cat had any."

The story she told was so brutal and ugly I wanted to puke. Ralph rubbed his eyes and shook his head sadly. "I'm really sorry to put you through all this, Tanya, but once Detective Fraymore finds out about what you've told us, he's going to be asking the exact same questions."

Tanya nodded. "I guess I knew he would," she said. "Amber and I went for a walk this afternoon while you all were at the hospital. I realized then I'd have to tell somebody. If it was only me, I wouldn't, but with Amber ..." She paused and shrugged. "Well, I guess I have to face it sometime. And in a way, it's easier than I thought. It's like I'm two different people—the girl all those awful things happened to and somebody else, the person I am now. It's like acting. If you live a role long enough, you start believing it, and none of what I told you ever happened. I shut it out of my mind, and it doesn't exist."

"What about your parents?" I asked. "Do they? Still exist, I mean?"

"I don't know. I don't care."

"Jeremy and Kelly told me that your parents died in a house fire when you were small, that you ran away from your guardian."

"No," she replied quietly. "That's a lie. I made it up because it was easier to pretend they were dead than to accept them for what they really were. Over in eastern Washington, in the town of Goldendale, there was a girl about my age whose parents did die that way—in a house fire. I remember reading about it in the newspaper and wishing it could have been my parents who died instead of hers. I wanted to be her so much that finally I was. I stole her story and turned it into mine."

"You're not from Goldendale at all?"

"No. Walla Walla. My father was a guard at the prison. My mother cooked in the school cafeteria."

"What are their names?"

Tanya's story had led her through a landscape teeming with emotional land mines, yet through it all she had maintained her composure. Now a note of genuine alarm crept into her voice.

"Do you have to bring them into this? I don't want anything to do with them—nothing. I don't even want them to know I'm still alive."

"Someone will have to contact them," I said. "If we don't, Fraymore will. As soon as he tumbles to the Daphne Lewis/Martin Shore connection, he's going to be on your case. Believe me, his questions are going to be a hell of a lot tougher than Ralph's."

Tanya seemed to consider my words before she answered. "Roger and Willy," she said finally. "Their names are Roger and Willy Tompkins."

"Would they still be in Walla Walla?"

"Probably." Tanya nodded. "I don't think they'd ever leave."

"And your name?" I asked. "The official one on your birth certificate?"

"Roseann Charlene Tompkins," Tanya answered. "I always hated it. My father chose the name, and I couldn't wait to get rid of it."

We had been sitting on the picnic bench for far too long. Ralph Ames stood up and rubbed his back. "How did that happen?" he asked. "What was the chronology that took you from Roseann Tompkins to Tanya Dunseth?"

"Some kids run away to join the circus. I ran away to make movies. I stayed with Elise and Jacques for two years. It worked for me. Eventually, I did get to be an actress. Except when we were making a movie, they left me alone. I had a place to live, enough food to eat, books to read. Nobody bothered me."

"You made more than one movie? How many?"

Tanya shook her head. "I don't know. Ten maybe? But if Fraymore recognized Martin Shore, then he has the very first one."

"Why? How do you know?"

"Because that's the only one where Jacques didn't wear a mask. I guess he was afraid someone might recognize him."

"No wonder," I put in. "He was a cop."

"A cop?" Tanya echoed, her eyes widening. "Really?"

"He got drummed off the force in Yakima when they found out he was distributing pornography. I don't think anyone ever realized he was making the flicks and starring in them as well."

Suddenly, surprisingly, Tanya Dunseth started to giggle. Within moments she dissolved into semihysterical laughter.

"What's the matter?" I asked when she was finally able to talk again. "What's so funny?"

"You mean all that time he was really a cop?" she asked, wiping tears from her eyes and gasping for breath.

"Yes," I answered. "Why does that make you laugh?"

"Whenever we were doing it, I always pretended I was making it with the Lone Ranger," Tanya answered. "I don't know why that made me feel better. Maybe I was crazy. Maybe I am."

"You were a survivor," Ralph cut in. "Playing games like that with your tormentor is a well known survival technique. Don't ever fault yourself for it. It's what they teach POWs to do in order to maintain their sanity. You stayed with them for two years?"

Tanya nodded. "One day they gave me five thousand dollars and told me to leave town. I don't know why. Maybe they were about to be raided. I bought a bus ticket and came here."

"To Ashland? Why?"

"I always read about Ashland, even when I was little. I knew they did plays here. It seemed like the place to go if I wanted to be an actress. I gave myself a brand-new name—Tanya O'Brien, came here, got my GED, and started taking drama classes at Southern Oregon State College. And I started trying to work my way into the Festival. I did everything—sold tickets, mopped floors, worked the concession stands, sewed costumes. It took a while, but finally I started getting parts."

"That's when you met your former husband?"

"I didn't realize it at the time, but Bob was just like my father— mean. He had a bachelor of fine arts. I didn't. When I started getting parts, it made him crazy and meaner. When I got my first speaking part, he beat me up the night before the opening. I went onstage the next night wearing a pound of makeup. Then, when he found out I was pregnant, he beat me up again and left town. At first, I felt deserted, but when I had time to think about it, I was relieved he was gone. It was the best thing that could have happened for me or for Amber."

Ralph stopped pacing. "Have you ever told anyone else about this?" he asked quietly.

"No."

"Not a roommate or a friend? Not even your ex-husband?"

"No. No one."

"Do you have any enemies?"

"Other than my father and my ex-husband? No."

"And you don't know of anyone else here in Ashland, maybe someone else here at the Festival, who might share your . . ." Ames stumbled. ". . . your, uh . . . unfortunate background . . . someone else who may have her own grudge against these two and who is systematically trying to shift the blame to you?"

Tanya shook her head. "No. I get along great with everybody. Ask anyone. No one here ever gave me any trouble."

It wasn't difficult to understand Ames' line of questioning. The idea of Shore having another victim inside the Festival had already crossed my mind. I added my own twist. "By the way, where is your ex?" I asked.

"He jumped off the 1-5 route. He burned out and isn't doing West Coast theaters anymore. For a long time now, I haven't heard anything about him, and I don't want to know."

"He doesn't pay child support?"

"Are you kidding?"

I'll admit, with someone like Robert Dunseth, asking about child support was strictly a rhetorical question.

Ralph shook his head. "I don't think it would be him, anyway, Beau. It has to be someone with a grudge against all three—Tanya, Daphne, and Martin Shore. Did Martin Shore try to contact you once he got to town?"

Tanya shook her head. "Not that I know of. I never received any messages, either at work or here at home."

"What about Daphne?"

"No. I never saw her until the party."

"Where did you go after you left the Members' Lounge?" I asked.

"Detective Fraymore wanted to know the same thing."

"I'm sure he did. What did you tell him?"

"I went home."

"How?"

"I walked."

"All the way to the farm? It's a long way—several miles."

"Not that far. Besides, I was upset. I needed to think."

"Did anybody see you?"

She shrugged. "I don't know. Maybe."

"So you don't have any kind of alibi for when Martin Shore was killed?"

"I guess not."

"Did Gordon Fraymore ask you about that?" She nodded. "Did he ask the same question about any other time period?"

Since I couldn't very well come out and ask Fraymore the question directly, I was trying, in a roundabout fashion, to establish an approximate time of death for Daphne Lewis.

Tanya shook her head. "He only asked me about Saturday night. And I told him the same thing I just told you."

Out front, Sunshine resumed her hoarse barking. A car engine switched off, but I didn't pay much attention, until the back screen door slammed open. An agitated James Renthrow appeared in the doorway.

"There you are, Tanya. They're coming. I heard them talking about it on the police scanner on my way over."

"Who's coming?" Tanya asked.

"The cops," Renthrow answered breathlessly. "Detective Fraymore and the rest. They're coming to Live Oak Farm right now. It sounds like they've got a warrant for your arrest."

The other shoe had fallen. It was only because of James Renthrow's electronic eavesdropping that we had even a moment's advance warning.

With a stricken expression on her face, Tanya turned to Ralph. "Are you really my attorney, Mr. Ames? You're right. I do think I need one. What am I supposed to do now? Will you come with me?"

Ralph nodded. "I'll come to the station, but not in the same car. When Detective Fraymore shows up, go with him quietly, without any protest or fuss. They'll read you your rights. Whatever you do, answer no questions. After they book you, you'll be allowed one phone call."

As he spoke, Ames pulled a scrap of paper from his wallet and scribbled something on it. "Here's the number of Beau's car phone.

Memorize it. When they allow you that one call, dial that number. I'll be waiting outside. Again, I'm your attorney. You're not to answer any questions without my being present, understand?"

Tanya nodded. "What about Amber?"

"Don't worry," Ralph said. "We'll take care of her. If nothing else, Beau can pack up her things and take her back to Oak Hill for the time being. Someone there will know what to do. Beau probably does himself. He's just rusty."

But Tanya Dunseth wasn't looking for temporary measures. "I'm not talking about just tonight," she said urgently, clutching desperately at Ralph's arm. "Promise me one thing."

"What's that?"

"If I go to jail or prison, you won't let my parents get Amber. No matter what. I'd rather she were dead."

"Believe me," Ralph Ames declared. "I'll see to it." He turned to me. "Give me the keys to the 928, Beau. Tanya and I will go down the road and head off your friend Fraymore before he has a chance to come into the yard."

"What about me?" I asked. "Shouldn't I come along?"

"Not on your life," Ralph answered. "I have the protection of professional privilege. You don't. I don't want Gordon Fraymore knowing you were privy to this entire conversation. Maybe this good man here . . ." Ralph waved distractedly in Romeo's direction. "What is your name, sir?"

"Renthrow," Romeo answered. "James Renthrow."

"Well, then," Ralph said, "maybe Mr. Renthrow will be kind enough to give you and the baby a ride into town. Come on, Tanya. Hurry."

With that, Take-Charge-Ralph led an uncomplaining Tanya away. Moments later, the engine of the Porsche roared to life, and they were gone.

Romeo turned to me. "What now?" he asked.

"We do as we're told," I answered. "We find a diaper bag and pack same."

One of Tanya's housemates, the deep brown one I had seen baking herself to a cinder on the front seat of the old Chrysler, directed us to Tanya's upstairs room. There, with Romeo's help, I pulled together what looked like a relatively complete baby kit. For overnight or longer.

After that, we woke Amber up and carried her out to James Renthrow's fire-engine-red VW Bug with the proper Shakespearian vanity plate of 2BRNOT2B. His scanner was still tuned to police frequencies when we got in the car, but there was nothing on the air about the arrest of Tanya Dunseth.

"Nice of you to take care of Amber this way," James Renthrow said, in his melodic sounding accent, as we headed for Oak Hill. "Not everyone would take in somebody's baby like that, especially with Kelly so badly hurt and all. You seem to have more than enough to worry about on your own."

It seemed like that to me as well. "Most people don't have friends like Ralph Ames," I returned darkly.

I admit to being moderately grumpy when I said it. I was glad someone had noticed and appreciated it, even if it was only Romeo. With Kelly still hanging in limbo, I did have certain troubles of my own. Not only that, I was more than slightly bent out of shape by Ralph's high-handed attitude. He took off in my car, leaving me stranded and having to beg rides from total strangers. Then, of course, there was Amber.

It was easy for Ralph to wave his wand magnanimously and say he'd take care of something when, in actual fact, some other poor chump was the one who'd be left holding the bag.

To say nothing of the baby.

12

Again I found Alex waiting on the front porch. She met us at the car to give me a quick update. Karen Louise was fine. Kelly had been moved from Recovery to a private room where her condition had been upgraded to serious but stable. She had not regained consciousness. In other words, we still weren't out of the woods.

Inside, the Oak Hill B & B was alive with activity. Bed-and-Breakfast establishments don't usually supply evening meals, but this wasn't a usual circumstance. Florence made pot after pot of coffee, regular and decaf. She served that along with plates heaped high with salvaged wedding cake to an informal gathering that threatened to last all night. Most drop-by visitors were friends of Kelly and Jeremy's, people who had expected to attend a wedding. They came instead to express dismay and to glean progress reports on Kelly and the baby.

Word of Tanya Dunseth's arrest preceded us. When James Renthrow and I arrived with Amber in tow, the response was enthusiastic and immediate. Maybe there's something in that old line about no people like show people. The people gathered in Florence's spacious living room, Tanya and Jeremy's fellow cast members, were very much concerned, and they wanted to help. Someone started a sign-up sheet for volunteers to take turns watching Amber. Most mentioned they'd be happy to care for Karen Louise as well. It warmed me to know help would be available for Kelly once her out-of-town relatives returned home.

Florence had been busy doing more than just making coffee and serving cake. Calling in some of her B & B chips, she had found lodging for everybody, although not at a single location. At that time of year, last-minute accommodations in Ashland are the exception, not the rule. Still, Florence had managed.

Alex and I were scheduled to stay where we were. Dave and Karen ended up at someplace called the Auburn Street Cottage, where, I was told, although the shower was tall enough to stand up in, it was also outdoors—across a long backyard and concealed behind a lacy curtain of green growing vine. Scott and Ralph Ames shared a double room at the Ashland Hills.

There was a considerable fuss when Romeo and I first showed up, me carrying Amber and James Renthrow packing the diaper bag. Within minutes Alex personally took charge of the child. Since Alex's underhanded scheming had precipitated this current crisis, that seemed only fair. I repaired to the kitchen, where I found Dave Livingston bird-dogging the phone. He poured two cups of coffee, kept one for himself, and handed the other to me. We both leaned against the kitchen cooking island to drink it.

"I hear Kelly's condition has been upgraded," I said.

He nodded. "The doc says it'll be several days before we know if there's any residual damage—paralysis, memory loss."

My stomach knotted at the prospect. We stood in silent commiseration—two fathers caught in the aftermath of disaster—agonizing about an injured child, fearing the worst but stubbornly hoping for the best. Dave, a likable, ordinary guy, seemed as frazzled as I felt. His concern for Kelly mirrored my own. Realizing that—in the face of hearing Tanya's appalling story, of knowing there were some other awful fathers out there in the world—made me feel incredibly lucky. And grateful.

I remembered then that I hadn't seen Mrs. Livingston as I came through the house. "Karen's still at the hospital?"

Dave shook his head. "I took her back to our place so she could rest. I'm waiting for Jeremy to call here when he's ready to leave the hospital. There's no phone in our room."

"You don't have to do that," I told him. "Karen's not the only one who needs rest. When Jeremy calls, I'll go pick him up. I wanted to peek in on Kelly anyway."

Dave examined my face, checking to see if I meant it. "You're sure it's no trouble?"

"None at all."

"All right then," he agreed. "Thanks. I don't like leaving Karen alone for very long."

I almost told him not to worry about Karen, but it was none of my business. When Dave left a few minutes later, I helped myself to some cake and wandered back through the house. Alex and Florence were making phone calls and trying to find a crib. Boris, Florence's gray tomcat, meandered through the room, took one look at Amber, and departed for parts unknown. Natasha, Oak Hill's tiny dust mop of a dog, stood her ground and regarded the child with wary curiosity.

The house seemed crowded, noisy, and overly hot. I ventured outside to the front steps and gazed up at a dazzling array of stars. When puny human frailties overtake me, stars can help put things in perspective, although stargazing in Seattle is a relatively rare occurrence.

I was still outside when the phone rang. Moments later Alex appeared at the door to tell me that Jeremy was ready to leave the hospital. She handed me the keys to Ames' Lincoln. I found Jeremy waiting for me, pacing up and down the sidewalk outside the hospital entrance. Although official visiting hours were long over, I parked the car. "How're things?" I asked.

"Better," he said. "Lots better than they were."

"Wait here a sec, if you don't mind, Jeremy. I'd like to see for myself."

He nodded. "First room on the left, just beyond the nurses' station."

I walked down the hall, ready to battle any nurse who tried to stop me. None did. Kelly lay sleeping, her long blond eyelashes resting on pale, bruised cheeks. Trying to see beyond the marks on her face and the bandages on her head, I recalled her as an impish little girl, sweet and innocent only when she'd been in bed asleep. Now she was asleep again, and I hoped to God she'd wake up. Trouble or not, I sure as hell didn't want to lose her. Biting back tears, I rushed from the room.

Jeremy waited in the car, sitting with his eyes closed, leaning wearily on the headrest. He didn't look up as I climbed into the car and switched on the ignition.

"I'm still scared, Mr. Beaumont," he said doggedly. "And I feel so damn helpless."

It might have been only three days since I'd first met him, but Jeremy no longer seemed like a kid to me. Maybe we both were growing up. Tragedy had temporarily scrubbed the wedding, but I sensed Jeremy Todd Cartwright III was a keeper. Bearing that in mind, it wouldn't do to have him calling me Mr. Beaumont for the rest of our lives.

"We're all scared, Jeremy," I assured him. "And by the way, call me Beau, would you? Everybody else does."

He sat up then and glanced in my direction. "Having a baby . . . I just never thought about it that much before. You have to take her home, feed her, take care of her, read to her, teach her things, help her grow up. How do you know what to do so you don't hurt her? What if she gets sick? I mean, being a father is just overwhelming, isn't it?"

"I'll say," I agreed, with remarkable restraint.

We were quiet, both of us presumably musing about the responsibilities of fatherhood. At least, that's what I was doing. When Jeremy spoke again, though, he changed the subject. "I hear they arrested Tanya. Do the cops really think she killed both those people?"

"That's the general idea."

"Not Tanya," Jeremy said decisively. "Never in a million years. She wouldn't do such a thing. She's one of the kindest people I know. She won't even kill a spider. She carries them outside. I've seen her do it."

Jeremy didn't know even the barest surface of Tanya Dunseth's real story, and I wasn't at liberty to tell him. There's a pervasive belief that the kinds of abuse suffered by Tanya Dunseth provide a fertile breeding ground for many of society's psychopathic killers. And there's a common tendency to forgive the trespasses of those once-tormented children. I had learned that myself when it came to Anne Corley.

To Jeremy I said, "Not killing bugs doesn't necessarily translate into not killing people, but Tanya claims she's innocent."

"What's going to happen to Amber in the meantime?" he asked.

"She'll be all right." I explained our hastily arranged child-care program.

Jeremy shook his head. "It's not fair. Tanya's worked so hard. Now she's going to lose everything, probably even Amber."

"We're working on the problem," I said.

And "we" were. My use of the plural pronoun was accidental. I realized only after the fact that I actually meant it, that I was now a committed member of the Save Tanya Dunseth Movement. Roped into the program reluctantly at first, now I qualified as a full-fledged volunteer along with Ames and the people who offered to baby-sit.

I asked Jeremy if he wanted to come by Oak Hill and visit with some of his friends, but he declined. He was scheduled for *Majestic* Tuesday afternoon. He wanted to get some rest.

The idea of rest—of crawling into a bed and actually sleeping—seemed uncommonly sensible. In fact, I was more than ready for an entire night's worth of serious shut-eye myself, but it didn't turn out that way. To begin with, Ralph was back at Oak Hill when I returned from the farm.

I asked how things were going, and he gave me a surprisingly dour response. "Not so good."

"Why? What's the matter?"

"Fraymore found a note in Daphne's sweater pocket signed by Tanya. It says to meet her at the house after the play. Or maybe it says after *Juliet.* I'm not sure, because I didn't see the note itself. Fraymore is sending it out for fingerprint analysis."

"Does Fraymore know about the rest of it? About the Daphne-Shore connection and that bastard in Walla Walla?"

Ralph nodded. "Tanya told him. I figured we'd be better off telling him before he learned about it himself. Not that it made any difference. The arraignment's sometime late tomorrow."

"Any hope of posting bond?"

"What do you think?"

"I agree," I told him. "It was a dumb question. Not even Ralph Ames is that much of a miracle worker." Ralph greeted that with a sickly smile.

"What about Child Protective Services?" I asked. "When do you think they'll get into the act?"

"I've held them off for the time being," he said, "but I don't know for how long."

All in all, it wasn't an uplifting conversation. Later that night when I tried to go to sleep, Ralph's comments kept replaying themselves in my head, giving me something constructive to worry about. The two of us together hadn't been able to save Anne Corley, and I doubted we'd be able to rescue Tanya, either.

The other obstacle to sleeping was Amber. Florence of Oak Hill is a miracle worker in her own right, but only up to a point. She hadn't been able to conjure a crib out of thin air on such short notice. There was a second bed in the Iris Room—a twin—but it had no sides. There's a good reason cribs and playpens are made the way they are. It's hard to keep a rambunctious two-year-old confined to a bed with no rails.

So Amber Dunseth slept in Alex's and my queen-sized bed. With us. Between us, actually.

"I'm sorry," Alex said as we lay in bed with a restless and still wide-awake child wiggling between us. "I shouldn't have inter-fered, especially not when you already had so much going on."

Amen, I thought. I said, "It has been one hell of a day."

"Do you think Ralph will be able to help Tanya?"

"I doubt it."

"Oh," she said.

Any more than I had with Jeremy, I wasn't free to tell Alex the details of the harrowing story Ralph and I had heard from Tanya. I had no right to. If she chose to reveal that part of her history to others, that was her choice. It wasn't up to me to make that decision for Tanya Dunseth, not even with Alexis Downey.

"Couldn't Ralph do one of those plea-bargain things?" Alex asked much later. "They're in the news all the time. Maybe Tanya suffers from some form of post-traumatic stress syndrome, and it caused her to go temporarily insane."

On the face of it, temporary insanity really wasn't totally out of the question for a change—if she had done it, that is. But I kept going back to Tanya's insistence that Martin Shore hadn't hurt her, that he and Daphne had, in their own dreadful way, made her life better. They had rescued her from a hellhole of unremitting abuse.

I could understand how the shock of seeing Daphne Lewis might trigger the return of Tanya's loathsome memories and allow her to see into a murky past she had obscured in an effort to survive. Yes, it must have been terrible to recall all those years of pain and degradation. But if Tanya really was the kind of person who avoided killing spiders, why would she set out to murder the very people who once helped her? What was the point?

If she was going to go against her own beliefs and kill someone, why mess around with Daphne Lewis and Martin Shore when she could instead go after someone who really deserved it—like her father, for instance?

With those conflicting thoughts circling in my head, sleep became more and more elusive. When I dozed at all, it was on tiptoes for fear of crushing Amber. Several times I woke up in a panic and lay there listening for the sound of her breathing, afraid that something had happened to her while I slept. Once or twice a baby knee or elbow dug deep into my gut and shocked me awake. How do pregnant mothers ever get any sleep?

So much for yet another romantic night in Ashland, Oregon, I told myself grouchily around 4:00 A.M. Next time, we could just as well bring Hector along. That cat is trouble, but at least he's trouble of a predictable nature. When everything else seems strange and out of control, it's nice to have something you can count on, something whose behavior you can predict with reasonable accuracy.

In a universe awash in uncertainty, there's reassurance in knowing that some things in life are unchanging, that they respond in an entirely preordained fashion, even if it's only to bite a chunk out of your naked toes.

The one good thing about lying awake most of the night was that it gave me lots of uninterrupted thinking time. Since Tanya Dunseth was already in jail, it would seem I should have focused on her, but for some reason my thoughts turned again and again to Guy Lewis. Why had he suddenly checked out of the Mark Anthony? Was it before or after Daphne Lewis died in the basement at Live Oak Farm?

Between five and seven, I finally slept. At seven, Amber landed squarely on my chest and giggled uncontrollably at my startled "Oomph!" Alex and I were both still groggy, but Amber was wide awake and ready to play. She missed her mother, but she was willing to accept these two slow-moving folks as tolerable substitutes.

The child struck me as a happy-go-lucky, well-adjusted little kid who had no fear of strangers. What that said to me was that Tanya— despite her straitened circumstances and her own ill-used childhood—had somehow provided her child with a world peopled by a collection of trustworthy adult care-givers. Alexis Downey and me included.

It was a considerable challenge corralling Amber and bathing her before we were all due to go downstairs for breakfast. When Alex, kneeling wet-handed beside the bathtub, passed me an armload of squirming, towel-wrapped toddler, I forgot how short the bathroom ceiling was and rapped the top of my head a good one in the process of taking her. I whacked myself hard enough that I saw stars, but I didn't drop the baby.

Minutes later I carried a fully dressed child downstairs while Alex grabbed a quick bath for herself. In order to avoid complicating breakfast preparations, I took Amber out on the porch to play. We were there when Live Oak Farm's decrepit Econoline van turned into the yard and stopped. Jeremy Cartwright climbed out.

After returning Amber's gleeful greeting, he went around to the back of the van and emerged carrying a high chair, which he set on the porch beside me.

"It's Amber's," he said. "It'll make mealtimes easier."

Bless Jeremy's thoughtfulness and consistent good sense. For someone who wore Birkenstocks, he wasn't bad.

"Thanks," I said. He turned down an invitation to breakfast, saying that Kelly was awake and he was headed to the hospital to see her.

"You actually talked to her? How'd she sound?"

"Much better," he said. "But I want to see for myself."

I was trying to decipher the workings of the unfamiliar high chair when Florence appeared at the front door saying I was wanted on the phone. "Who is it?" I asked. "Kelly?"

"It's a man," she answered. "I think he said his name is Peters."

Ron Peters was my partner in Homicide before an on-duty accident robbed him of most of the use of his legs. A less stubborn man might have taken his disability pension and run, but Ron had fought his way back onto the force and into full-time active duty, first with a long, boring stint in the Media-Affairs Division and now, much more happily, as a special assistant to Captain Anthony Freeman, head of I.I.D., Seattle P.D.'s Internal Investigations Division.

"Hey, Ron," I said. "How's it going?" I had taken the call with Amber balanced gingerly on one hip the way I had seen Tanya hold her. Except my hips aren't shaped quite the same way. As soon as I tried to talk, Amber slid down my leg.

"Why don't you tell me what's going on?" Peters demanded.

Where to start? I wondered. With Kelly and Jeremy and their almost-but-not-quite wedding? With the brand-new granddaughter I had barely seen? With Tanya Dunseth and a double homicide? With Kelly's serious fall that had landed her in a hospital?

"Not too much," I said. "Just enjoying a little R and R."

"That's not what I heard," Peters replied pointedly.

Right about then Florence's Natasha made an appearance. Amber greeted the animal with a delighted squeal. "Dog! Dog! Dog!"

The ungodly racket in my ear meant she was also screeching directly into the telephone's mouthpiece. "What's that?" Ron demanded. "Where are you—a day-care center? Sounds like you're locked in a room with a whole tribe of ankle-biters."

"There's only one child here at the moment," I answered, hoisting Amber again. "Hang on." Alex appeared just then and took charge of the wiggling Amber, carting her off to breakfast.

"That's better," I said with a relieved sigh. "Now that I can actually hear you, what were you saying?"

"I said it sounds as though you've been busy."

"Not really. How are things up there?"

"Interesting," Peters replied. "Captain Freeman dropped a bomb on my desk a little while ago. He suggested I handle it first thing."

A tiny stab of anxiety flickered through my mind. Peters didn't sound quite his usual self. "Maybe you'd better call in the bomb squad," I quipped uneasily.

It was a joke, but Peters didn't laugh. "It's not that kind of bomb," he said. "What I have in my hand is an official interdepartmental complaint, actually two-in-one. It's from both the Jackson County Sheriff's Department and from the Department of Public Safety in the city of Ashland, Oregon."

"An official complaint? You're kidding! What does it say?"

"According to one Detective Gordon Fraymore, you are hereby requested to cease and desist from interfering with him and his counterpart at the Sheriff's Department in their common pursuit of their official duties in the investigation of a recent double homicide, blah, blah, blah. How does that grab you?"

"Why that ungrateful . . ."

"He goes on to say that you have been obstructing justice in that you have failed to promptly report meaningful information to him in connection with those same two above-named cases. Is that true?"

"Well . . ." I hedged.

"Tony says cut it out. He says you're on vacation, so act like it. All right?"

"All right," I returned, taken aback and properly chastened.

"Good," Peters said, sounding more himself. "Now, with that out of the way, why don't you tell me what's really going on?"

I told him more or less the whole story while Oak Hill's breakfast went forward without me. It's fair to say Ron was astounded when he learned that the chief suspect's daughter was the "ankle-biter" who had screamed in his ear at the beginning of our conversation.

"No wonder Detective Fraymore thinks you're interfering. I can see where he might pick up such a crazy, unreasonable idea." Actually, so could I.

"Well," Peters said finally, "are you going to follow orders and stay out of it or not?"

"Most likely not," I answered. Since I was talking to Ron Peters, I could just as well be honest. "And neither will Ralph Ames," I added. "He's volunteered to be her defense attorney."

"Great," Peters said. "The brass is going to love that."

"I don't see what any of this has to do with them. After all, I *am* on vacation. Not only that, Ashland is a good eight hours away from the Public Safety Building."

"You're forgetting the power of the press," Ron said. "The papers are full of it. 'Prominent Seattlelite Murdered in Ashland.' Guy and Daphne Lewis are big news here in Seattle. The murder made the front page of this morning's Northwest section. Tony is serious when he says you're to butt out."

I didn't like Tony Freeman or anyone else issuing orders to me while I was on vacation. My hackles stood on end. "Freeman's got a hell of a lot of nerve," I said, sounding surly even to me.

"He's going by what Gordon Fraymore said," Peters reasoned.

"Oh, him. Fraymore's had it in for me from the moment I set foot in this town. I haven't done anything wrong, so far. For that matter, I'm beginning to wonder if Tanya Dunseth has, either. Gordon Fraymore thinks he's built himself an airtight case, and I think Fraymore's a jackass."

"You always did keep your opinions to yourself," Ron observed.

He may have been making fun of me, but I was thinking on my feet. Fraymore's letter, one way or another, had brought the situation in Ashland to the attention of Seattle P.D. Now, with Ron on the phone, I had a chance at some semi-official lines of inquiry—if I could manage to reel him in.

"I wonder . . ." I said tentatively.

"Wonder what?" Peters asked, going for the proffered bait like a half-starved fish, exactly as I knew he would.

"If someone else is using Tanya Dunseth as a fall guy."

"Fall guy or fall woman?" Peters returned. He spent so long in Media Relations that politically correct language has become second nature.

"Are you saying she's being framed?"

"Possibly."

"By Detective Fraymore?"

"Not deliberately. He's a jerk, but he's only doing his job. He wants to clear the case as soon as possible, and he has what seems on the face of it to be pretty conclusive evidence. But what if someone else is handing him that evidence, someone we don't know about?"

There was a long silence on the other end of the line as Peters considered. I knew it was only a matter of time.

"Who?" he asked.

"Guy Lewis maybe?"

Ron whistled. "Are you serious? As in king of the chemical toilets? You think he's the one pulling the strings?"

"I take it you already know him?"

"Only what it said in the paper up here this morning. Chemical toilets may not be all that glamorous a racket, but there must be good money in it. According to the article, he and his late wife were big benefactors on the local arts scene. You want me to see what I can dig up on him?"

I knew I had Ron Peters then. I had sucked him in the same way Alex and Ralph had cornered me. Other than Ron's impossible affinity for natural foods, he's a pretty squared-away guy. When we worked together, we got along well because we were a matched pair of unconventional mavericks—typical homicide dicks.

"What do you want to know?" Ron asked.

"Everything."

"Make it easy. How about some hints?"

"Look into Guy Lewis and his wife. Both wives, actually. And you might see if you can turn up any current connections between Daphne Lewis and Martin Shore."

"The way you say that, it sounds as though there were some connections in the past," Peters said.

"You got it. Shore and Daphne were equal partners in a porno ring over in Yakima."

"No joke! Guy Lewis, too?"

"No. I'm thinking Guy found out about it only recently."

"And it disturbed him enough to want to get rid of them?"

"Seems plausible."

Over the phone, I heard the scribble of pencil and paper as Ron made notes. "Anything else?" he asked.

"Actually, there is. Check out a prison guard over in Walla Walla—a guy by the name of Roger Tompkins. I'd like to know what he's up to."

"You've got it," Peters said cheerily. "That's all?"

"One more thing. You take *Consumer Reports*, don't you?"

"Every month."

"Would you see which companies manufacture the best high chairs and car seats? We're talking top-of-the-line here. I want names and model numbers both."

"Car seats. You mean for little kids?"

"Yes."

"I presume these are for Amber, the one who was yelling her head off a few minutes ago," Peters said. "Interfering is one thing. Aren't you going off the deep end?"

"They're not for Amber," I replied. "They're for Karen."

"Karen? Your ex-wife? She's not having a baby, is she?"

"Not my ex-wife. My granddaughter. Kelly's baby."

"Granddaughter!" Peters echoed. "Wait a minute. How the hell did you end up with a granddaughter? You never told me Kelly was married."

"She isn't," I answered.

There was a long pause while Peters assimilated that information. "Oh," he said at last. "Well, how about telling me what *else* is going on?"

Just then the call-waiting signal buzzed on Florence's line. "Nothing much. I'll explain it all later. I've got to go now. This is a business line. I can't keep it tied up any longer."

"Wait a sec here," Peters bristled. "I've got one more thing to say to you." He sounded as if he meant it—call-waiting be damned!

"What's that?" I asked innocently.

"Did anyone ever tell you you're one closemouthed son of a bitch?"

"No," I told him. "I don't believe anyone's ever mentioned it before. You're the very first one."

"The hell I am!" he growled, and slammed down the phone.

I tried clicking the switch hook, but the caller had already given up. Feeling guilty, I headed into the dining room in search of breakfast leftovers.

I still don't understand why Ron Peters was so offended. If I had tried to tell him the whole story of my romantic interlude in Ashland, Oregon, we would have been on the phone for days.

13

Around ten, two young women from the Festival appeared. One came to take care of Amber. The other was a temporary fill-in as Oak Hill's upstairs maid. Although I'm sure they were both just scraping by financially, neither would accept any payment. The substitute maid told Florence that she should fill out the time card as though Kelly had come to work herself. Nice people.

Cut free from our self-inflicted baby-sitting chores, Alex and I stopped by the hospital to see Kelly. The room had been fairly dark the night before. This morning the curtains were open, and the entire place was alive with flowers.

Some of the arrangements were obvious refugees from the canceled wedding. A few were commercial-type baskets, including a huge one from the board of directors of the Oregon Shakespeare Festival. But the ones that got to me most—the ones that put a lump in my throat—were the numerous amateurish but thoughtfully put together, homegrown variety in simple cut-glass vases. This astonishing array covered every available horizontal surface. It was as though all the gardeners of Ashland had collectively taken their green thumbs outdoors early that morning and plucked their flower beds clean of every colorful bloom.

When it comes to flowers, I don't know much beyond the basics, which is to say roses. And some of the bouquets actually contained roses, but most of the flowers in that vivid, assortment I couldn't have named on a bet.

Looking at them ranged everywhere and spilling out into the hall, I didn't think it possible that the people of Ashland would shower someone as new to town as Kelly with that kind of abundant affection. What I kept forgetting, though, is that Ashland is small-town America. In a place like that, people don't have to know someone personally in order to give a damn.

Don't get me wrong. I like Seattle, but Ashland was showing me that my home turf isn't necessarily the only place to live.

Kelly was asleep when we first arrived. Alex waited around a while, then Dinky came to pick her up, and the two of them set out for Medford to do some shopping. I sat beside Kelly's bed watching and thinking.

I knew that beneath the swathe of bandages the doctors and nurses had shaved off a huge patch of her long blond hair. If anything, the bruises on her face had grown darker overnight. But hair grows back. Bruises heal. The important thing was that she was still alive and most likely would recover.

A few minutes later, Kelly's eyes blinked open. At first she looked around with the dazed, puzzled expression of someone who can't remember quite who or where she is. Then her gaze settled on my face, and she smiled. Her hand sought mine, held it, and squeezed. No paralysis, at least not in her arms. I breathed a small prayer of thanksgiving.

"Hi, Daddy," she whispered. "How long have you been here?"

"Just a couple of minutes."

"Why didn't you wake me? Have you seen the baby?"

I nodded. "She's perfect. She looks just like you did when you were born."

Kelly's lips were dry and cracked. Positioning the straw, I helped her take a sip of ice water from a glass beside the bed. "Jeremy told me what you're doing for Tanya," she said. "That you're helping her and taking care of Amber. Thank you."

I didn't want to take credit where it wasn't due. I certainly didn't merit thanks. "It's all Alex's doing," I said.

Kelly closed her eyes. I thought she was sleeping again, but a moment later her blue eyes fluttered back open. "Jeremy told me there was someone dead in the basement, some woman. I couldn't understand it. Who was she? Why was she there?"

"Her name is Daphne Lewis. She was from Seattle."

"If she was there and I saw her, why don't I remember? Why is it all blank? I remember eating lunch, and the next thing is waking up here in the hospital."

My own nightmarish remembrance of Daphne Lewis dangling on the end of the rope was still far too fresh. "It's a blessing you can't remember, Kelly, something to be grateful for."

"But it seems weird to have that part of my life gone just like that. Erased. I keep thinking if I just concentrate . . ."

"Let it go, Kelly," I advised. "Forget it. If you're going to concentrate on something, focus on getting well so you can get out of here, go home, and take care of Karen."

Kelly went right on as though I hadn't said a word. "Daphne Lewis?" She frowned. "Who is she, and why do the police think Tanya killed her? That's the dumbest thing I've ever heard."

I gave up avoiding the issue and tried answering questions. "Tanya knew Daphne Lewis years ago. There's enough evidence connecting them to arouse Detective Fraymore's suspicions."

"But Tanya's so nice," Kelly argued. "You don't know her the way I do. She's not violent. She would never kill anyone, no matter what."

It was more or less the same thing Jeremy had said. Clearly, there was much about Tanya that neither Kelly nor Jeremy suspected, and it wasn't my place to tell them otherwise.

"Kelly," I said reprovingly. "Remember the other day? You told me to stop playing detective. Now I'm telling you the same thing. I'm not on duty here. Neither are you. Your only job is to get well."

Kelly nodded and then winced, as though even that small movement pained her. "All right," she said. "I'll try."

About then I spied Grandma Karen Livingston out in the hallway. The nurse had told us to limit both visits and visitors so as not to tire the patient. With that in mind, I told Kelly good-bye and got up to leave. Karen caught me outside the room.

"Dave went to pick Scott up from the motel," she said. "We're all going home today."

"So soon? I thought you'd stick around for a while, maybe help with the baby until Kelly gets back on her feet."

"No." Karen shook her head emphatically. "I can't do that. We have to go. I just wanted to thank you for all you've done."

I felt like shaking her. What the hell could be more important than being there when her daughter was in the hospital? But since Karen was supposedly being conciliatory, I did the same.

"If the wedding is rescheduled for later this summer, will you come back?"

Karen met my gaze for a moment, then she looked away. "Maybe," she said.

Maybe? I couldn't believe what I was hearing. Kelly was Karen's only daughter, and yet she couldn't do any better than a lame "maybe" when it came to attending a wedding? Karen slipped away from me into Kelly's room before I had a chance to reply,

Instantly furious, I stomped out of the hospital. Here I was bending over backward to get along. Why, then, did Karen have to be so damn difficult? The wedding Jeremy and Kelly had planned had been blown apart by circumstances far beyond their control. What would it hurt if our granddaughter was two months old or six months or even a year when the wedding took place? Call me an old-fashioned, romantic fool, but I still thought her parents deserved a real wedding to celebrate their marriage. I couldn't understand why Karen Livingston didn't agree.

I was pacing up and down the sidewalk in front of the hospital when Dave drove up with Scott in the car. We all sort of milled aimlessly around in the parking lot for a while, struck suddenly dumb and shy by all the important things that needed saying but couldn't quite be said. I made my good-byes and took off before Karen came outside. I no longer trusted my ability to keep a civil tongue in my mouth.

With Alex off shopping in Medford and with Amber safely under control, I found myself at loose ends. I didn't have anything special in mind as I drove over to the Ashland Hills looking for Ralph Ames. My expectation was that the two of us would do some of what today's young people call "hanging out."

When I knocked, Ralph came to the door with a cellular phone stuck to his ear, held there by a shoulder to free up his hands for a yellow tablet and pen. I saw at once that hanging out was out of the question. Ralph was far too busy.

In a mad frenzy of activity, he had created the most technologically up-to-date, instant hotel-room office imaginable. His portable fax was hooked up and running, ringing and groaning as it coughed out sheet after sheet of burned-smelling, heat-sensitive paper. Ralph himself was hard at work transferring notes from the yellow tablet to his handy-dandy laptop computer. Periodically, he would have to lunge over to the wall and disconnect the fax from the phone jack in order to use the modem on his computer.

"How did people ever function with only one telephone line?" he demanded irritably over his shoulder when a harried receptionist somewhere left him sitting on hold.

"This may come as a shock to you, Ralph, but people actually survived on this planet before there were any phones at all," I told him. "How much good does all this high-tech stuff do, anyway?"

"Not much so far," he conceded, "but I'm just starting. What gives with you?"

Ralph carried on his part of the conversation, asking and answering questions, without ever taking his eyes off the glowing computer screen. He reminded me of one of those weirded-out video-game addicts. I probably should have taken the hint and left him to his work, but I was feeling nervous and anxious for some reason. I didn't much want to be alone. In that frame of mind, distracted and preoccupied company was better than no company at all.

"Karen, Scott, and Dave just left," I said forlornly.

"I know," Ralph returned. "I was here when Dave picked Scott up. He was staying with me, remember?"

I had somehow forgotten that detail. "Scott's in summer school now," I continued. "Dave probably has to get back to work. I can understand that. What I can't fathom is why Karen couldn't stay on any longer to help out. It wouldn't kill her to bend a little bit now and then."

"Maybe she had something important to do back home," Ralph suggested.

"Sure she did," I agreed sarcastically. "What's more important than being here when her daughter needs her? How about taking care of her only grandchild when her only daughter is damn near at death's door? What's more important than that? A hot bridge game? Maybe a tennis tournament?"

Ralph's fingers paused over the keyboard while he looked me full in the face. "Are we feeling a little testy today?"

"I guess."

"What's eating you?"

"Everything and nothing." Ralph kept looking at me, but his fingers started moving again, speeding over the keyboard with incredible dexterity without his having to look at either the screen or the keys. Ames is now and always will be a far better typist than I am.

"By the way," I added. "I talked to Ron Peters in Seattle today."

Ralph's nimble fingers never missed a stroke. "What did he have to say?"

"I'm in some kind of hot water as per usual. Fraymore sent an official letter of complaint to Seattle P.D. in regard to my continued interference with his homicide investigation. Tony Freeman in I.I.D. handed the problem over to Ron."

Ames shook his head. "That was fast. Fraymore must have written it and faxed it overnight. I had a feeling our behavior was offending the local constabulary. Don't feel picked on, Beau. Gordon Fraymore would complain about me, too, if he could just figure out where to send the paper."

Somehow, knowing I wasn't the only target for Fraymore's ire did make me feel a little better.

"I take it you've had your hands slapped?" Ralph asked.

"Officially, yes. Peters passed along Tony Freeman's verbal message, which was, 'You're on vacation. Act like it.' "

"And unofficially?"

"Ron's going to dig around up there in Seattle and see what, if anything, he can find out that might be of help."

"I've always liked Ron Peters," Ralph said. A moment later, he paused in his typing and frowned. "What are you up to today?"

"Not much. I guess I'll hang out at the hospital. Worry."

"I've got some legwork that needs doing, but I don't want you to wind up in any more trouble."

"Legwork's something I'm good at. If you've got something for me to do that will keep me occupied, let me at it. We'll worry about trouble later."

"You're sure?"

"What kind of legwork?" I returned.

Ralph reached over and shuffled through an already impressive stack of rolled-up fax-generated paper. Pulling out one sheet, he handed it to me. "I don't have time to chase this down myself. It's going to take all morning to prepare for the arraignment. On the other hand, I don't see how Fraymore could possibly object to your doing this, since it has nothing whatsoever to do with the murder investigation, per se." He paused and then added, "It may end up having some bearing on our defense, however."

Glancing down at the paper, I was riveted by what I saw there—the names Roger and Willy Tompkins, along with a street address in Walla Walla.

"You want me to go see them?"

Ralph nodded.

"To talk to them, or to punch that guy's lights out?"

"Talk," Ralph said. "Definitely nothing but talk. We've got to learn whether or not these people will try to make any kind of trouble when it comes to sorting out long-term custody arrangements for Amber. If they'll be reasonable, so will we. If they try to make things difficult, I'll blow them clean out of the water."

"Long-term custody?" I asked. "That sounds like you think we'll lose and that you've already given up."

"We have to be prepared for every contingency," he returned darkly. Ralph Ames is not a man prone to discouraging words. Clearly, things weren't going well.

"Fraymore's evidence is that solid?"

Ralph nodded. "It's solid all right. And there's no reason for him to lie to me about it."

"Have you given any thought to the possibility that we might be dealing with a carefully planned, well-thought-out frame?"

"Frame?" Ralph repeated.

"I spent all night thinking about it, and I talked it over with Ron. There's something about this whole thing that doesn't ring true. It's too pat."

"You think Fraymore's crooked?"

"No. I didn't say that. Misguided, maybe. Overzealous, perhaps. What if he's being suckered by somebody else?"

"All I can say is that somebody went to a hell of a lot of trouble," Ralph replied.

"But wouldn't you?" I asked. "If you wanted to get away with murder, you'd do whatever was necessary."

We were both quiet for a few moments. Finally, Ralph shook his head. He wasn't buying it. Tired of arguing, I let it go.

"How's Tanya holding up?" I asked finally.

"All right, except . . ."

"Except what?"

Ames shook his head. "It's hard to explain. I can't quite put my finger on it. She seems almost drifty and vague at times, as though she can't quite grasp the reality of all this, as if it isn't quite getting through. Other times she's totally on track."

"She's probably just feeling overwhelmed," I suggested.

"Maybe," Ralph agreed. "But there's something else that bothers me. I've thought about it ever since last night. I was there in the room when she told Detective Fraymore the same story she told us. I listened to the whole thing again, Beau. It was almost verbatim. Like a prepared speech."

"All of it?" I asked.

"Word for word."

I felt a slight tinge of worry. Most people don't use the exact same words to tell a story the second time. There are always some changes, some slight variations. Unless what's being delivered is a canned speech, lines of dialogue delivered by a consummate actress. Were Ralph Ames and J. P. Beaumont being played for suckers one more time?

In my present mood, that question wasn't one I cared to sit around contemplating. I got up and walked over to the telephone jack.

"If I can commandeer the phone away from your fax machine for a few minutes, I'll see what kind of connections are available between here and Walla Walla."

Armed with my Frequent Flyer number, I started checking for flights. What I found out in a nutshell was that you *can* get to Walla Walla from Ashland, but it isn't necessarily easy. There are really only two decent connecting flights per day—one in the early morning, which I'd already missed, and one in the late afternoon, which required an overnight stay. I went ahead and booked that one. With Amber most likely spending another night in the room with Alex and me, I couldn't see that it made a hell of a lot of difference.

I had no more than finished booking the flight and putting down the phone when it rang again. "Should I answer it?"

Ralph shrugged. "Go ahead. If it's for me, find out who it is and take a message."

"Hello."

"Beau, is that you?"

It was Ron Peters, calling from Seattle. I had told him where Ralph was staying in case he couldn't locate me, but I was surprised to have him call back so soon.

"What's up?"

"I thought you'd like to know that I've just solved the mystery of where Guy Lewis disappeared to."

"You found him? Is he back home in Seattle?"

"Not quite. He never made it this far," Ron Peters answered. "In fact, he never made it past Medford."

The way he said it made it sound permanent. Not another murder, I thought. "Don't tell me. Is he dead?"

"No, but it's a miracle he isn't. God knows he should be. The Medford cops and the state police acting together picked him up at six o'clock Sunday morning, drunk as a skunk, and driving his Miata northbound on southbound I-5 at ten miles an hour. He blew a point-two-nine on the breathalyzer and was so out of it that they took him to a hospital to dry out instead of throwing him in the drunk tank."

I was thunderstruck. How could Guy Lewis end up that smashed within eleven hours of our attending an N.A. meeting in the basement of that Ashland church? "Good work, Ron," I said.

"Wait a minute. You haven't heard the half of it. By Monday evening, he was sober enough to post bail. He was about to be released from the hospital, when that cop you told me about, Detective Fraymore, showed up to tell Lewis that his wife had been murdered. As soon as he heard, he went into some kind coronary arrhythmia. It must not have been all that serious, but they kept him there under observation. He's been in the hospital ever since, but he's due to be released late this morning or early this afternoon."

Fumbling for paper and pencil, I jotted down the name and address of the hospital in Medford. "Have you had a chance to do any checking on the rest of it?" I asked. "Anything on either Shore or Daphne?"

"You want it all, and you want it right now, don't you? I'm working as fast as I can, Beau. I can only do so much. Try practicing a little patience."

I'm nothing if not an ungrateful wretch. "You're right, Ron. This is great. It's a big help."

A few words later, we hung up, and I gave Ralph the news. He didn't seem surprised or even all that interested when I told him, but then he hadn't spent the first part of Saturday evening at the N.A. meeting with a then-sober-and-proud-of-it Guy Lewis. I had. After ten years of sobriety, what had blown him off the wagon?

Ralph and I talked a minute or two longer, then I told him I was going to head back to Oak Hill, tell Florence I'd be away overnight, pick up an extra key, and leave a note to that effect for Alex. I didn't mention the hospital address on the piece of paper I'd shoved in my pocket. I didn't say I might go there to see Guy Lewis, because at the time I left Ralph's room at the Ashland Hills, I still didn't know for sure I would.

For one thing, if Gordon Fraymore ever found out I went to see Guy, my ass would be in a sling for certain—not only with Fraymore, but also now with straight-shooting Tony Freeman back home in Seattle. Freeman wasn't the type to rave and carry on, but when he said, "Act like you're on vacation," he expected people to pay attention.

As I left Ashland heading north, Guy Lewis bothered me more and more. What would make somebody fall off the wagon after being sober that long? I wondered. God knows I had come close to slipping myself that very day. In retrospect, I could see how emotional overload about Kelly and Jeremy had almost sucked me into a relapse, but I had pulled myself back from it. In the past two days, even though things had continued to spiral downward, I hadn't been in nearly the same jeopardy of taking that first drink as I had been when I ventured into the smoky bar of the Mark Anthony. Guy hadn't been as lucky.

That brought me to another question. How long had Guy Lewis been sober? Ten years stuck in my mind. Something about his first wife leaving him about the same time he dried out.

Between Saturday night and six o'clock Sunday morning, something had pushed Guy Lewis off the edge of a very steep emotional cliff. Old habits die hard, and he had set out to drown his sorrows. In those few hours, he had downed enough booze to require a doctor's care just to regain consciousness. I don't call that slipping. It's more like crashing and burning.

Had Lewis been drinking at the party? I didn't remember smelling booze on his breath when we chatted in the Members' Lounge or seeing him drinking hard stuff later on at the Bowmer, although he could have been. Drunks are cagey that way. They drink and drink, and it's all invisible—up to a point.

Whatever caused it, once he was drunk, he must have decided to leave town, with or without Daphne in the car. Again the question came to mind—was Daphne Lewis still alive at the time Guy headed north?

I was in a 928 equipped with a working cellular phone, so I dialed Ron Peters' extension at the department in Seattle. He didn't answer, and I didn't dare leave a message on his voice mail—not after being told in no uncertain terms to butt out.

And then another thought hit me. Peters had said that when Fraymore came to the hospital to deliver the bad news about Daphne, Guy had suffered some kind of coronary disturbance. That meant one of two things. The first choice was the most obvious: News of his wife's murder had so shocked Guy Lewis that his heart went gunnybags on him.

Option number two was that Guy already knew Daphne was dead because he personally had something to do with her murder. If that was the case, finding himself trapped in the same room with the man sworn to find his wife's killer might very well have scared the living piss out of him. It would have scared me.

So which was it? Number one or number two? As optometrists are so fond of saying: Which is clearer? This? Or this? I didn't have an answer right then, but I was going to find out.

I'm learning. When I pulled off the freeway in Medford, I stopped at the first gas station and asked for directions. I didn't want to waste any time at all being lost.

14

I've heard stories about people who age overnight, but Guy Lewis was a true flesh-and-blood example—the first one I ever observed with my own eyes. I found him sitting in a wheelchair in the lobby at Rogue River Medical Center. His skin was sallow; the muscles and skin of his body seemed to have collapsed in on his bones.

"Hello, there, Guy. Could you use a lift?"

He looked up at me out of dull eyes that had no spark of life left in them. "Oh, it's you, Mr. Beaumont. I'm waiting for a cab. I can walk, but I have strict orders from that idiotic nurse over there not to step out of this thing until the cab gets here."

"Where are you going?"

"The Red Lion," he said. "Out along the freeway. I screwed up the undercarriage on my Mazda. They had to order in a special part from L.A. It'll be ready later this afternoon."

"If you want, I can take you wherever you're going."

He nodded gratefully. "I'd sure appreciate it. This place makes my skin crawl."

We canceled the cab dispatch. I brought the Porsche around, and a very brusque, businesslike nurse supervised Guy Lewis' transfer from wheelchair to automobile. The man breathed a sigh of relief when the door closed, effectively shutting the nurse out and us in.

"You saved my life," he breathed. "If I'd been stuck in that lobby for another ten minutes, I would have gotten up and gone looking for the nearest bar."

"We both know that's a bad idea," I told him.

"Yes," he said. "I guess we do."

On the way to the hospital, I had considered dozens of possible ways to begin asking the necessary questions, but that was before I saw how frail Guy seemed. How could a man who looked as though he would be bowled over by a strong breeze hold up under one barrage of questions after another—not only from me, but also from Gordon Fraymore? Studying him, I wondered if the incident of arrhythmia was more life-threatening than I'd been led to believe.

"What brings you to Medford?" he asked, eyeing me suspiciously. "Twelfth-stepping?"

I shrugged, uncomfortable with his use of A.A. jargon. I hadn't come calling on Guy Lewis in a single-minded effort to save him from Demon Rum.

"After a fashion, I suppose. I have a plane to catch later on, around five. That left me with an hour or two to kill."

"How did you know I was here?"

"One of my friends in Seattle. The story about Daphne was in the papers up there this morning. I don't know how he found out about you."

When Guy heard my answer, he made a strange, strangled sound—a choking, hiccuping noise. I looked at him anxiously, thinking maybe the heart problem had returned. Instead, he slouched against the far car door, sobbing.

At last he pulled himself together. "She's dead," he said brokenly. "I don't know how I'll get through all this—making the arrangements, planning a funeral. Some things you never expect to do. Look at me. I'm twenty-three years older than she was, and overweight besides. I don't exercise, and I've had a heart condition for years. I'm the one who should be dead."

With that he broke down again. To hear Guy's anguished sobs and see his quaking body was to experience misery made manifest. Daphne Lewis might have had much to answer for in this life, but her passing had left behind a man stricken by the rampant paralysis of grief. It was impossible not to be touched by his overwhelming suffering—touched and awed.

I believe younger people—those in their twenties and thirties—assume passion will more or less disappear over time. They expect that, with age, raw emotion gradually slips out of our lives, gliding silently from view the way a molting snake abandons the shell of last year's useless skin. Here was Guy Lewis—a heavyset, balding man in an improbably gaudy orange Hawaiian shirt—weeping uncontrollably. At his age—the far end of fifty—one might expect anguished passion to surface as only a rare comic anomaly.

But there was no pretense in the sorrow that etched Guy's face, no playacting in the way he huddled miserably in my car, no phoniness to his hurt. For all Daphne's faults, Guy Lewis had loved his second wife—loved her wildly, withholding nothing. And that's when I realized something about his arrhythmia episode—something an empathetic doctor might possibly have already recognized. What had been observed medically on high tech EKG monitors was nothing more or less than the outward symptom of a newly broken heart.

When we arrived at the Red Lion, Guy was still in no condition to talk, so I left him in the 928 under a shaded portico and used my own AmEx card to check him in. I explained to the big-eyed young desk clerkette that Mr. Lewis had lost his wife and that the remainder of the check-in procedures would have to be handled when he was better able to deal with them.

As soon as we made it into the room, Guy disappeared into the bathroom for a much-needed shower, while I called room service to order coffee and sandwiches. I know enough about the internal workings of hospitals to realize that they routinely plug you full of decaf and call it the real thing. It's no wonder people come out of hospitals feeling worse than when they went in. They're all suffering from severe caffeine withdrawal.

When Guy Lewis emerged from the shower, he may have felt better, but his looks hadn't improved. The room-service food was already waiting on the table. He sat down in front of one of the two cracked-pepper meat-loaf sandwiches. He looked at it distractedly, making no move to pick it up. I poured a cup of coffee and bodily placed it in his hand.

"Drink some of this," I said. "It'll do you good."

Mechanically, like a child doing as it's been told, he took a sip and swallowed it. The steaming brown liquid could have scalded his tongue with second-degree burns, and he wouldn't have noticed. He slammed the cup back into the saucer with such force I was surprised it didn't shatter into a million pieces. Coffee slopped in all directions.

"That's part of what's killing me," he said hoarsely. "Its going to come out now, isn't it?"

"What's going to come out?" I asked.

"All the rumors."

If ever there was a time for feigned innocence, this was it. "What rumors?" I asked.

"There are all kinds of stories about Daphne's past. Some of them are true. But no matter what they say, she wasn't a gold digger who was only after me for my money. She liked the money fine. Who wouldn't? And she may have had her little flings now and again, but Daphne loved me, dammit! I know she did."

"I'm sure she did," I agreed.

"I don't want to talk about it," he continued as though I hadn't spoken. "I hate the very idea but I have to. I need to talk to someone. Whatever I tell you is in confidence, isn't it, the same as if I said it in a meeting?"

That was putting it to me. "Yes," I said.

"Years ago, when Daphne was a struggling young woman, she got her start making movies. I guess you could call them naughty movies."

Calling child pornography "naughty" is like calling television
"intellectual." The two words don't belong in the same sentence.
I would term the coupling of a middle-aged man and a prepubes-
cent girl vile or repulsive, to say nothing of illegal. I wouldn't say
it was naughty. I wondered if Guy Lewis had ever seen any of the
movies in question. And I questioned whether or not he knew
about Daphne's role in the forced servitude of Tanya Dunseth and
the production of Dinky Holloway's videotape. If he didn't yet
know any of those awful details, he would shortly.

"It must have been at least fifteen years ago now," he continued.
"Daphne and I have been together for ten. This was long before
that."

I added up the numbers in my head. They didn't exactly tally
with what Tanya had told us, but I let it pass.

"Now, according to Detective Fraymore, it's all going to come
out in the open. He as good as told me there's nothing I can do to
stop it. That young woman in jail—the one who played Juliet, as
a matter of fact—was in some of those same kinds of movies.
According to Fraymore, there was a connection of some sort between Daphne and this Tanya person. Fraymore says Tanya just all
of a sudden freaked out and started killing people."

"What about the man who was killed? Was he involved in the
movies, too?"

Guy Lewis' eyes darkened. "I don't want to talk about him. You're
a police officer, Mr. Beaumont, so I'm sure you'll understand this
if I tell you. I believe that man was somehow blackmailing Daphne.
Maybe he and that Tanya did it together. I don't know. I just know
that when I saw them together . . ."

His voice trailed off. By sheer force of will, he bit back another sob.

"When you saw who together?"

"Daphne and Martin Shore, talking together, when we first went
to the party at the Bowmer. I just flat lost it. They were off in the
dark theater, sitting with their heads so close they must have been
necking. They didn't think I saw them. I knew about Shore, of
course. Daphne had told me all about him long ago. They started

out as partners and were even married for a short time. But that was all in the past. At least, I thought it was. Then, when I saw them together like that, acting so cozy, I don't know what got into me. I went crazy. That's when I hit the sauce.

"You saw the bar at the party. There was plenty of booze to choose from, and I chose it all. When we left the party to walk back to the Mark Anthony, I was already drunk and plenty pissed. Daphne and I ended up in a terrible fight. For a while, we walked on opposite sides of the alley, screaming insults, but I don't think anyone noticed because of all the sirens and fire trucks down on the street."

"That must have been when the accident happened, and when Martin Shore got killed."

"That's right," Guy agreed. "I suppose it was, but I didn't know that at the time. By then I was too drunk to know anything, and I probably wasn't much fun to be around, either. There was a message waiting for Daphne at the hotel. When she told me she was going for a walk, I accused her of all kinds of terrible things. I told her she was probably going to meet with Martin Shore up in the park, that they'd go off in the bushes and fuck like a pair of dogs."

He blushed then, recalling those awful words. For a moment, with the ruddy color back in his cheeks, he looked more like himself—the way he'd been on Saturday night when the two of us crossed the street together before the plays. The color faded, almost as fast as it had appeared, leaving him washed-out and sallow.

"I'm sorry I said those things now," Guy said softly. "It hurts like hell that the very last thing I ever said to her was so hateful and mean. I'd take it back if I could, but right then, more than anything, I wanted to hurt her. I said if she walked out of the lobby not to bother coming back, that I'd leave Ashland and go home without her. She probably thought I was bluffing—that I was too drunk to try it—and she was right. I was too drunk, but I did it anyway. That's how I ended up here."

He paused, tracing shapeless forms in the splotches of spilled coffee on the tabletop, connecting the dots with streaks of brown.

"I really did leave her," he went on distractedly. "In my mind, I was leaving for good, but I had no idea I was abandoning her to a murderer. Jesus! What a creep I am! What an incredibly worthless, no-good creep! Where was I when she needed me? I'll tell you where I was—being arrested and carried into a hospital because I was too goddamned drunk to walk!"

Guy Lewis' deep voice quavered, shaken by the intensity of his own self-loathing. "If she's not alive," he added softly, "I don't much care if I am, either."

Veiled threats of suicide are fairly common in those kinds of circumstances. When someone says they don't want to go on living after some unforseen tragedy, it's always easy to stand outside the circle of their pain and give worthy advice. "You don't mean that," and "You'll get over it," and, worse, "Life goes on," are only a few of a thousand empty-minded statements that devalue the shattered treasures of someone else's heart.

Daphne Lewis might have been a consummate scam artist and an unfaithful wife to boot. The things she did might have been reprehensible and criminal both, but she had been the single light in Guy Lewis' life. Without her, he was virtually incapable of continued existence. The rest of the world might have mocked him and called Daphne his "trophy wife," but to Guy Lewis, she had been a rare jewel, a prize worthy of the game at whatever price it cost him.

"How did you meet her?" I asked.

"At the Rep," he said, "at one of the first fund-raisers after we opened the Bagley Wright Theater back in the early eighties. Daphne and Monica, the girl who used to have Alex's job, knew one another from somewhere, although I can't recall now just where. Monica was the one who introduced us.

"It was love at first sight, for me anyway. Unfortunately, I was still married to Maggie at the time. That was a big problem. But someone who deals in chemical toilets gets used to dealing with shit, one way or another. It's godawful. It's messy, but somebody has to do it. My father made a fortune at it, and so have I. I figured if I had to spend some of what I call my hard-earned turd money just to get rid of Maggie, I would. And I did, too. She fought me every step of the way, and her lawyer drove a hell of a hard bargain, but I figured Daphne was worth it—and she was."

As he warmed to the telling, some of the color and animation returned to Guy Lewis' pathetic cheeks. Just talking about Daphne seemed to make him feel better. I felt sorry as hell for him. He wouldn't be able to talk about her like this forever, because I suspected I knew some dark things about Daphne Lewis that were going to poison the well of his treasured memories.

"You said you thought your wife was being blackmailed?"

Guy nodded. "I never balanced a checkbook in my life," he said. "That's why God gave us accountants. But I'm one of those guys, if you ask me what's in my wallet, I can tell you within five bucks. Same way with my bank accounts. I'm not tight. I've met men who are. They make a lot of money and then can't stand to spend it. Or can't stand for their wives to spend it. Not me. I say, 'If we've got it, use it.'

"Daphne had a real hard life until she met me, God bless her. I wanted to give her everything she ever wanted. I wanted her to have fun. She got a real kick out of having plenty of money. Used to be, if a big chunk disappeared out of the household accounts, something would come back in—a piece of bronze sculpture she liked or a painting maybe. She liked those damned abstracts best. Once she bought a whole damn garden and had them move it into our yard a brick at a time.

"In the last year or so, three big lumps of money evaporated completely. I didn't ask her about it, because I figured maybe she was getting me something for my birthday. I was afraid to ask, afraid I'd wreck the surprise. But now I don't think that anymore. Do you?"

His direct question caught me off base. "How much money?"

"Right at a hundred-fifty thou, give or take."

I shook my head. "No, Mr. Lewis," I said. "There may have been a surprise, but I wouldn't hold my breath waiting for a birthday present."

He nodded sadly. "That's what I thought," he said.

Picking up the coffee cup, he swilled down the remainder of its contents and then took an almost unconscious bite of his sandwich. "Tell me about Tanya Dunseth," he said, chewing thoughtfully. "Know anything about her?"

"Not much."

"Fraymore says she was in some of the movies Daphne and Martin Shore made." Guy paused and took another bite. "That's how people are going to remember Daphne now, isn't it?"

"What do you mean?"

"That she was involved in those movies once."

"Some people may," I hedged.

"I know better," he returned. "Don't try to placate me by telling me any different. Daphne did a lot of good for charities in Seattle. No matter what anybody thinks, she was a hard worker. What I do isn't very pretty, but the nonprofits like having my money on their balance sheets. Daphne was glamorous as hell. Having her with me made me almost ... well, legitimate. And I did the same for her. We could go places together that wouldn't have let either one of us in by ourselves. But now that Daphne's dead and gone and can't defend herself, those same society dames who used to suck up to her will throw her to the wolves. They'll probably still want my money, though," he added bitterly.

"Why is the world like that, Mr. Beaumont? Why do people love to find someone like Daphne—someone beautiful or a little different, someone they can smear or tear to pieces?"

"Guy," I said, "if I knew the answer to that, you can bet I wouldn't be working as a homicide detective."

"No," he agreed, "I don't suppose you would."

Listening to Guy's version of the story, I wondered where the truth lay. Had Daphne been carrying on with Martin Shore the whole time or was she being blackmailed by him? If not him, who else was a likely candidate? How much did Guy Lewis know about Daphne's real past? How many other kids besides Tanya had been victimized by taking a starring role in one of Martin Shore's movies?

Given what I had learned from other sources, I tended to agree with people who would say the fates meted out to both Martin Shore and Daphne Lewis were nothing if not just desserts, but sitting closeted in a darkened hotel room with a grieving Guy Lewis, I saw no reason to tell him that. He didn't deserve it. And somewhere in the world there might be a Mrs. Martin Shore who didn't deserve it, either.

The phone rang, startling us both. I think Guy expected me to answer it. Instead, I picked it up off the nightstand and brought it to him. From hearing only one side of the conversation, I surmised that the fully repaired Miata had just been dropped off. The desk clerk wanted to know if Mr. Lewis wanted her to bring the keys up to his room or should she keep them down at the desk. He told her to keep them and that he'd be down to pick them up later, when his four o'clock appointment arrived.

"What appointment?" I asked, when he got off the phone.

"That detective, the one from Ashland. What's his name?"

"Fraymore," I supplied. "He's coming here?"

"Didn't I tell you? He still has some questions to ask."

The last person I wanted to run into right then was Gordon Fraymore. If he found me in Guy Lewis' room, he'd be ripped, and rightfully so. Worried, I glanced at my watch. Three forty-five didn't leave much time. I stood up. "I'd better be going," I said.

"Fraymore asked about you, by the way," Guy Lewis added.

"About me? How so?"

"He wanted to know how the two of us met. I told him about the Bentley. He seemed to get a real kick out of it."

"I'll bet."

"He also asked how we happened to hook up in Ashland. I didn't want to talk about the meeting, so I told him we met during the Green Show."

By chance both Guy and I had told the same story. Two wrongs don't make a right, and two lies don't make the truth, either—

especially not in a murder investigation when the detective already knows better. In homicide-cop mentality, Fraymore was busily adding up provable lies and stirring them into a bubbling vat of conspiracy.

"What did he say to that?"

"Nothing much."

I was almost out the door, but mention of our meeting brought up another question in my mind. "How was it that you and Daphne happened to be down here in the first place? Was it something you had planned for a long time?"

"Oh, no," Lewis answered. "It was completely spur of the moment, one of those surprise deals. Daphne sprang it on me just the first of last week, although she must have had the tickets earlier than that. I think she and Monica Davenport must have dreamed up the idea in order to get to spend some time together, although if I know Monica, she probably had an ulterior motive. She's just like Alex—always looking for a way to relieve a fellow of a little hard-earned cash."

There were other things I wanted to know, other questions I wanted to ask, but I didn't want to risk hanging around any longer and running into Fraymore. If he drove up and caught sight of the Guard-red Porsche out in the parking lot, I was dead meat. There aren't that many 928s racing around in southern Oregon. Not only that, it was time to go catch my plane.

Guy Lewis followed me to the door. The food and talk had done him some good. His coloring was better. He seemed steadier on his feet. Outside the room, Guy surprised me by reaching out and grabbing me in a powerful, bearlike hug.

"I've been twelfth-stepped a couple of other times in my life," he said, "Some were real hassles. You know—guys coming over to preach in your face and set you on the straight and narrow. At least that's how it seemed at the time. You really listened to me today, Mr. Beaumont, and I want you to know it helped. It helped a lot. I appreciate it."

I drove away from the Red Lion carrying a heavy load of J. P.

Beaumont special-reserve guilt. I had gone on an intelligence-gathering mission that Guy Lewis had understandably mistaken for a legitimate twelfth-step call.

He had told me a lot—far more than I deserved to know. And as I drove toward Medford's Jackson County Airport, I realized that—preserving the confidentiality of a meeting—I wouldn't be able to use any of it.

15

For outlying towns in the Pacific Northwest—the isolated Pull-mans, Wenatchees, and Walla Wallas—Horizon Air's busy fleet of small planes fills a very real need. In some markets around Washington, Oregon, and Idaho, those diminutive planes consti-tute pretty much the only air-travel game in town. Seeing Horizon's fleet of DeHavilland Dash 8's parked in tight clusters at Seattle's C-concourse and dwarfed by the much larger 747s and 767s, I'm always reminded of a swarm of hornets. But they do fly.

When the Medford-Portland-Seattle shuttle came in for a landing, I thought I'd died and gone to heaven. The plane was one of the new Dash 8's. I couldn't believe my luck. At six-three and 185 pounds, I can ride in a Dash 8 in relative comfort. My good fortune lasted only as far as Portland. There, I was herded onto a sardine-can Metroliner for the rest of the trip to Walla Walla. An hour or so in a Metroliner puts a permanent crick in my neck and creases in both knees, but it beats walking. Just barely.

Summer comes late to the Northwest. In terms of heat, the end of June is only the very beginning of hot weather, but during this relatively dry year, fire season was already under way. We flew east along the Columbia River, maneuvering around an immense pillar of smoke that rose from an uncontained fire burning out of control in the Mount Hood Wilderness area.

No doubt some anonymous forest-service official was busy at his computer totaling up numbers and figuring out accountability, trying to decide if this particular blaze should end up on the "natural" or "man-caused" side of the forest-fire ledger. That was a moot question for the unfortunate animals who had once called that corner of old-growth forest home. Rather than cause, they worried about effect—about battling for bare survival and searching for some new place to live.

In a way, those poor hapless creatures were not unlike Guy Lewis. He, too, had been laid low by complicated events he could neither explain nor fathom. When trees disappear, the animals don't have the time or energy to investigate the cause of destruction. The same for Guy Lewis. Daphne was dead, murdered. Unlike many in his situation, the grieving widower apparently had little curiosity about who had killed her. Just like those ill-fated squirrels, deer, and other wildlife scrambling desperately to escape the raging inferno far below the moving shadow of my plane, he was too numb, too paralyzed, too traumatized, to think linearly.

I, on the other hand, like that fire-counting minion from forest-service officialdom, live in the accountability sector, the cause-and-blame sector, the let's-find-out-why-this-happened department. It's a mind-set, a way of life, that doesn't go away just because your calendar or Tony Freeman says you're on vacation. So I sat in the plane and tried to force what I had learned about the two murders into some kind of meaningful whole.

That didn't work very well. Nothing connected to this case turned out to be quite what I expected. My interview with Guy Lewis was a prime case in point. After hearing him talk openly in the N.A. meeting about his deteriorating second marriage, I was struck by the depth and obvious sincerity of his grief.

Maybe society had jokingly referred to Daphne as his trophy wife; maybe people had derided the king of chemical toilets for being a rich old fool—laughed at him because Daphne led him around by the gonads. But Guy Lewis' relationship with Daphne was no joke to him. He had cared for her deeply and still did. Even though she was dead, Guy was fully prepared to stand up for her—to defend her memory in public if necessary despite the posthumous disclosure of Daphne's none-too-savory past.

And the lady did have a past. That set me to wondering about Daphne herself, about whether or not Guy Lewis' feelings for her had been reciprocated. Daphne had divorced Martin Shore, yet she had somehow managed to keep him hanging around on the sidelines, an arrangement my mother would have referred to as having your cake and eating it, too.

What kind of tortuous, winding path had carried Daphne Lewis from the modeling-scam/porno-queen days of her presumably first marriage in Yakima to the position of sought-after society matron in well-heeled Seattle? There's a hell of a climb between those two extremes, and I'm not just talking about the Washington Cascades, either. How had Daphne managed to travel the distance from point A to point B, and what had she done in between?

A cool $150,000 was missing from the Lewis family financial coffers. Guy suspected Martin Shore and Tanya Dunseth had conspired together in some kind of scheme to blackmail Daphne. As far as I was concerned, that sounded like a bad case of wishful thinking on Guy's part. Believing a complex conspiracy theory was probably a way for him to discount the disturbing reappearance of longtime rival Martin Shore.

I tried to compare the two vastly different versions of the Daphne Lewis/Tanya Dunseth story. Things didn't quite add up. The chronology continued to be slightly off. Tanya claimed to be twenty-five years old. She also had told us that the Martin Shore video had been filmed when she was fifteen. Guy Lewis, on the other hand, maintained that he and Daphne had been together for a full ten years, and that her moviemaking days had ended years before that.

Which story was true? One wild card in the deck was Daphne herself. She was, after all, a con artist—a professional liar. There was always the possibility that the original story she told Guy—the one she used to land him—was an outright lie. For instance, she might have said she was out of the movie business when she was still in it up to her long-lashed eyeballs. She could also claim to have broken off with Shore when that wasn't the case.

My first instinct was to trust Guy's story, as far as it went. His version of life with Daphne was punctuated by easily verifiable facts—public records of marriages and divorces, events hosted and attended, etc. Tanya's version had been short on actual dates. She had told us the Martin Shore movie had been filmed when she was "around" fifteen.

When people toss out the word "around" in that fashion, they're usually hedging, giving themselves the benefit of the doubt. "Around" allows for a certain amount of slippage in either direction and makes corroboration difficult.

Based on that analysis alone, it was far more probable that Guy Lewis' version offered more of the truth, but again, only insofar as he knew it. Prior to ten years ago, however, when it came to what Daphne had told him, all bets were off. Between Daphne and Tanya, I didn't know which one to believe.

I was aware of a growing sense that something was basically wrong with Tanya Dunseth's story. It's like a tooth going bad. At first, the only thing that bothers is maybe a slight twinge when a chunk of cold lettuce wraps itself around the surface of the tooth. It's not that serious, and it goes away, but that first shock of cold is symptomatic of something worse going on—something ominous beneath the surface and out of sight that says a root canal is coming.

Right now, some of the surface details of Tanya's story were cracking and moving apart. I worried about what implications that held for the foundation—the parts underground we didn't know and couldn't see. I didn't like noticing. After all, it was only the beginning of a hunch, but if it proved correct, that meant Ralph Ames and yours truly had once more been led down the primrose path by yet another pretty face.

People who labor long in the accountability sector are trained not to leap to hasty conclusions. Hunches aren't necessarily bad. Modern technology aside, well-played human hunches are responsible for most of the successful crime detection that goes on in this country. But homicide cops who don't want to become laughingstocks don't flaunt their untried hunches in public. They keep them quiet while they go about checking details and verifying facts as much as possible. Only after that process is complete do they haul out the result and run it up a flagpole for all the world to see.

So when I got off the plane in Walla Walla, I didn't go straight to the nearest public phone booth, dial the Ashland Hills, and leave a message for Ralph Ames saying "Watch out, we're being played for suckers. I abided by the unofficial rules of accountability behavior—and got both Ralph Ames and J. P. Beaumont royally screwed over in the process.

The landing approach in Walla Walla took us within sighting distance of the gray-walled state prison—the Walls of Walla Walla, as they're called. It was odd to realize that I was visiting a town of approximately thirty thousand people, and the only folks I knew there were convicted felons. My connection to most of them was that of a police officer sending a never-ending parade of inmates up the river both literally and figuratively.

The state prison in Walla Walla is a repository for the worst dregs of Washington's society—murderers, rapists, drug abusers, robbers, and burglars. In fact, part of my job is making sure the prison system runs at full capacity. My current errand, however, brought me in search of Roger and Willy Tompkins, two supposedly well-respected local citizens, who currently and in the past had lived their lives well outside the confines of the prison's walls. Where was the justice in that?

Why should someone like Roger Tompkins—a man who had spent years routinely violating and terrorizing his very own daughter—be one of the keepers instead of one of the keepees? Why had he worked as a prison guard when he himself deserved to be a regular inmate just as much or more so than many of the people he guarded?

Extreme moral outrage doesn't leave a whole lot of room for playing happy-go-lucky tourist. I took possession of the one rental car available—a stripped-down Ford Tempo. I found my way to the local TraveLodge, checked into a room, and then asked the room clerk for directions.

Walla Walla is a relatively small town, and the desk clerk was a clean-cut young man in his early twenties. Since I'd been told Willy Tompkins worked in the high school cafeteria, I decided to go ahead and ask the clerk about the couple to see if he, by any chance, knew someone named Roger and Willy Tompkins. It turned out he did.

"Oh sure," he said, when I mentioned the Tompkins family. "Everybody knows them. I believe the old man's retired now. She's been a cook at the high school forever."

So far, so good. Then the young clerk readjusted his carefully knotted tie and threw me a curve. "I played baseball with their grandson, Walter. I don't believe Mrs. Tompkins ever missed a single home game in four years of ball. She was there rain or shine, win or lose. I always thought they should have given her a letter every time they gave Walt one."

The phone rang, and the clerk turned to answer it. I walked away from the desk feeling half-sick. What grandson? One old enough to be almost the same age as Tanya? I remembered her speaking at length about her father and her mother, but she hadn't said a word about brothers and sisters, nor had she mentioned a nephew—a contemporary—being raised in the same town and/or household right along with her. From the way she told the story, I had assumed that she must have been raised as an only child. It seemed as though the kinds of things that had gone on in that disfunctional family would have been far more difficult to control or conceal with the addition of even one more family member, to say nothing of several.

I drove to the address Ralph had given me. To all intents and purposes, this was Main Street U.S.A., home of *Ozzie and Harriet* and *Father Knows Best*. The Tompkins house turned out to be a well-maintained bungalow set in an immaculately kept but tiny yard. Sunset was still almost an hour away, but already the house was wearing its evening face with pooling halos of lamplight glowing through curtained but open windows.

Funny, I thought. The place doesn't look like a candidate for House of Horrors.

As I pulled up to the curb, a late entry in the evening's neighborhood lawn-mowing detail chattered noisily into action. Neatly covered trash cans lined the street, awaiting a morning pickup. Squaring my shoulders, I started toward the house. When I pushed it slightly, the rust-free gate sprang open without an accompanying squeak. Everything about the place—from the carefully edged walkway to the newly varnished, old-fashioned screen door—exhibited pride of ownership and careful attention to detail. It wasn't at all what I expected.

I felt edgy walking up to the door. I believe most child molesters—"chesters," as they're called in prison parlance—are basically cowards. Otherwise, they wouldn't victimize helpless children. That doesn't mean they aren't dangerous, however, or that they won't turn on you if cornered or provoked. Some of the most vicious dog bites are inflicted by basically cowardly animals who find themselves trapped in unfamiliar situations. Cowardly people operate the same way.

Boarding the plane in Medford, I hadn't wanted to fight my way through airport security while carrying my automatic. Instead, I had checked it with my luggage. By the time I stepped onto the Tompkinses' wooden porch in Walla Walla, however, I was happy to have it with me—to feel the familiar weight of the weapon under my jacket and against my ribs. I couldn't shake a surge of uneasiness as I realized I was totally on my own—out of reach and hailing distance of any kind of help or backup. My 9-mm automatic and I were it.

Moments after I rang the bell, the door was answered by a straight-backed African-American woman whose age I would have guessed to be somewhere around sixty. "Yes?" she said without opening the screen door. "What can I do for you?"

"I'm looking for either Roger or Willy Tompkins."

She squinted at me, regarding my face through glasses that were probably designed primarily for reading. There wasn't anything threatening or antagonistic in her manner, only the understandable wariness of a householder whose evening quiet has been interrupted by an unexpected and unknown visitor.

"Who are you?" she asked.

Vacation or not, old habits die hard. Although my standing as a Seattle P.D. detective carried no more weight in Walla Walla than it did in Ashland, I dug into my coat pocket and extracted my official I.D.

"My name's J. P. Beaumont," I said. "I'm with the Seattle Police Department. As I said, I'm looking for either Roger or Willy Tompkins."

The woman turned back into the room. "Roger," she said. "Maybe you'd better come here. This man's a police officer, but he won't tell me what he wants."

A tall but slightly stooped, gray-haired black man appeared behind her. "What's this all about?" he asked.

My mind reeled. This man was Roger? I must have made a mistake. Maybe I had given the desk clerk the wrong address. How could red-haired, green-eyed Tanya Dunseth's parents be African-American? It didn't make sense.

"I'm looking for Willy and Roger Tompkins," I stammered quickly. "I want to talk to them about their daughter. I believe her name is Roseann."

Sometimes when progress demands demolishing some stately old building, work crews will record the event for posterity. After first lacing the interior of the structure with explosives, they'll capture on film the moments just before and just after detonation. At first dust flies, but the building itself seems untouched. Then, gradually, details change—the facade shifts out of focus—and the entire building begins to crumble.

The same thing happened to the old woman standing before me. Her face went slack, her features slightly fuzzy. She sagged back against the man behind her. He tried to catch her but only succeeded in cushioning the severity of her fall.

He knelt beside her, cradling her head and stroking her face. "Willy," he said. "Willy, wake up. Are you all right?"

Willy? I thought. This can't be Willy! I must be losing my mind.

The screen door was still closed. I had not been invited inside. At first, I was too stunned to do anything but look on helplessly through the door. Moments after she fell, the woman's eyes flickered open. The man started to help her up, but somehow his feet became entangled in a throw rug, and they both went down in a heap. That was all I could stand. Uninvited, I wrenched open the screen door and tried to help lift them to their feet.

Holding Willy between us, Roger and I guided her to a nearby couch. She had twisted her ankle and now could barely put any weight on it. Once seated, she turned on me, leveling a hard, tear-stained stare in my direction. When she spoke, however, her words were directed strictly to her husband.

"Roger," she said, "you get this man out of my house, and you get him out now!"

"But, Willy," he objected, "your ankle's swelling like crazy. We should probably carry you to the doctor." He stood up, went back over to the door, and retrieved her wire-rimmed glasses from where they had fallen. Wiping them on his shirt, he handed them to her.

"We're not doing anything at all until that man is gone," she insisted flatly. "Not one thing."

The old man looked at me helplessly. "We'd best step outside," he said.

I was already apologizing before we ever reached the front porch. "Obviously, there's been a terrible mistake. You're Roger Tompkins?"

He nodded. "As far as I know. Have been for going on seventy years now."

"That means the person who claimed to be your daughter was lying."

"You've met someone who says that?" He sounded shocked.

"Yes, a young woman down in Ashland, Oregon. She told us that she was Roseann Charlene Tompkins from Walla Walla, Washington. She said you were a guard in the prison."

"I was, until I retired a few years back."

"She said your wife was a cook at the school."

"That's also correct. Willy retired from there just this past month."

"I'm so sorry to have disturbed you, Mr. Tompkins, and to have upset your wife. Obviously, this young woman can't possibly be your daughter. She's a red-haired Caucasian."

"There's a better reason than that," Roger Tompkins returned with restrained dignity. "Our daughter is dead."

"Dead?" I repeated, sounding like an insubstantial echo.

Tompkins nodded. "Roseann died back in 1968. She was a change-of-life baby—our last one. She was only four months old when she died. That's why Willy's so upset. I'm sure she thought it was someone playing another one of those ugly pranks. We had phone calls about it at the time—some of 'em pretty bad—people saying we must have killed her, that kind of thing. Back then nobody talked about Sudden Infant Death Syndrome. People know more about it these days. It's been a long time, but I don't think Willy ever got over it, not altogether."

In all my life, I don't remember ever feeling more the heel. And stupid besides. Tanya Dunseth had seen Ralph and me coming a mile away. Her heartrending tale of monstrous abuse had left us putty in her hands. Even I—a prizewinning chump if ever there was one—could see that Roger Tompkins was no monster.

"I'm sorry to have disturbed you, Mr. Tompkins, and to have brought your painful ordeal back to the surface. I had no idea."

"No," Roger Tompkins said kindly. "I'm sure you didn't. Who is this troubled young woman, anyway? Why would she do such a thing?"

"That," I declared hotly, "is something I intend to find out. She's obviously gone to the extent of learning as much about you as possible. For instance, she knew your address and where both you and your wife worked. It's an old stunt people pull when they have something to hide. They go back through old newspaper files and assume the identity of a child who died at an early age but at approximately the same time."

"In order to get a Social Security number, wouldn't she need a birth certificate? You said this girl is white. As you can see, Willy and I most certainly are not."

"Actually, Mr. Tompkins, it's even more complicated than that. She was using an entirely different identity for official purposes, and it turns out that one's fake, too."

We had walked out to the street and were standing beside my rental car. Roger Tompkins clicked his tongue. "How truly unfortunate," he said thoughtfully. "Circles within circles, wheels within wheels. To spin a trail of lies like that, she must be very disturbed."

"You could say that again," I said. "You certainly could. Please express my sincere apologies to your wife. I hope her ankle isn't hurt too badly. I'd be happy to help take her to an emergency room if you wanted."

"Oh," Roger Tompkins answered with an easy smile, "that won't be necessary. She'll be fine. We'll go to the doctor tomorrow morning if need be. Willy's a pretty tough old bird. We both are. We've had to be."

I hadn't a doubt in the world that was true.

Beside myself, I headed back to the TraveLodge. Wheels within wheels all right! There was no way to make sense of the tangle of lies Ralph and I had been fed, but one thing was certain. Tanya Dunseth was not to be trusted.

Was she the murderer? Maybe. Most likely, in fact, especially the more I thought about it. Why else would she have spun this web of fabrication? Only people with something awful to hide build those kinds of complicated but phony constructs around them.

Ralph Ames had told me that even if Tanya Dunseth was guilty, he was prepared to defend her to the best of his personal and professional capability. You'd better gear up, my friend, I thought. You've got your work cut out for you.

I made it back to my room in what was probably record time for Walla Walla. My rented Tempo didn't come with a cellular phone, so I waited until then before I tried calling Ralph. He wasn't in. I tried again half an hour later and every thirty minutes thereafter, from 9:00 P.M. until midnight. He finally answered the phone at 12:25.

"Where've you been?" I demanded peevishly. "I've been trying to reach you for hours."

"I just came back from the Bowmer," he said. "Alex and I went to see *Romeo and Juliet*. It is wonderful and Alex didn't mind seeing it again. For such a young woman, Tanya really is an exceptional actress."

"Tanya!" I exploded. "Tanya Dunseth was in tonight's production?"

"What other Tanya would I be talking about?"

"She's out of jail and back playing Juliet?"

"That's right. Her landlady and I posted bail for her around four-thirty this afternoon, just in time for her to make the eight-thirty curtain."

"Jesus Christ! You've got to be kidding."

"Beau," Ralph said calmly. "Of course I'm not kidding. What's gotten into you? Are you upset about something? Is something wrong?"

"You could say something's wrong," I returned morosely. "Just wait until I tell you."

And I did.

16

Once he heard what I had to say, Ralph was as thunderstruck as I had been. "We've been nailed but good, haven't we?" he said. "No doubt about it. What do we do now?"

That was a switch—a real first—Ralph Ames asking me for advice. "Don't do anything until I get back, except try to keep her from skipping town. By the way, where is she now?" I asked.

"Back at Live Oak Farm, as far as I know, although I'm not sure we can count on her staying put for long. If she takes off, all those people out there will be on the street."

"How come?"

"Because Marjorie Connors signed over the deed to Live Oak Farm to bail Tanya out of the slammer."

"Why'd she do a thing like that?"

"Why else?" Ralph returned. "Misplaced loyalty, most likely. Marjorie Connors volunteered, just like all the rest of us. There's a lot of that going around these days."

"I don't understand how come they let her out in the first place. If Fraymore's evidence is that good . . ."

"My guess is the Festival probably pulled in a marker or two. If there's any political pull in this county, they own it. Remember, it's the height of the season. They wanted Juliet back if only temporarily. Fraymore gave me some advance notice. He told me prior to the hearing that they might allow bail, but I didn't think it would happen, purely as a matter of economics. Then, out of the blue, Marjorie turned up with a guarantee for the whole amount, and that was that. It was damned nice of her."

"Stupid, you mean."

"Well, yes. That, too. I can't help but feel sorry for Mrs. Connors. She's been hoodwinked even worse than the rest of us.

"Don't worry about Marjorie Connors," I told him. "She is perfectly capable of taking care of herself. The woman's gone out of her way to amass a collection of somewhat troubled kids, Kelly Beaumont included. People who make a hobby out of rescuing orphaned wildlife or patching up injured birds are bound to get bitten or pecked on occasion."

I doubt Ames was listening to me. "Now that you mention it, is it possible Mrs. Connors knows the truth about Tanya?" he asked.

"Why would she?"

"Try this. If Tanya were to confide in anyone, wouldn't Marjorie Connors—the woman who kept her from being thrown into the streets—be the logical choice?"

"Hold on, Ralph. Tanya Dunseth doesn't do *truth* or logic either, for that matter. If she told Marjorie anything at all, you can bet it will be some far-fetched sob story designed to elicit the greatest amount of sympathy. You can ask, but I'll bet money what Marjorie knows has very little bearing on the truth—whatever that might be."

"You mean every story is a variation on the same theme, so she can suck other people in as well."

"You've got it. I personally don't give a damn how many people she cons, and I don't care how many lies she tells. My main concern isn't whether or not she's a liar, but whether or not she's a killer. If she is, my worry is that you and I may be helping put her back out on the streets so she can do it again."

There was a pause. "In other words," Ralph Ames said, "once a homicide cop, always a homicide cop. You don't like walking on the other side of the street, do you?"

"Don't joke around, Ralph. I've spent a lifetime putting killers away. It galls me to think I've been busting my tail to turn one loose."

"Maybe she really is crazy," he suggested thoughtfully. "I believe you said Mr. Tompkins called her 'disturbed.' We talked about it before. That's why they allow insanity pleas."

"An insanity plea may work like a charm," I told him, "but I don't want anything to do with it. There's too much risk."

"I can see you're going to have to give it some thought, Beau. As for me, I said I'm going to try to help her, and I will."

Shortly after that, I rang off and tried to go to sleep. Even though I had barely slept for days, it still didn't work. I tossed and turned for hours. Periodically, I'd sit up and look at the clock, thinking it must be almost morning, but only fifteen or twenty minutes would have passed since I last checked. Sometime during the night, I reached a decision.

It wasn't necessarily a logical decision. I didn't have to worry about proving anything beyond a reasonable doubt, because it was strictly personal—an internal verdict, not something happening in a court of law. In those painful midnight proceedings, J. P. Beaumont weighed both guilt and innocence, analyzing Tanya Dunseth's complicated fabric of lies. I thought about questions of opportunity and motivation. I pondered the connections between her and the two victims and weighed Tanya's access to the murder weapons.

When my middle-of-the-night hearing ended, somewhere close to three in the morning, I decided that Tanya Dunseth was too damn hot for me to handle. If Ralph Ames wanted to defend her or help her cop a plea, that was strictly up to him—but I wouldn't be involved. I wanted out. And once I finally reached that conclusion, I was able to sleep.

The next day I was up and out so early that I arrived at the airport a full two hours before my scheduled departure. I figured once I reached Ashland would be time enough to tell Ralph that I was bailing out on him. I didn't figure he would give me that much grief over it, but I worried about potential repercussions from the Tanya Dunseth cheering section, both Alex and Kelly.

I worried, too, about whether or not Gordon Fraymore had learned I was AWOL from Ashland. What was it he had said?—If I were you, I wouldn't leave town. Fair enough. Detective Gordon Fraymore was definitely not J. P. Beaumont.

I flew into Medford from Portland aboard a Dash 8 called, appropriately enough, *The Great City of Medford*. Once back in my 928 with my cellular phone handy, I figured I had returned to civilization. I picked up the phone and dialed Ron Peters. He answered after only one ring.

"It's about time I heard from one or the other of you," he complained. "I've been calling all over and haven't been able to raise either Ralph or you. I even talked to Alex. She said she didn't know where you were and didn't particularly care. What happened? Did you two have a fight?"

"We didn't have a fight," I said. "I got called out of town. What's happening?"

"I've managed to pick up some information for you," Ron said. "Is now a good time?"

"It's fine. Shoot."

"For one thing, I tracked down that prison guard in Walla Walla. Everything official says he's a real straight shooter. He's retired now. So's his wife. For many years, she's been a cook in the high school cafeteria over there."

Ron Peters was up in Seattle doing what he could to help. I didn't have the heart to tell him that his information was yesterday's news.

"What else?" I asked.

"Martin Shore was a sleaze, but you already knew that. Here's the surprise. Years ago, Shore was married to Daphne Lewis, and the two of them ran a lucrative kiddie-porno ring out of Yakima. It got busted up about the time Shore was kicked off the force over there. They had split up shortly before all hell broke loose. After they split, Daphne somehow managed to go straight. Later she hooked up with Guy Lewis, while Shore started working in Seattle as a private eye."

"Any current connection between them?"

"Between Daphne and Shore? Could be, but I haven't found one yet."

Networking has always been Ron Peters' strong suit. Nonetheless, it was amazing that, sitting stuck in a desk-bound wheelchair in Seattle's Public Safety Building, he had learned almost as much as I had, with considerably less trouble and at far less expense. Knowing that made me humble.

"You've been working overtime," I said.

He laughed. "You know me. I'm a big one for using inside sources. That Ashland cop, Fraymore, has asked Seattle P.D. to cooperate with his investigation. Right now, they're looking into a possible blackmail angle. All I've had to do is ask a few discreet questions."

"And know who to ask," I added. "Anything else?"

"That's about it, except for some clippings I've come up with on Guy Lewis. The guy's a real publicity hound. He ends up with his picture in the paper almost as often as the mayor, along with whichever wife is currently in vogue. Does he have a complex or what?"

"If you'd made your family fortune with chemical toilets, maybe you'd be defensive, too."

"Maybe. Anyway, I have a whole fistful of society-page-type clippings and several photos of him and his two wives. Separately, of course. Naturally, Daphne Lewis and Maggie Lewis don't appear in any pictures together. If you'd like my unsolicited opinion, and judging by the photos alone, Guy did lots better in the looks department the second time around."

"I suspected as much."

Ron Peters laughed. "I've got a picture of Maggie Lewis and a puppy she picked up at a Humane Society benefit. The dog's better-looking than she is. Want me to send you this stuff?"

"How much is there?"

"Ten, twelve pages."

Even though I personally was out of it, and even though I didn't see that it would do much good, I didn't want to sound ungrateful. "Please. Fax it on down to Ralph so we can take a look at it."

"What about the information from *Consumer Reports* on the car seat and high chair?"

"Fax that, too," I told him. "And thanks."

"No problem," he said. "Glad to do it."

Once I reached Ashland, I drove straight to the Ashland Hills. All I wanted to do was tell Ralph I was out of it, that he was on his own, but Ralph's rented Lincoln wasn't in the parking lot, and no one answered the door when I knocked. I took a turn around the coffee shop in case he was there having breakfast, but when I couldn't find him, I headed back to the Oak Hill B & B. Maybe he was joining Alex for breakfast.

It turned out Ralph wasn't there, either. Alexis Downey was. So was Amber Dunseth. I found Alex sitting in the sun on the back deck watching Amber play with some stuffed animals. Alex didn't seem exactly overjoyed to see me.

"It wasn't nice to take off like that without letting me know," she said. "Given the chance, I would have gone along."

I was struck by her obvious irritation. The day before I had left Ashland in my single-minded work mode, intent only on the jobs at hand—of seeing Guy Lewis and hurrying on to Walla Walla to do what was needed there. Like detectives everywhere, once I'm immersed in a case, there isn't much room left for personal consid- erations. It's part of my nature and one of the things that makes me good at what I do. It's also something that drives people around me crazy. It's a leading factor in statistical studies of police-officer divorces—mine included.

Dummy that I am, it hadn't occurred to me to invite Alex along on the trip to Walla Walla, much less that she might have wanted to go.

"Walla Walla's not all that much fun," I said, in hopes of worming my way out of the doghouse. "Besides, you enjoyed going to the play with Ralph, didn't you?"

"That's not the point," she observed coolly. "You forget, I see plays all the time. I thought we came here to spend time together."

Touché. I tried changing the subject. "Have you heard from Ralph this morning? I stopped on my way here, but he wasn't in."

"Naturally, you went to see Ralph first," Alex returned. "Here." She picked up Amber and angrily thrust the child in my direction. "You take care of Amber for a few minutes while I take a bath and cool off. All the actors and technical people have a required meeting at the Elizabethan this morning. There wasn't anybody else to take care of Amber. Jeremy dropped her off again a little while ago."

Carrying both the child and a collection of toys, I trailed Alex into the house, through the dining and living rooms, and up the stairs. Amber had spent the night with her mother, and I was in more trouble than I thought.

"Alex, what's going on?"

"Going on?" She paused in the doorway and spun around. I fully expected the door to slam shut in my face.

"I'll tell you what's going on, Mr. Beaumont. This may come as a surprise to you. It certainly does to me. I think I'm jealous, dammit, and I don't know what to do about it."

I was standing there in the hallway, holding Amber with one arm while stuffed toys leaked out of my other arm and spilled down my leg. How could anyone be jealous of someone like that?

"Who are you jealous of?" I asked in genuine dismay.

She shrugged. "I don't know. With Kelly and Jeremy and your whole family here—and now with all this business about Tanya— I feel like I'm on the outside of your life looking in. It's not very pleasant. I don't like it."

"But, Alex, you *asked* me to help Tanya, remember?"

"I know, that isn't fair, is it?" she agreed, her voice near tears. "If you're doing what I wanted, it's not right for me to feel lost and abandoned. I hate being unreasonable!"

I finally gave up and dropped the rest of the stuffed animals. Then I reached out and pulled Alex to me in an awkward, sideways, one-armed hug. "Go take your bath," I said. "We'll talk about all this when you're finished. Maybe by then you'll feel better."

She disappeared into the bathroom. I put Amber on the bed,

then went back into the hallway to retrieve the scattered toys. I had no more than closed the door to the hallway when the bathroom door opened, and Alex popped her head out.

"I have one question," she said.

"What's that?"

"Can we have dinner tonight? Just the two of us?"

By then I was prepared to grovel if that was what it took to earn my way back into Alex's good graces. Dinner was easy.

"You bet," I said, meaning every word, not knowing that life was about to throw me another curve and that dinner with Alex that night would be a physical impossibility.

"Where would you like to go?" I asked.

Alex turned away from the bathroom door, leaving it slightly ajar, enough so that I caught a glimpse of naked leg as she climbed into the tub. "Oh, I don't care. Someplace nice where we can talk. Dinky says there's a new French restaurant that's very good. It's called Monet's. We could try that."

"Wherever you want to go will be fine," I said.

With Amber playing contentedly on the bed beside me and in the comfortable intimacy of a bathroom/bedroom conversation, I slipped into a nodding doze. It wasn't quite like being married, but it was very nice.

Downstairs I heard the distant ring of a telephone, but it didn't cross my mind that it might be for me until I heard footsteps hurrying up the stairs. Someone tapped on the door. "Mr. Beaumont," Florence asked. "Are you in there? Telephone."

It was exactly like being married. I got up and opened the door. "Who is it?" I asked.

"Jeremy. He says it's urgent."

Thinking Kelly might have suffered a relapse, I bounded down the stairs to take the call. "Hello."

"Mr. Beaumont, I'm glad you're there."

"What is it? What's wrong?"

"Have you seen Tanya?"

"Tanya!" I heard the rising irritation in my voice. I was worried about Kelly, and here he was asking me about Tanya Dunseth. "I haven't seen her anywhere. Why?"

"There's a mandatory meeting here at work. We're all required to show up. Anyone who isn't present is liable to be fired. I offered Tanya a ride in earlier when I brought Amber, but she said she didn't need one. She isn't here, and no one has seen her, but I know she doesn't want to lose her job. Would you mind running out to the farm to see what happened? Maybe a car broke down or something. They won't call roll until just before the meeting ends at twelve. If she's here by then, I'm sure it'll be fine."

If I were as hard-nosed as I'd like, I would have said, "Forget it." I would have told Jeremy that Tanya Dunseth's problems had nothing to do with me. But the kid had a heart as big as all outdoors. I couldn't very well turn him down.

"All right," I agreed crossly. "I'll go check."

Back upstairs Alex, wrapped in a thick peach-colored towel, was out of the bathroom. "What's going on?"

"I've got to go out to the farm for a few minutes," I said.

"How come?"

"Because Tanya's AWOL from the meeting, and Jeremy's afraid she'll be fired. He wants me to bring her to the Elizabethan before they finish taking roll, although if she's on her way to the slammer, I don't know why anyone should worry about her losing her job."

"Go ahead and go," Alex said, giving me a playful push toward the door. "Hurry." Obviously, she was feeling better. She offered me a quick kiss on my way by, and I took it happily.

I hurried out to the car, but as I drove past the Ashland Hills, that old incurable stubborn streak reasserted itself. Here I was, one more time, rushing around trying to save Tanya Dunseth from herself. How about doing something for me for a change? I thought. Why not stop off long enough to pick up my faxes? Maybe Alex and I could run up to Medford that afternoon and order the high chair and car seat.

It was only eleven. If I arrived at the farm a minute or two later, it wouldn't make any difference. I could still have Tanya at the Elizabethan long before they took attendance.

I swung into the parking lot, expecting to see Ralph's car, but I didn't. However, a maid's cart stood parked outside his room, blocking open the door.

With a nod to the maid, I darted inside, collected the stack of faxes, and stuck them in my pocket. Without even bothering to look through them, I hurried back to the Porsche and headed for Live Oak Farm.

When I pulled into the yard, a blue Mazda Miata with Washington plates was parked directly in front of the steps. What the hell was Guy Lewis doing here? I wondered uneasily.

After parking between the Mazda and the house, I jumped out of the Porsche and locked it, all in one motion. Then I bounded up a set of newly completed steps. In the course of several days, I had been to Live Oak Farm a number of times. Always before, Sunshine had been there to greet and/or fend off new arrivals. This time the old dog was nowhere in sight. Despite rising midmorning heat, the house seemed unusually deserted and forlorn with the windows closed and the doors shut. It felt odd. I was filled with a sudden sense of foreboding, as though the house were somehow sitting there holding its breath, waiting for something to happen.

The push button for the bell had been removed and the wires taped. I knocked. No one answered. I knocked again. Still nothing—no sound of movement inside, no barking dog.

Finally, I reached down and tried the knob. It twisted easily in my hand, and the door swung open. "Hello," I called. "Anybody home?"

As soon as the door opened, I smelled it and knew what it was. Gas. And not just any gas, either. Liquid propane. The whole house reeked of it.

My first thought was to get away. I lived with propane for years out at Lake Tapps, and I know how volatile that heavier-than-air compound can be, how treacherous if let loose into the atmosphere. I don't remember turning or going back out through the door. Without noticing how I got there, I found myself standing in the middle of the porch with my heart pounding frantically in my chest.

And that's when I remembered seeing the propane tank, around back near Amber's enclosed play yard. I remembered all about those tanks well. There would be a shutoff valve on top.

I raced to the end of the porch, hitched my legs up over the rail, and dropped to the ground, landing heavily on my heels. I touched down hard enough to know I'd have to pay for my folly later, but right then, my only thought was to get to that shutoff valve as fast as I could.

I pounded down the side yard. As I passed the basement door, a feeble male voice cried out, "Help! Please help me!"

My God, someone was in there—trapped in the basement. But the only thing I could do—the only thing *to* do—was to run on past, and hope to God that I made it to the shutoff valve in time for both of us.

17

As I struggled to twist the stubborn shutoff valve, my mind sifted through the smidgen of information I could remember about liquid-propane gas, about what it is and how it behaves. LP gas remains liquid only when contained within highly pressurized tanks. After passing through a regulator, it is converted into gas that can then be used to run everything from outdoor barbecues to family clothes dryers.

While still contained in a tank, the mixture, too rich to burn, is relatively harmless. But once released, it grabs hold of any and all neighboring oxygen molecules to create a much leaner and much more volatile mixture. In that condition, even a single spark can set it off. When it goes, it burns at a temperature of 3,500 degrees.

Any fire can be frightening, but 3,500 degrees present a daunting possibility. The very idea scared the hell out of me.

Because propane is heavier than air, it tends to flow like moving water when let loose, pooling in gaseous clouds in low-lying areas, but responding to thermals and drafts as well. I knew that if the upstairs of the house was permeated with the stuff, the basement would be full of it. Propane isn't poisonous, but it displaces oxygen.

Not only was the person in the basement in danger of being blown to bits, he was also at risk of suffocation—even if no explosion occurred.

When I finally finished closing the valve, I knew I had lessened the danger somewhat. At least the gas concentration couldn't grow any worse. But that was small consolation. Being killed in a small explosion offers no appreciable advantage to dying in a larger one.

"I'm coming," I called as I ran back through the side yard. "Hang on."

I listened, but there was no answering response. Turning off the valve had occupied only a matter of seconds, but it was possible I was already too late.

I looked despairingly at the solid wood of the basement door where Gordon Fraymore's crime-scene tape had all been removed. My heart fell when I saw the official-looking padlock was still safely in place. If I tried breaking it, would I risk an explosion-detonating spark? I sniffed the air.

Propane itself is odorless, so an evil-smelling sulfur-based compound, ethyl-something-or-other, is added as an odorant at a ratio of about 1 to 80,000, giving the gas its distinctive, carrionlike stench and making it readily detectable. Even outside the door I caught a whiff of the stuff. If the smell was everywhere, so was the propane. Beads of cold sweat trickled down the inside of my shirt, watering the hairs that pricked erect beneath my collar.

I tugged tentatively on the padlock and was astonished when it fell open in my hand. The top had been sawed in half and then repositioned in a way that made it look as though it were still intact. With a single motion, I pulled it off the hasp and threw it down in the grass behind me before wrenching open the door. Immediately, a cloud of propane filled my nostrils as gas trapped in the basement caught the updraft and boiled up into my face.

Looking down the stairs—the same stairs where Kelly had fallen only days before—I saw the figure of a man slumped against the banister at the bottom landing. Taking a deep breath of outside air, I plunged down the stairway.

"Come on," I urged, grabbing the man by one shoulder and shaking him. "Wake up. We've got to get out of here."

Guy Lewis' head lolled limply from side to side. He was out cold. Only when I tried to raise him to his feet did I realize that both hands were tied to the banister.

Last year, Scott gave me a Swiss Army knife for Christmas. I keep it on my key ring so it's always handy. Groping in my pocket, I found the knife and fumbled it open. By then I was beginning to feel dizzy. I stood up, raising my head out of the pooled propane, and took another breath.

I knelt back down and concentrated my whole being in the blade of that knife. The cutting edge is tiny, but I keep it razor sharp. It didn't take more than a few seconds to hack through the gnarly strands of rope, but it seemed forever. I felt myself growing dizzy again, but I resisted the temptation to grab another breath of air. There was no time.

When the little blade finally severed the rope bindings, Guy Lewis fell over and would have tumbled all the way to the hard-packed earthen floor, if I hadn't grabbed him by the shirt and held on.

Guy must have outweighed me by a good fifty pounds, but some-how I hauled him—deadweight that he was—up the stairs and out the door. Then, walking backward, I dragged him through the side yard. His heels scuffed matching trails in the grass. In front of the house, the Mazda and the Porsche were parked side by side. I pulled Guy around the cars until we were on the far side of the Miata. I figured if the house did go up, having the two cars between us and it would provide a little bit of cover and help shield us from the full force of the blast.

When I stopped, I eased him down on the ground and knelt beside him. Starting to come around, he squinted up into the overhead sun.

"Beaumont!" he choked. "Thank God you made it in time. What about the girl? Did you get her out, too?"

"The girl? What girl? I didn't see any girl."

"Tanya. Isn't that her name? Tanya? She's in there somewhere. I don't know where. You've got to find her."

My mother had seen to it that I spent almost every miserable Sunday morning of my childhood imprisoned in one interminable Sunday school class after another. I know all about turning the other cheek, but this was ridiculous.

"You want me to go back in there?"

"We can't just leave her to die, can we?"

I looked at the house. There was no movement around it, nothing to indicate that it was a deadly powder keg waiting for the slightest spark to blow it into oblivion.

"How do you know she's inside?" I asked.

"She said she would be," Guy Lewis said. "She told me."

Mrs. Reeder, my English teacher from Ballard High School, used to complain bitterly about faulty pronoun reference. "Faulty pronoun reference indicates faulty thinking," she would say.

At the time, I should have thought to ask Guy Lewis, "She who? Who are you talking about?" But who worries about grammar at a time like that? Besides, I was far too busy fighting my interior ethical battle to pay that much attention to Guy Lewis' exact words.

I did not want to help Tanya Dunseth. My first reaction, plain and simple, was: "Like hell! Why should I risk my life and limb? No way, José! Let Tanya find her own damn way out."

At best, she was a liar and a cheat. At worst, she was a two-time killer with yet a third and fourth attempted homicide chalked up on the scoreboard at that very minute. But when I made no effort to move, Guy Lewis began struggling to his feet.

"If you won't go, I will," he said determinedly. Even though he was still gasping and wheezing, he strove to right himself.

"Never mind," I said in disgust. "I'll go. You stay here and keep your head low." I started away, then had another thought. I turned back to him. "Do you have a cellular phone in that Miata of yours?"

Lewis shook his head. "No. Why?"

"I do. In the 928. Here are the keys. Whatever you do, don't start the engine. It'll set off a spark and blow us to kingdom come. Once you're inside all you have to do is reach inside and hit the power button on the phone to turn it on. Call nine-one-one and let them know we've got a serious problem out here. Tell them to stop all traffic, not to let any but emergency fire and police vehicles down Live Oak Lane. Got that?"

With Guy nodding in understanding, I set off for the house at a brisk trot. I didn't want to be winded when I got there. On the front porch, I inhaled another deep clear breath before opening the door.

I had no idea where to start. I had walked through the house to collect Amber's things from Tanya's upstairs room, but other than that one straight-through shot, the entire house was unfamiliar. I was afraid I'd have to race through the whole place to find her.

I dashed first through the main rooms of the ground-floor level—the living room, dining room, kitchen, and utility room—seeing no one. I came back into the living room and paused there prior to starting up the stairway to the second story. That's when I noticed a pair of glass-paned French doors in a wall just to the left of the front door.

In my hurry to get inside the house, I had darted past without even noticing them. Now, though, when I looked through the doors, that's where I found Tanya Dunseth, lying facedown on an outdated couch—the old-fashioned folding kind my mother used to call a davenport.

Coming into the side room, I realized it had once been a formal parlor now converted to an in-home office complete with book-shelves, a regular desk, a movable computer workstation, easy chair, and couch. As soon as I opened the doors, the stench of gas was far more powerful than it had been elsewhere in the house. Because the room was smaller than the others and totally closed off, the invisible gaseous cloud had risen to a higher level. Tanya was lying on the couch, not the floor, but the bluish tinge of her skin told me that she was suffering from oxygen deprivation.

"Tanya!" I called.

She didn't move. One bare arm trailed off down the front of the couch with the tips of her fingers almost touching the face of an ugly old dial-type telephone that sat on the floor only inches from the couch. Had I been thinking with my brain instead of my lungs right about then, I might have noticed the significance in the location of that museum-piece telephone. Instead, I had only one purpose and focus in life—to grab Tanya Dunseth up off that couch and get us both out of there. Fast!

I tried picking her up, hefting her once to test the weight of her in my arms. She was solid enough, but much lighter than Guy Lewis. Compared to hauling him, Tanya was easy. Holding her in front of me, I headed outside. When I reached the doorway, I kicked open the screen door.

Guy Lewis stood beside the Porsche, leaning heavily against it, as if the exertion of scrambling around the cars and making the phone call had worn him out. When he saw me, though, he smiled and gave me a thumbs-up sign. I don't know if it was for my finding Tanya or if it was because he had managed to make the call. Maybe both.

I had been holding my breath for a long time. Now, as I stumbled down the steps, I gasped fresh air into my oxygen-starved lungs. We're home free, I thought. We made it.

To this day, I'm still not sure if I actually heard the beginning of that abortive telephone ring, or if it was only my vivid imagination. Maybe the noise I heard was just the ringing in my ears—the pounding of my own overworked heart. Later, the arson experts told me, whether I heard it or not, the clapper in that old-fashioned ringer provided the needed spark—the only one necessary to set off a huge conflagration.

I was on the ground, carrying Tanya and moving away from the house as fast as I could, when the explosion hit. The force of the concussion jarred Tanya out of my arms and sent us both sprawling and plunging head over heels, rolling us along like a pair of wind-driven tumbleweeds.

I was already halfway across the road when the explosion occurred, but even that far away, an incredible blast of heat seared the backs of my eyeballs. I landed facedown. I stumbled to my feet and turned around, staring up at the steeply gabled roof. For an eerie, soundless moment, the entire surface of the roof seemed to rise in the air a good foot or so. It hovered there for what seemed like forever, then it settled gracefully back down—like a huge comforter falling back on a bed—in what appeared to be its original position.

My first thought then was that the worst was over. But I was looking at the roof. I hadn't noticed the burning sofa that had come shooting out of the house through a gaping hole that had been blown clear through the front outside wall. Propane burns hot and clean. Unless it soaks into some combustible material, it won't do a sustained burn. Unfortunately, the upholstered couch provided just the right kind of material to hold the gas and burn like crazy.

Tanya and I were some distance beyond the cars. Guy Lewis had been knocked to the ground, but he was struggling to regain his footing at the same time I caught sight of the burning couch on the porch. My first thought was that maybe we could get to it and somehow put it out, but before my body could respond and put thought to action, a series of secondary explosions echoed through the house, rocking it on its foundations.

Those several blasts shook the already weakened structure so severely that some of the supporting columns on the front porch, weight-bearing beams designed to hold up the second story, tottered out of their moorings, came loose, and crumpled. It was like watching a line of dominoes fall. As the columns collapsed, the added weight crushed the construction jack that valiantly had held up the one still-unrepaired corner of the porch. When the jack went, the floor above it disintegrated in a long, slow-moving wave, taking with it the rest of the porch. The burning couch dropped out of sight into a void.

Now the house stood naked in a cloud of dust and rubble. For several seconds, it seemed to ripple, like distant desert mountains viewed through waves of shimmering heat. And then, with a thunderous groan and the collective screech of a thousand tortured nails, the loosened roof began to fall. The sound was so wild and fierce it might have been the death cry of some living thing.

Pieces of roof avalanched down to the place where the broken porch was no more. Careening down, it rained wood and shingles and broken glass everywhere. Finally, when it stopped—when there was nothing left moving—I was struck by the terrible stillness all around me. In that silence, I realized Guy Lewis had disappeared. So had both the Miata and the Porsche. All three, two cars and the man, were buried beneath a mountain of debris. Meanwhile, from where the porch had once been, I saw the first ominous curlings of smoke.

What should I do? I was torn. I know now how emergency medical personnel must feel when they make the triage call—the life-and-death decision you can spend the entire rest of your life-time second-guessing, rationalizing, debating, or justifying.

The choice was mine alone to make. Guy Lewis had been moving when I last saw him. Chances were he could fight his way free of the rubble, but I had no idea how long Tanya had been deprived of oxygen. She lay flat on the ground beside me, still limp, still unmoving, still blue, but a thin stream of blood flowed from a tiny cut on her face. With oxygen deprivation, seconds, not minutes, mean the difference between survival and death; recovery or per-manent brain damage.

Guy Lewis had wanted her saved—had begged me to save her. I had to try.

Incapable of walking, I crawled over to her on my hands and knees. I checked her airways and began administering CPR. Know-ing from experience that adrenaline can fuel a man, giving him fleeting but inhuman strength, I held back deliberately, hoping not to break her ribs or do more damage in my desperate attempt to revive her.

I don't know how long I worked at it. A minute? Two? Several? There was no sense of time. Behind me, I heard the ominous crackle of hungry flames biting into tinder-dry wood, but I concen-trated solely on what I was doing. At last Tanya's breast heaved, and her eyelids fluttered open.

By then the heat was more intense. I pulled her to her feet. "Come on. We have to move farther away."

She tried to take a step or two, but then she stumbled and fell.

I had caught my second wind, so I picked her up and carried her again, running another twenty or thirty yards beyond where we had first come to rest. There, I felt I could lay her on the ground in relative safety.

"Stay here," I ordered. "Don't move."

She nodded weakly and made no effort to rise. I turned back toward the house, thinking that now maybe I'd go drag Guy Lewis from the wreckage. But even as I looked, I realized that the fire was much worse than I expected. It was already too late.

The burning couch had landed on what was left of the shattered porch, and the aged wood exploded in flame like so much tinder-dry kindling. Fed by fallen cedar-shake shingles, the entire front of the house was now a roaring inferno. Not only was the house itself fully involved; so was the pile of wood and rubble that had rained down on the two parked cars. On the parked cars and Guy Lewis.

I started forward, screaming at the top of my lungs. "Guy! Guy Lewis! Can you hear me? Get the hell out of there now. It's going to blow!"

The next explosion came even as I screamed out the warning. The gas tank of the Miata must have been broken or damaged by a falling beam. The Mazda went up first in a giant, eye-singeing fireball. I stood there stunned—seeing the flames, feeling the heat of them, and knowing for sure that Guy Lewis was a dead man. There was no way to get him out. No way to help.

My only hope then, as now, was that maybe Guy Lewis was already dead by the time the flames reached him. Otherwise, wouldn't he have screamed or cried out? Wouldn't I have heard him? Or were my ears still too damaged and traumatized by the noise of the preceding explosions? I don't know. Won't ever know.

I wonder about that sometimes in the middle of the night when I'm lying wide awake, when I'm haunted by the idea that it's my fault, my responsibility, that Guy Lewis is dead. After all, I'm the one who sent him on the fool's errand. He was out of danger and would have been perfectly safe if I hadn't sent him to the car phone to make that deadly 911 call.

Maybe it's a good thing that I'll never know for sure.

By then I could hear sounds of sirens in the background. I knew help was coming, but it would be too little and far too late. The second rocking explosion took me by surprise. For a moment, I was too disoriented to realize exactly what had happened, but finally I did.

The Porsche had gone up in a roar of flames. Anne Corley's beloved Guard-red 928—my 928—was a thing of the past.

Filled with a surge of blinding anguish and bellowing with rage, I spun on my heel and went looking for Tanya Dunseth.

18

Fortunately, the medics reached Tanya Dunseth before I did. They carted her off to the relative safety of the hospital. For a while, I was part of a small crowd that stood around gaping and watching the fire and the fire fighters who were dealing with it.

Even though there was no point in trying to save the house itself, there was still plenty for the overworked fire fighters to do. For one thing, they set up a safety perimeter and kept everyone well on the other side of it.

Since no one knew how much propane remained in the tank, there was still some danger of another BLEVE. A Boiling Liquid Expanding Vapor Explosion, the fire fighter's worst nightmare. When BLEVEs happen, they are eruptive killers that take out both fire personnel and unsuspecting bystanders.

The farmhouse itself was clearly a total loss, so they let that burn to a cinder while attempting to keep the flames confined to that one building. Because of the tinder-dry conditions in the surrounding grasslands and forests, they didn't want the fire to get away from them; to spread to outbuildings or to that collection of junked cars with its supply of highly combustible dead tires.

Being careful to stay out of the way, I nonetheless spoke to several police officers—Jackson County sheriff's deputies this time. This may have been rural Pacific Northwest, timber-and-wine country, but they let me know that a professional arson investigator from Medford, a guy by the name of Darryl Dandridge, was already en route to the scene. Although it would be days before the ashes cooled enough for sifting, the investigator would be taking statements from any and all eyewitnesses.

Soon after Dandridge arrived, one of the deputies took it upon himself to introduce us. As a consequence, he started his investigation with me. In the course of answering the series of questions, I soon realized that Darryl Dandridge was working on a theory about how the fire might have been ignited by someone who was outside the house at the time. When I happened to mention the presence of that old-fashioned telephone, I thought the guy was going to haul off and kiss me. Darryl acted as though I had handed him an outright gift.

Once he explained the mechanics of it, we both realized that someone who *wasn't* Tanya Dunseth must have been involved. There was no way to tell for sure about Tanya's possible involvement. If she was part of it, whoever placed the call couldn't have known that Tanya had been overcome by the gas and was about to become a victim of her own fire. If she wasn't, then she, too, had been an intended victim.

I spent almost an hour talking with the arson investigator. About the time we finished, a 1967 Mercury Montego convertible pulled into the yard. Gordon Fraymore, dressed in khaki shirt and pants and wearing both a fishing hat and vest, climbed out of the car. He spoke to several people—fire and police personnel both—before sauntering over to me.

He raised his head to peer closely at my face through thick bifocals. "We'd better get you into town to have that hole in your cheek stitched back together," he said.

I remembered noticing blood much earlier, but bleeding is one of those curious things. If it isn't too serious and if you ignore it long enough, it eventually goes away.

"I understand you need a ride," he added.

I nodded. I didn't want to talk about the loss of my Porsche. Compared to the loss of a life—compared to Guy Lewis' death—losing a car is nothing. Yet it hurt. Because of all the 928's connections to my past, it hurt far more than I wanted to acknowledge.

Without a word, I followed Fraymore back to his car, and we both got in. The Montego was a classic car in cherry condition with a flawless, cream-colored convertible top and an ink-blue body that was polished to a mirror shine. It takes time and effort to keep a car up that way for twenty-five or thirty years. I chalked one up for Gordon Fraymore.

"Your day off?" I asked.

"Was," Fraymore answered gruffly. "Isn't anymore."

The engine turned over responsively as soon as he started it. Driving carefully, gingerly, he threaded his way back out through the gradually diminishing collection of emergency vehicles.

"She did it again, didn't she?" he said with a grim shake of his head. "I hope you and that fancy lawyer friend of yours are proud of yourselves."

"Can it, Fraymore," I returned wearily, too tired to argue or put up much of a fight. There was no point in bringing up the arson investigator's theories. "The judge is the one who let her out on bail. The possibility was offered. All Ralph Ames did was take advantage of it."

"Right," Fraymore said. "It may have worked the first time, but let me assure you, it won't again. Her bond guarantee is a pile of ashes. I've submitted a request to the judge and prosecutor that he revoke Tanya Dunseth's bail and that we take her back into custody as of right now. I've posted a round-the-clock guard at her room in the hospital. When she gets out of there, she goes straight back to jail on the original charges—to say nothing of a whole brand-new set. You got that?"

"Got it," I said. No argument there.

A police barricade had been set up at the turnoff to Live Oak Lane. Ralph Ames' Lincoln Town Car was the first vehicle stuck on the other side. I wanted to stop and talk to him—bring him up-to-date—but Gordon Fraymore wouldn't hear of it.

"He'll find out where you are soon enough," the detective said to me. "Right now, I want to talk to you. I want you to tell me what you know and what went on. From the very beginning."

It wasn't a simple assignment. There was lots to tell, and it took a while, especially since I began with my trip to Medford and Walla Walla the day before. I believe in the anonymity of A.A., but once someone is dead, I don't think it makes that much difference. Besides, I didn't think Guy Lewis would mind. So I told Gordon Fraymore about my conversation with Guy. I also told him in detail of my meeting with Roger and Willy Tompkins.

I confess there's one thing I avoided telling him. It was a deliberate oversight. I told him about how Guy Lewis was caught in the explosion because he was standing beside my car, but I failed to mention that I had asked him to use my cellular phone to make a call. I already blamed myself for it. Why add an official inquiry into the mix? It wouldn't have done any good.

We were interrupted by the arrival of a young ER physician. It took almost an hour for that beardless youth of a doctor—the same one who had sewed up my wrist—to clean and stitch shut the jagged cut along the top of my jawbone. It wasn't until after that when I finished telling my story to Detective Gordon Fraymore.

As I gradually ran down and shut up, I discovered that Fraymore was sitting there, staring down at the floor and spinning his hat in his hands while the brightly colored lures on his hatband whirled into a kaleidoscope of colors.

"So we still don't know much of anything more than we did before, do we?" he grumbled.

"About why she did it?"

"That's right."

"Nope. Not much. And if we ask her, most likely she'll spin us another set of yarns."

"That's my guess, too." Fraymore sighed and rubbed his forehead. For a man who had planned to spend the day fishing, he wasn't having much fun. He still wasn't catching anything.

Fraymore stood up. "I'm going to go talk to her all the same. By the way, your daughter came through the lobby in a wheelchair while you were in with the doc. She wants you to stop by her room and see her before you leave. Do you need a ride?"

"No," I said. "I can call. Someone will come get me."

He walked as far as the door. "I suppose those kids of yours lost everything in the fire?"

"Pretty much," I said.

He clicked his tongue. "Too bad," he said sympathetically, sounding as though he meant it.

When I got to Kelly's room a Nursing—No Visitors sign was posted on her closed door, so I went to the nearest public rest room and cleaned up as best I could. The ER folks had scrubbed my face clean, but the rest of me was a mess. I could easily have passed for one of the homeless, down-on-their-luck vagabonds who line up daily under the Alaskan Way Viaduct back home in Seattle, waiting for a handout of food and a place to spend the night. My clothing was sooty and dirty and reeked of smoke and sweat. The sleeves of my jacket had protected my arms from the incredible heat, but some of the hair had singed off my head and the backs of my hands. I literally stank.

After washing up, I went back to the lobby and found a chair. That's where I was sitting, almost half-asleep, when Ralph Ames walked in a few minutes later. He looked brisk and dapper. His clothes were unwrinkled, and there wasn't a hair out of place. I'm surprised sometimes that the two of us manage to remain friends.

"There you are," he said. "They told me you wouldn't be done until about now, so I spent the time working. I've notified the insurance company about the Porsche. They're making arrangements to have a temporary rental brought down for you to use."

"Good." I sat back and relaxed. I should have known Ralph would be hard at work sorting things out.

"And I've found an apartment for Kelly and Jeremy," he added. "It's over in the little town of Phoenix—not the most convenient location in the world; it means a twenty-minute commute to Ash-

land, but that's the best I could do on such short notice. A couple
of the other kids from the farm will be within blocks of the same
place, so at least they'll be able to carpool.

"From what she said, I believe Marjorie's going to go ahead and
let them continue using her van for the time being. It's not worth
much, but Jeremy seems capable of keeping it running. That's what
they need more than anything else—a running vehicle."

"You've talked to Marjorie?"

"Several times. In fact, I met with her this morning. The two of
us were having a late breakfast at the Mark Anthony when the
explosion went off. We were talking about your visit to the Tompkins family and the patchwork of lies that came out as a result of
your visit there. We were trying to decide if it would be wise for
Marjorie to rescind her part of the bail-bond guarantee, especially
since it would seem Tanya has avoided telling the truth whenever
it suited her."

"How's Marjorie Connors holding up?"

"About how you'd expect for someone who's just lost everything.
She's in shock, I think."

"I can't say that I blame her," I said. "So am I. Have you talked
to our friend Tanya?"

Ames shook his head gravely. "I haven't had a chance. I've been
too busy. She's back in custody, of course, although so far she's
just here in the hospital under guard. Fraymore tells me she's
claiming amnesia. Says she doesn't remember anything at all from
the time she was in her room getting ready to go to work until she
woke up in the hospital."

"How very convenient," I said, making no attempt to mute the
full effect of my intended sarcasm.

"At the moment, Alex is still looking after Amber, but that will
probably change. I expect the state will step in any minute. Since
we've found no responsible relatives to designate as guardians, it
will be out of our hands."

Maybe Ames was hoping I'd come up with some bright suggestion to the contrary. Admittedly, Amber was a cute kid, a great kid,
and I personally have very little faith in the ability of the state—

any state—to step in and provide even the most rudimentary of parenting. But I had reached the end of my rope when it came to trying to save the whole damn world. If Amber Dunseth was destined to become a ward of the state, so be it.

The longer I kept quiet, the more aware I was that Ames' eyes were watching me closely, searching my face. "What's going on, Beau?" he asked finally. "What's really going on?"

Isn't that what friends are for? I broke down and spilled my guts, told Ralph what I hadn't been able to tell Gordon Fraymore, about asking Guy Lewis to make that fatal call.

"So you're blaming yourself?" Ralph asked when I finished.

"Wouldn't you?"

"Guy Lewis did make the call," Ames replied slowly. "If he hadn't, the fire crews wouldn't have responded nearly as fast as they did. Had that fire escaped the house itself, it could have gone for miles, exploded into an ecological disaster."

"What are you saying?"

Ralph Ames shrugged. "Guy Lewis died a hero, Beau. Let it go at that."

That's one of the things I like about Ralph. He's pretty damn perceptive, and he hadn't even talked to Guy Lewis the way I had. Maybe the king of chemical toilets, that brokenhearted court jester with his murdered trophy wife, was indeed glad to die a hero's death and be done with it.

Down the hall, a bustling nurse emerged from Kelly's room carrying an armful of pink that she toted back to the nursery. With baby-feeding done for the time being, I could go into the room to see my daughter—a daughter who was, surprisingly enough, also a mother.

When I stood up and tried to walk, my heel spurs raged at me. I should have thought to ask the doctor for some anti-inflammatories, but I had forgotten, and by then it was too late. "I'm going to visit with Kelly for a few minutes," I said, limping away.

Ralph nodded and waved. "Sure," he said. "Go ahead. I'll wait here and take you back home when you finish." He sniffed and wrinkled his nose. "You could use a shower."

Kelly had heard all about the fire and knew about the cut on my face as well. Relieved to see me, she looked altogether better. "My doctor says I'll probably be able to go home day after tomorrow. After what happened today, with the fire and everything, I didn't see how I could. But Jeremy says Mr. Ames has already found us another place to live. He's pretty wonderful, isn't he?"

"Who's wonderful, Jeremy or Ralph Ames?"

Kelly looked at me and smiled. "Both, actually," she said.

I knew then that looks weren't deceiving. She really was getting better.

We didn't talk long, just enough to touch base, for each of us to assure the other that we were both all right. Then I went back out, and Ralph Ames gave me a ride to Oak Hill B & B. A somewhat familiar-looking Lincoln Town Car was pulled up next to the house.

"Isn't that the same one Dave and Karen used?" I asked.

Ralph shrugged. "Could be," he said. "I don't know how many Lincolns they have at the airport in Medford, but it's probably not an unlimited number."

A man from Budget was waiting for me to sign off on the paperwork on the car. Afterward, he and Ralph left together. Alex stood in line until I finished up with the car-rental business before she had her crack at me.

Women are funny that way. When something bad happens, they can't seem to decide whether to hug your neck because they're glad to see you or chew your ass because you're a stupid jerk who never should have pulled such a dumb stunt in the first place. She took the ass-chewing option, but it was probably the nicest bawling-out I've ever had.

When it was time for me to go take my bath, Alex disappeared into the kitchen to finish feeding Amber. I didn't want to talk about Amber or what was going to happen to the child within the next day or two. Some things are better left unsaid.

Out of habit, I undressed the same way I always do—emptying my pockets one by one onto the dresser and bedside table. The last thing I took out were the faxes from Ron Peters that I'd been carrying around with me all day long.

I filled the tub as full as I dared and dumped in a handful of bath gel. I felt a little silly crawling into a tub full of bubbles, but silly gave way to luxury as the hot-water soak relaxed the muscles I'd strained and pulled trying to drag Guy Lewis and Tanya Dunseth out of harm's way. In the end, I lay there with my eyes closed, enjoying every moment of it. Finally, though, when my skin was wrinkled and shriveled and when the water grew too tepid, I climbed out and toweled myself dry.

Then, with the towel still draped around me, I sat down on the edge of the bed and picked up the faxes. My intention was simply to glance through them. Before I came upstairs, Alex had made it clear that she was still holding me to the promised dinner. She had even located a substitute baby-sitter. At that point, I didn't have a thought in my head of standing her up.

Ron Peters had said he was sending ten or twelve pages. In actual fact, there were eleven. Seven of them were strictly text, with several articles from various sources pasted together on the same page. Because of the nature of fax machines, particularly gray-scale resolution, the reproduction on the four photos wasn't high quality. The print in the various articles and in the captions under the photos was legible enough, but the pictures themselves were primarily unrecognizable blobs of light and dark.

So I settled for scanning the articles and reading the captions on the pictures—Daphne and Guy Lewis at a benefit for the Bagley Wright Theater, Daphne and Guy picking up the keys to the Bentley, and Guy mugging with actors from the Rep at some special event for Children's Hospital. The last picture in the batch was of Margaret Lewis at a Humane Society auction holding a puppy named Sunshine, the high-priced golden Lab she had just adopted.

My eyes stopped moving. So did my brain. Sunshine? The caption said "Sunshine"! I read it again, and the name hit me like a swift slap in the face! Another dog named Sunshine? Or could this be the same Sunshine I knew—the cataract-blinded, stiff old dog who formerly held sway on Marjorie Connors' front porch? If so, what the hell was she doing in a newspaper photo with Maggie Lewis?

I held the paper up to the bedside lamp and tried to squint some details into the fax-generated globs of light and dark. The woman in the picture was very heavyset and wearing a dark-colored dress, probably an evening dress of some kind, but there was no way to discern a single detail about the woman herself. The specific features of her face had been scrubbed away by a technology that allows for amazing speed at the expense of detail. The puppy was a vaguely dog-shaped blob superimposed on the much darker surface of the woman's clothing.

A wave of gooseflesh ran down my leg. If Sunshine was Live Oak Farm's Sunshine, then was Marjorie Connors also Maggie Lewis? For the second time that day, I felt as if I couldn't quite gather a lungful of air. This time the disability had nothing to do with liquid-propane gas displacing oxygen.

Dropping the towel, I scrambled into my skivvies, pants, socks, and shoes. I was still buttoning my shirt as I scurried downstairs. I raced into the family room and commandeered Florence's telephone and phone book both. Luckily, Ashland is a small town. In Seattle, homicide cops can't afford to have listed telephone numbers. In Ashland they do.

Gordon Fraymore's wife answered the phone and made it quite clear that she didn't appreciate having her husband called away from his evening meal, especially on his day off.

"What's up?" Fraymore asked, when he learned who I was.

"How well do you know Marjorie Connors?"

"Some," he said guardedly. "Why?"

"I think you'd better come over here right away," I said. "I believe we have a problem."

Alex came through the room and asked me what was going on. "I'll tell you in a minute," I said. "First I need to call Ralph."

The Ashland Hills operator told me Ralph was in the dining room. Someone would have to go find him. While I waited, I could hardly contain myself. Was that what this was all about, then? Was Marjorie Connors nothing more than a woman scorned who had enlisted Tanya Dunseth in a long-term, complex, and exceedingly lethal form of revenge? It was hard to believe, but I was beginning to believe it was true.

I took the picture out of my pocket and examined it again. The news photo wasn't dated, but if it was from late in her marriage to Guy Lewis, that meant Sunshine would be twelve to fourteen years old. And it also meant that Sunshine was Maggie Lewis' Achilles' heel. The woman might have changed everything else about herself—her name, her friends, her past—but she had cared too much to leave the dog behind. Or to change the old dog's name. Or to put Sunshine down.

And then I finally understood why, on that particular day, Sunshine had been missing from her customary place on the front porch at Live Oak Farm. Marjorie Connors had taken Sunshine along to meet Ames in order to save the old dog's life.

Ralph Ames came on the line. "What's happening?" he asked cheerfully.

"Three questions," I said. "Who initiated the meeting between you and Marjorie Connors this morning?"

"She did. She called early, right around seven. She asked if we could get together later on, sometime between ten and noon at the Mark Anthony. Why?"

"Next question. Did she have her old dog with her?"

"Sunshine? As a matter of fact, she did. She talked to the desk clerk about it. He agreed that the dog could sit with us as long as we stayed in the lobby. Beau, what's going on?"

"One last thing. When the house blew up, they say people heard it for miles. Did you?"

"Well, of course."

"Was Marjorie with you—at the time of the blast, I mean?"

Ralph Ames paused for a moment. "Why no, now that you mention it, I don't believe she was. I believe she had just excused herself to go to the ladies' room."

"Bingo!" I said. "I've gotta go, Ralph. Gordon Fraymore is just now driving into the yard."

19

Fraymore and I sat in his Mercury outside Oak Hill B & B while I told him in considerable detail everything I knew—or thought I knew—about Guy and Daphne Lewis. And about the fact that there was a good chance the woman everyone in Ashland knew as Marjorie Connors was, in actuality, the original, cast-off version of Mrs. Guy Lewis.

I wasn't sure how or when it happened, but somehow, in the course of revealing this new information, Fraymore and I moved away from our former mutual antagonism into a spirit of grudging cooperation. He listened carefully to everything I said, nodding occasionally.

"Could this friend of yours in Seattle send down the original of that picture so I could have a look at it?"

"I'm sure he'd be happy to," I answered. "If he shipped it counter-to-counter, we'd have it by midmorning."

I looked down at the seat, instinctively searching for the presence of a cellular phone. The Montego didn't have one. "That's all right," Fraymore said, starting the engine. "We'll call from my office."

When Fraymore had arrived at Oak Hill, I had expected to talk to him for several minutes and then go right back inside. I assumed that once I gave him the information, it would be up to him to take action. Fraymore, however, seemed disinclined to let me loose. I certainly hadn't planned on going along with him, but as we drove toward his office, I still expected I'd return in plenty of time to keep my dinner date with Alex.

After calling Ron Peters and making arrangements for him to ship the photo, I again expected to head back home. Nothing doing. Instead, Fraymore picked up the phone and made a series of off-hand, almost casual calls. In Seattle, the first one would have been an official inquiry to the Department of Motor Vehicles. Then, armed with the suspect's vehicle license number, an all-points bulletin would have been issued.

This, however, was Ashland, a place where people knew their neighbors. Without having to consult Motor Vehicles, Gordon Fraymore already knew the kind of car Marjorie Connors drove. He directed his officers to be on the outlook for an '85 brown-and-tan Suburban with a permanently dinged right front-door panel and a rearview mirror that was attached to the frame of the car by massive amounts of duct tape.

Within minutes of passing along this somewhat folksy description, Fraymore's small-town law-enforcement grapevine located the vehicle in question. A downtown church—the same one where the N.A. meeting had been held the previous Saturday—was hosting a hastily organized emergency potluck dinner to feed and collect donations for the burned-out victims of the Live Oak Farm fire. According to Gordon Fraymore's informant, Marjorie Connors was believed to be in attendance.

The detective assimilated the information and stood up abruptly. "It figures she would be," he said, nodding in satisfaction. "It would call too much attention to her if she wasn't. Let's go." He headed out of his office, and I followed.

"Where to? The potluck?"

"Not just yet. We'll start with the hospital. I want to talk to Tanya Dunseth one more time."

"Tanya," I echoed. "Why her? She's never told the truth, not once in her life."

"Maybe she's been telling some of the truth all along," Gordon Fraymore said with a thoughtful frown. "Maybe we just weren't smart enough to pick up on it."

We? There was that the fateful word "we" again. I let the questionable usage pass. Obviously, I was included in whatever was going down, but Fraymore said almost nothing on the way to the hospital. When we reached Tanya Dunseth's room, he motioned for me to follow him inside.

Tanya, wearing a hospital-issue gown, lay on her raised bed watching a mute television set.

"Hi, there, Tanya," Gordon Fraymore said easily when she glanced in our direction. "Mind if we ask you a couple of questions?"

"What kind of questions?" she asked.

Strictly speaking, Tanya should have thrown us out without giving us the time of day. Most homicide suspects, from casual killers to perpetrators of fatal domestic violence, know the drill all too well. Few of them are first-time offenders. They've been picked up before for something, although their previous offenses may not have been murder. Some of them know more about their rights than the cops who arrest them. Habitual offenders can and do recite the Miranda warning without the necessity of any prompting.

Since she didn't send us packing, it crossed my mind that maybe Tanya didn't know all that much about the process, at least not from personal experience. I was sure Ralph Ames had given her strict orders not to answer questions without his being present. But then he wasn't charging her for his services. Free advice is always easy to ignore.

"Do you know why we're here?" Fraymore asked.

Tanya shrugged. "I suppose it's the same as this afternoon. You think I killed Guy Lewis. You seem to think I killed everybody."

Her direct reference to the investigation was an answer in itself.

It's the kind of forthright response that usually comes from suspects who are actually innocent. Guilty ones generally affect an air of total mystification. They can't think of a single reason why an investigator might possibly come to them asking questions. They have zero idea what has happened or what the investigation might concern.

"Did you?" Fraymore asked straight out. Ralph Ames would have been outraged and rightly so. Tanya answered all the same.

"No," she answered firmly. "I did not. I didn't even know the man. Why would I kill him?"

"You knew his wife," Fraymore prompted.

Tanya nodded. "I knew Daphne, but not him."

"How did you hook up with Marjorie Connors?" The abrupt change of subject stymied Tanya momentarily.

"Marjorie? Why are you asking about her, and what do you mean, 'hook up'?"

"Just that. She didn't advertise in the paper for people to come live with her, so how did you end up out on her farm?"

"She came to me."

"When?"

"I don't remember exactly. I was pregnant with Amber at the time. I was about to be evicted because I couldn't afford my rent. I didn't know what to do or where to turn. I knew her slightly from working with her in the theaters. One day, out of the blue, she offered to help me."

"Sort of like yesterday when she showed up with enough money to post your bond?"

Tanya looked at Fraymore long and hard before she nodded. "Sort of like that, yes."

"What did she say?"

"Yesterday?"

"No. Back then, when you first met her."

"She said she was new to town, but that she was thinking of starting a co-op, an inexpensive place for young actors to live. She said she had heard I might need a place like that."

"Did she ever tell you where or how she heard about you and your predicament?"

"No. We never discussed it, but someone must have mentioned it to her."

"You and your daughter were her first tenants out at the farm?"

"Yes."

"What about the other young people who lived there—the ones who came later? Did she go looking for them the same way?"

Tanya shook her head. "Not really. I helped her find most of them. I posted notices on the bulletin boards at the Festival and at the grocery stores in town. Word gets around."

I was in the room, but I wasn't sure why. Fraymore's manner made it clear he regarded me as nothing more than a piece of furniture. Nonetheless, I paid close attention. I could more or less see where he was going with this line of questioning. The fact that Tanya claimed Marjorie had actively recruited her could have been significant, especially since all the other roomers had turned up by sheer happenstance. But whether or not that was credible depended on whether or not you believed a single word Tanya Dunseth uttered. I, for one, didn't. Not by a long shot.

"Let me ask you this," Gordon Fraymore continued. "Did she ever ask about your past?"

The whole time we had been in the room—the whole time Tanya had been answering Fraymore's questions—her manner had been casual and composed. She had carried her part of the conversation as easily as if she had been fielding questions about the changing weather. Now there was a subtle change in her demeanor. She blinked and shifted her position on the bed. In an interrogation situation, that kind of body language shift sends out a clear signal of distress on the part of the suspect. It means the questions are circling in on something important.

"No, why?" Tanya asked, feigning carelessness, but even her stage-trained voice evinced a slight tremor.

"She never asked you about what you did before you came here? Never asked about your career in the movie business?"

"Nobody knew about that!" Tanya shot back at him. She sat up in bed and glared at Gordon Fraymore while cracks spread across the surface of Tanya Dunseth's smooth veneer. The striking change in her reminded me once more of her reaction when Daphne and Guy Lewis had walked into the Members' Lounge.

Gordon Fraymore nodded in my direction, acknowledging my presence in the room for the very first time.

"I believe you know Mr. Beaumont, here," he said. "Why don't you tell Miss Dunseth about your visit with Roger Tompkins in Walla Walla last night."

Tanya's eyes panned from Fraymore's face to mine. She seemed to gather herself into a smaller package while her fingers dug into the bedclothes. "I don't want to hear," she said defiantly. "Go away."

I was on. Fraymore had turned the spotlight full on me—with no advance warning and with no cue cards to tell me what he wanted me to say.

Stalling, I cleared my throat. "I'm afraid my visit with Mr. Tompkins was very upsetting to them both, to him and to his wife," I said, "especially since their daughter died back in . . ."

"Get out!" Tanya interrupted. "Get out now! I don't have to talk to you without Mr. Ames here. He told me I didn't."

"But, Tanya . . ." Fraymore began.

With no warning, Tanya grabbed her plastic water glass off the nightstand and fired it in the general direction of Gordon Fraymore's head. He ducked out of the way. The glass missed his head, but it sprayed him with water before bouncing off the wooden door directly behind him. At the sound, the uniformed guard burst into the room, only to dodge out of the way of the next missile— the water pitcher itself—which flew on out into the hall and was followed shortly thereafter by a tissue box and the emesis basin.

"Get out! Get out! Get out!" Tanya shouted.

The guard started to draw his weapon, but Fraymore stopped him with a quick shake of his head. "It's okay," he said. "She's just a little upset."

Upset? I couldn't believe my ears, but Fraymore herded both the guard and me out of the room before I had a chance to object. We were met in the hallway by an irate nurse.

"What in heaven's name is going on in there?" she demanded.

"It's nothing," Fraymore said decisively. "She'll be all right once we're gone."

Nothing? I looked at him in astonishment. As far as I know, assaulting a police officer is a felony in every state of the union. Only when we were outside in the parking lot did he speak again.

"I wanted an impartial observer. What do you think?"

"I don't understand any of it."

"What don't you understand?"

"If she wasn't involved in the murders, why is she still lying through her teeth about her parents?"

Fraymore stopped beside the Mercury. "Makes you wonder, doesn't it?"

"What now?"

"You packing?" he asked casually.

Gordon Fraymore was talking guns, not suitcases. I nodded. "Why do you ask?"

Without answering, he opened the trunk of the Montego and rummaged around in it, eventually hauling out a Kevlar vest, which he handed over to me.

"We're going to stop by that potluck supper and pay a call on Mrs. Connors. You'd best put this on."

If I were anything other than a crazed homicide cop, I would have told him to put the damn thing away, that a good woman was waiting for me to take her out to dinner, and that it was his job, not mine, to pay a courtesy visit on Madam Marjorie Connors. Instead, I slipped out of my jacket and started unbuttoning my shirt.

"Lead the way," I said.

We drove through last-minute, pre-theater traffic and reached the church at ten after eight. Several cars were just then in the process of leaving the parking lot. Only a few vehicles remained, including an aging Chevrolet Suburban, brown and tan, with its mirror held on by layers of duct tape. Sunshine, her long leash attached to the front bumper, lay on the pavement directly in front of the truck. She was sound asleep.

"Are you a betting man?" Fraymore asked.

"Not particularly."

"Ten to one that thing's loaded with suitcases and boxes."

"No bet," I said.

And it's a good thing I didn't. When I hopped out of the car long enough to press my face against the darkened glass on one of the back panels, I saw that the back of the Suburban was packed to the gills. Among the suitcases and boxes was a fiberglass airline doggie crate. Both Marjorie and Sunshine were leaving town.

I returned to the Montego and leaned in the window. "You called that shot," I said.

Fraymore kept his eye on the entrance to what I knew to be the church social hall. He nodded. "Looks like we got here just in time," he said. "Get in. We'll park and wait."

By eight-fifteen traffic on the main drag had reduced appreciably as most playgoers settled into their seats. I was glad of that. For a cop, staging any kind of armed confrontation on a busy street is a terrifying proposition.

"How do you want to handle this?" I asked. Since it was inarguably Fraymore's show, I intended to take orders from him.

"First we talk," he said.

"And then?"

"If she doesn't pay attention, we punt."

Great plan. Not long on strategy, but Fraymore was in charge; I was just along for the ride. I wasn't ecstatic about being stuck in a vehicle with no possibility of radio contact. If we ran into trouble, there'd be no calling for help or backup. All those anxious thoughts drummed through my head as we sat there, but for a change I surprised myself and kept my mouth shut.

Marjorie Connors and two other women came strolling out of the church basement about twenty-five after eight. The three of them ambled to the middle of the lot, where they stopped long enough to chat briefly and exchange hugs. I'm sure Marjorie must have seen the Montego parked nearby, but she gave no indication.

As soon as the other two women started toward their own car, she struck out for the front of the Suburban. She knelt beside the dog and began unfastening Sunshine's lead.

By then both Gordon Fraymore and I were out of the Montego. As we approached, Sunshine lurched to her feet. I expected another spurt of frail barking, but the dog kept quiet. Only when Fraymore was within a matter of feet did Marjorie appear to notice him, but instead of addressing him, she spoke to the dog.

"Come on, girl," she said, tugging on the leash. "Let's go for a ride."

"Evening, Marjorie," Detective Fraymore drawled. "I wanted to talk to you about the fire out at your place this afternoon. Do you have a minute?"

The woman's startling violet eyes met Fraymore's and held them without wavering. Meantime Sunshine hobbled forward. She stopped directly in front of Gordon Fraymore. Reflexively, and without bothering to look, he reached down and began to ruffle the old dog's lank ears. I should have tumbled right then, but I didn't.

"I don't have much time, or anything to say, either," she answered with casual unconcern. "As you know, I wasn't home when the fire started." She tugged on the leash again. "It's late, girl. Come on. It's a long drive."

Leading the dog, she walked around the Suburban and opened the door on the rider's side. Sunshine made one feeble attempt to crawl in by herself, but then she settled back on her haunches and waited patiently for help. Marjorie Connors leaned over, picked up the dog, and bodily boosted her up onto the bench seat. Then she closed the door and started around to the other side.

"We know all about you, Marjorie," Fraymore said, speaking slowly and deliberately. "Including the fact that you were once married to Guy Lewis."

Had I been Marjorie, that single all-encompassing revelation would have stopped me cold, but she didn't even break her stride. Straightening her shoulders, she thrust one hand determinedly into the pocket of her leather jacket and kept walking. Pure survival instinct, years of working the streets, warned me she had a gun.

"Please, Marjorie," Gordon Fraymore said haltingly, and with far more gentleness than I would have thought possible. "Please don't make me do this."

She stopped, turned around, and looked at him then. There was a moment—a vivid, electric, breathtaking moment—when everything I didn't understand suddenly whirred into focus like a scene in the viewfinder on one of those new electronic cameras. It happened when I finally allowed my senses to make the obvious connections—to see the abject way Gordon Fraymore was looking at her. When I let myself hear the heartbreak and desperate pleading in his voice.

Marjorie Connors and Gordon Fraymore were lovers.

And in that moment, when I realized the truth, I finally understood why Fraymore had dragged me along to the hospital, why he had issued me the bullet-proof vest.

For several seconds, no one moved. We all three stood there, frozen in place like life-sized pieces of art in public places. Marjorie's right hand never left her pocket. She kept her gaze focused on Fraymore's face, but she seemed impervious to the look of stark entreaty that was written there.

"I'm leaving now, Gordon," she said firmly, the way a mother speaks to a recalcitrant child. "We all have to do what we have to do. If you want to stop me, you'll have to shoot."

With that, she climbed into the Suburban, shut and locked the door behind her, and started the engine. She jammed the gearshift into reverse and peeled out of the parking place, then she sent the truck barreling forward. Fraymore and I were left standing in shower of gravel and a cloud of dust.

For another moment, Gordon Fraymore still didn't move. Ashen-faced, he stared after the fleeing truck, then slowly he let out his breath.

He sighed. "We'd better go get her and bring her back," he said grimly.

Several blocks away a fanfare of pealing trumpets from the Elizabethan announced the beginning of the outdoor show. Onstage there would be plenty of action and fighting. Fake blood would flow during well-choreographed swordplay, but no one would die. After the performance, all the players—the ones who survived the plot as well as those who didn't—would appear onstage for curtain calls and much-deserved applause.

Down here in the church parking lot, real lives were on the line. None of us would be using fake bullets. Ours were all too real. When the action was over, there was a better-than-even chance that one or more of us would be either badly hurt or dead. But we weren't worthy of pealing trumpets. And when the action was over, I doubted we'd be rewarded with a round of applause, either. It didn't seem fair.

"Why'd you let her go, for God's sake?" I demanded as we headed for the Montego. "Why didn't you try to stop her?"

Gordon Fraymore shook his head. "You saw it. She had a gun. I couldn't risk it, not here on the street in the middle of town. It's too dangerous. Someone else might get hurt."

That may sound like a lame excuse, but he was right. When you're confronted by that kind of situation, the safety of innocent bystanders takes precedence over every other consideration.

Back in the car, we tore across the parking lot toward the street, only to see Marjorie Connors' Suburban a good three blocks away, speeding south. Without benefit of either lights or siren, hot pursuit was out of the question.

After checking oncoming traffic, Fraymore turned carefully onto the street and followed the Suburban at a speed that gave little hope of our ever catching up. We were in the detective's lovingly maintained Montego. He drove the aging Mercury as if it were made of spun glass that would shatter at the slightest jar. Had we been in Fraymore's city-owned Lumina, it would have been a different story. Cop cars are disposable items, meant to be rode hard and put up wet.

While Fraymore drove, there was nothing for me to do but worry. "How dangerous is she?" I asked.

Fraymore didn't answer right away. "Three people are dead so far," he returned gloomily. "You tell me."

20

Riding in the car with Fraymore was an emotional nightmare. I knew exactly what he was thinking, what he was feeling, because I had walked in his shoes once. Dreading what was to come, I was scared witless, not just for me but for all of us. The situation was every bit as dangerous as walking into a house filled with highly volatile liquid-propane gas.

We followed Marjorie south and out of town, across the freeway, and past the turnoff to the charred remains of Live Oak Farm. She was speeding, but not as much as I would have expected. Even without hot pursuit, we maintained some visual contact.

"Are you going to stop and call for backup?" I asked as we passed what I knew to be both the last gas station and the last telephone booth on the outskirts of town.

"You *are* my backup," Gordon Fraymore responded.

I do ask stupid questions.

Outside the car, dusk was fast approaching. Fraymore flipped on the headlights. We swept out through rolling pastureland, around the end of what was evidently a small lake, then up a steep grade laced with switchback curves, and into the mountains, a lower spur of the Cascade Range. Neither the Suburban nor the Montego were particularly good at cornering on the steep, winding road. When Marjorie Connors increased her pace, Fraymore didn't, despite the fact that she was pulling well ahead of us. At times the Suburban's taillights disappeared completely in the deepening twilight.

"We're going to lose her," I warned.

Fraymore shook his head. "No. I think I know where she's going."

After that we rode for almost half an hour in absolute silence while paved road gave way to loose gravel. I don't know what Fraymore was thinking, but I was remembering the horror of finding Anne Corley at Snoqualmie Falls and quailing from what was to come with every atom of my being.

Beyond the fringe of oak trees and well into ponderosa pine, Fraymore turned left onto a dirt road that meandered off into the forest. By then it really was dark. A thick layer of pine needles littered the meagerly lit road before us. There were no visible tracks, no way to tell whether or not another vehicle had come this way for months on end, but Gordon Fraymore pushed on. In the reflected glow of the dashboard, his broad face was a study in grim determination and total despair.

To my credit, I didn't try to tell him everything was going to be all right. This was no time for sugar-coated platitudes. We both knew imminent disaster awaited us around each and every fast-approaching curve.

A half-mile or so later, Fraymore turned off yet again, this time onto a nearly invisible track barely wide enough to accommodate the width of his Montego. By then I found myself hoping he was wrong—that he didn't know Marjorie Connors nearly as well as he thought he did. With any kind of luck, we'd end up stuck out in these thick woods. It would fall to someone else to bring Marjorie Connors down—someone who, unlike Gordon Fraymore, didn't care so damn much.

But then, through a canyon of towering trees, the high beam of the Mercury's headlights bounced off the reflectors on the back of Marjorie's parked Suburban. Without thinking, I reached for my automatic and shifted it into a jacket pocket to make it more readily accessible.

Fraymore noticed. "Remember," he cautioned. "First we talk."

What else could he say? After all, he loved the woman.

"We already tried it your way. She drove off and left us. She's crazy, Gordon. The death toll already stands at three. You said so yourself. We can't let it go any higher."

Fraymore said nothing more, but I followed his lead and left the automatic in my pocket. When he shut off the engine, I felt naked and vulnerable, sitting there waiting for my eyes to adjust to the lack of light.

"There's a cabin off to the right on the other side of the Suburban," he told me, "about ten yards up a little path. Right around the truck there's a picnic table. My guess is that's where we'll find her. You go right; I'll go left."

"Any idea what she's carrying?"

"None whatsoever."

"Too bad," I said.

As I crawled out of the car and eased myself onto the ground, I couldn't help wondering why it is women never tell men the really important things about them—the life-and-death things. A woman lets you know how she likes her steaks, what she takes in her coffee, and whether or not she despises fingernail polish, but who needs to know that?

Gordon Fraymore may have known from the outset exactly where Marjorie Connors might go, but he didn't have the foggiest idea what kind of gun she might use to kill him. Or whether or not she would. Damn Marjorie Connors anyway!

I was halfway around the Suburban and wondering when I'd come face-to-face with a barking Sunshine, when I heard a sharp crack. I froze and held my breath, but it was only the crackle of dried twigs catching fire. Despite what I'd been through earlier that day at Live Oak Farm, the sound of a burning campfire was far more comforting than I would have thought possible. With the noise from the fire helping to conceal the sound of my approach, I edged around the front bumper to where I could see Marjorie toss an armload of wood onto a recently kindled fire laid in an outdoor river-rock fireplace.

The flickering light allowed me to locate Sunshine lying curled up nearby. She was close enough to the flames to take instant advantage of their spreading warmth. No doubt the higher elevation and much cooler temperatures were tough on the frail old dog's aged bones. I suspected Marjorie had started the fire more out of concern for Sunshine than to warm herself. Her regard for the dog was at once touching and revolting. How could she worry so about an ancient, worthless animal and yet show so little consideration for human life?

Finished stoking the fire, Marjorie retreated to the neighboring picnic table just as Gordon Fraymore emerged into the light from a pool of shadows. "Hello, Marjorie," he said softly.

She showed no surprise. "Hello, Gordy," she returned. "It's all right. I'm not going to shoot you."

"I'm not going to shoot" should join "Go ahead and shoot me" on the list of most overused famous last words, but Gordon Fraymore took them at face value. He stepped nearer the table. A pebble rattled under his foot, and Sunshine raised her head.

"It's okay, girl," Marjorie crooned reassuringly. "It's only Gordy."

Sunshine thumped her tail in a brief welcoming tattoo. Then, seemingly unconcerned, she wearily put her chin back down on her paws and closed her eyes while Fraymore edged even closer. I could see that his own gun was still holstered, the damn fool.

"What are you doing?" he asked.

"Waiting for you. Having a drink. Care to join me?"

"No, thanks. What's in the glass?"

A tall plastic glass sat on the wooden table in front of her. Next to it stood a bottle. "Gin," she answered.

"You don't drink," he observed.

"I do sometimes."

Their voices were so subdued and dispassionate, that I wondered if I had made up the other part, if I had only imagined the charge of passion arc between them, but when Fraymore asked the next question, his voice cracked with pent-up emotion.

"Why'd you do it, Marge?" he asked brokenly. "Why?"

"I was getting even," she answered with a shrug. "Guy threw me out. Once he saw her, he thought I was fat and ugly and old. You can fix fat, but there's not much you can do about old and ugly, is there. Guy dumped me on the garbage heap like an old shoe—and for a slut like that!"

"God in heaven! You didn't have to kill them."

Marjorie paused long enough to pour more gin into the glass. "Didn't I?" she returned scornfully. "If I didn't, who would? You must know what they were by now, or you wouldn't be here."

"It still wasn't up to you," Fraymore insisted doggedly. "Sooner or later, the law catches up with people like that."

"No, it wouldn't," she replied. "The statute of limitations ran out on most of Daphne's criminal activity long ago, and although you may not be willing to do it yourself, there's no law against ditching a worn-out wife."

Fraymore's massive shoulders drooped. "Why didn't you tell me what you knew? If you found out, it couldn't have been that much of a secret."

Marjorie picked up the glass and took a long pull on it. "Oh, it was a secret all right. They really covered their tracks. I found out because I made it my business to find out, because I made it my life's work. It took a long time. It took a lot longer to find the girl."

"What girl? Tanya Dunseth?" I asked. Speaking, I moved into the circle of light. I wanted Marjorie to know there were two of us— that she wouldn't be able to talk her way around Gordon Fraymore and get off scot-free. She dismissed me with barely a glance.

"As soon as I found Tanya, I knew she was a gold mine."

"As in blackmail?"

Marjorie regarded me over the rim of her glass. "That too," she allowed, "but also as bait. With Guy's theater connections, it was easy to get them down here when I wanted to."

"What about Tanya? Was she in on it?"

Marjorie smiled. "The only thing Tanya did was become an actress. Many of them do, you know."

"Do what?" I asked.

"Become actresses," she answered. "Incest victims become actresses so they can turn themselves into someone else, so they can live some other life. They often go a little crazy, too," she added with a laugh. "Tanya's crazy as a bed bug. You probably picked up on that."

For the first time, I noticed a slight slurring in her words, but I chalked that up to the gin. She was hitting the water-glass-sized tumbler pretty hard. In the course of that few minutes of conversation, she had drained it once and was filling it yet again. Once the alcohol hit home, I knew we'd have a roaring drunk on our hands. Subduing her and dragging her back to Ashland in Fraymore's ill-equipped Montego would be a real chore. I wasn't looking forward to it.

While she poured more gin, I saw a reflection on the table where firelight glinted off the pearl-handled revolver that lay on the table within inches of her glass. Armed and dangerous is bad enough. Armed and drunk is doubly so.

"You do understand what I'm saying, don't you?" she continued with amazing unconcern. I confess I had totally lost track of her train of thought, if any. In a situation like that, the whole idea is to keep the person talking. About anything.

"No, we don't," I said quickly, pulling Gordon Fraymore back into the exchange. "Why don't you try explaining it."

"Well," she said, her tongue much thicker now. She framed her words slowly and with some difficulty. "You seem like a smart man, Mr. Beaumont. I suppose you know what incest is."

"Tanya told us about her father," I said.

"Which one?"

"What do you mean?"

Marjorie giggled. "The real one or the ones she made up?"

"I'm not sure. We haven't quite sorted all that out."

"You don't need to. I already took care of him, too. The real one, I mean. He was for Tanya. Guy was for me. That's fair, don't you think?" She raised her glass in a mock salute.

Fraymore almost collapsed under the weight of her words. Obviously, there was another still-unnamed victim, someone else we didn't know about.

"How many are there, Margie?" he asked hollowly. "How many besides Guy and Daphne Lewis and Martin Shore?"

"That's all." She tossed the answer off with an air of nonchalance, waving her glass crookedly at him before taking another drink. "Three is all. Martin Shore's like the special of the week—two for one. I got 'em all down here and took care of all of 'em at once," she added with a giggle. "Like in that old story about the guy who killed all the flies on his bread. Remember that one? What's it called? 'Seven at One Blow,' I think. Yeah. That's it."

I was listening closely, trying to follow and make sense of her drunken rambling while at the same time keeping close watch on the gun. I was so preoccupied that I almost missed the crux of what she was saying as she edged closer to the terrible truth.

"Two for one," I repeated. "What does that mean?"

She looked at me and shook her head. "Mean to tell me you two smart boys still haven't figured it out?" She started to laugh in dead earnest then, pointing a taunting finger first at Gordon Fraymore and then at me. "Two big, clever detectives ..." she choked helplessly "... two whole detectives and you still ... don't know...."

"Don't know what?"

"The man's her father, stupid," she announced shortly, and laughed some more.

It was as though all the air had been sucked out of the already thin atmosphere around me. I hadn't seen Dinky Holloway's video and didn't care to. Gordon Fraymore had. His jaw dropped. "You mean Martin Shore is Tanya's real father?" he asked hoarsely. "Was Daphne her mother then?"

"Stepmother, but close enough. Before I stuck the knife in him, Shore kept asking me how I got hold of that tape, but I didn't tell him," she said before dissolving into yet another fit of drunken laughter. "Don' hafta tell 'em all my secrets."

"But she told us Martin Shore took her away from her real father, that he was the one ..."

"I already told you! Aren't you listening? She's C-R-A-Z-Y. As in *loco*." With effort she had spoken clearly for a moment, now she lapsed back into mumbling, dropping so many consonants it was difficult to understand her. The heavy dose of alcohol must have finally penetrated her brain.

I emerged from my stunned silence. "I thought Tanya was your friend, but you tried to kill her, too."

"I doan have any frien's, do I, Gordy? Not even you. Sunshine maybe. It's a bith ..." she attempted, but was not able to say the word. "It's a bi ... Can't say it, can I? Mouth won' work."

Once more her throaty laughter floated through the forest. The sound sent chills up and down my spine. I had warned Fraymore that I thought Marjorie was crazy. Here she was trying to tell us Tanya was, while her haunting, husky laughter provided inarguable proof that she was, too.

Gordon Fraymore dropped heavily onto the bench across from Marjorie, sagging forward across the table. "I don't believe it. Martin Shore was her real father?" He repeated the words as though he still couldn't accept them as true.

"Tha's righ'," Marjorie mumbled drunkenly, "... the real one. Izza a ... bi ... bi ... bitch, isn't it?" She laughed triumphantly when she finally managed to say the words properly.

With visible effort, Fraymore sat up and straightened his shoulders. "What all's in the glass, Margie?" he asked. "Is it really only gin?"

Marjorie's deranged laughter ceased abruptly. "Why'dya wanna know?" she demanded, pulling the glass toward her, guarding it from his hand. "I jus' wanna take a li'l nap. Time for a li'l *siesta*."

She moved abruptly to one side. For a single, heart-stopping moment I thought she was going for her gun. Instead, she flopped clumsily down on the picnic-table bench and closed her eyes. "Jus' lemme get a li'l sleep. Tha's all."

For several long seconds, neither Fraymore nor I moved. When Marjorie cut loose with a deep, lung-rattling snore, he reached across the table and swept up the gun. "Check her pockets," he ordered.

I hurried to comply. Inside her leather jacket, I found the sleeping pills, or rather, I found the brown plastic child-proof tube. It was open and empty. Without a word, I handed the container over to Fraymore, who held it up to the firelight. With a confirming nod, he wrapped it in a handkerchief and stuffed it in his pocket.

"Seconal," he said.

I put both hands under Marjorie's shoulders, preparing to lift her and take her back to the car. With the potentially lethal combination of booze and pills she'd ingested, we didn't have much time. Even if we took off right then and drove like hell, there was little chance we'd make it to the hospital before she went into either cardiac or respiratory arrest.

"You get her feet," I urged. "Hurry!"

"Sit down, Detective Beaumont," Fraymore said. "Sit down and let her be."

I couldn't believe my ears. "You mean we're not even going to try?"

"This is what she wanted," he returned gravely. "Her choice. I say we wait."

"How long?"

"Long enough."

He propped both elbows on the table and buried his face in his hands. What he was suggesting wasn't exactly aiding and abetting, but it wasn't preventing, either. Only Gordon Fraymore and I would ever know whether or not we had arrived at the campsite before it was all over.

"I don't want her to have to go to jail," he added raggedly. "I don't want her to have to stand before a judge and jury. We'll just say it's a failure to appear and let it go at that."

It was Fraymore's call, not mine. Cops are trained not to second-guess another guy's deal. Without a word, I lowered Marjorie's shoulders back to the bench and went around the table to sit next to Fraymore. He was crying openly by then. I couldn't fault him for his decision. When you're faced with impossible choices, one terrible alternative is probably as good as another.

"All right," I said. "We'll wait."

We sat there together for what seemed like forever. Every once in a while, Fraymore's shoulders would heave, and his whole body would shudder. I let him cry and didn't look over at him. A man deserves at least that much privacy.

Eventually, Fraymore stood up. He walked over to the fire and picked up one end of Sunshine's leash. "Come on, girl," he said softly. "Let's go for a walk."

With a weary but compliant sigh, the old dog sorted herself out and staggered clumsily to her feet. Fraymore walked slowly to the edge of the firelight, leading the limping dog. I knew what he was planning to do. My heart constricted, even though I couldn't fault him for that decision, either. I figured it was a kindness for both Marjorie and the dog—a fitting end for both of them to go together.

I waited in the dark another long while, expecting at any moment to hear the sharp report of Gordon Fraymore's heavy-duty .38. Despite spreading warmth from the fire, I was chilled. My teeth rattled in my head. A breeze sprang up. Off to the west, I was aware of vague flickerings of lightning as a heavy storm rolled in from the Pacific.

Then, finally, when I was beginning to wonder if Fraymore had fallen off a cliff and broken his neck, I heard the crunch of footsteps coming back up the path. He was still leading the dog.

"I couldn't do it," he said brokenly. "Call me a wimp if you want to, but I just flat couldn't do it."

He left the trembling dog standing beside me—between me and the fire—then turned and stalked off alone into the darkness. When I reached down to pat Sunshine, the coat on the back of her neck was soaked with moisture, even though the coming rainstorm was still miles away.

And sometime in between, silently and without any notice, Marjorie Connors—the discarded, crazed woman who had once been Maggie Lewis—stopped breathing and slipped peacefully into oblivion.

21

It must have been one-thirty or two when I got back to Oak Hill B & B. Under the circumstances, Fraymore couldn't very well take Sunshine home with him. I don't think his wife would have approved or understood, so I brought the dog home with me. It was raining like hell by then. I guess I could have left her on the front porch but somehow that didn't seem right.

Oak Hill's posted rules say NO DOGS ALLOWED, but Florence doesn't encourage babies, either, and we'd been dragging Amber around with us for days. In a case like this, I figured it was easier to beg forgiveness than it was to ask permission. So I smuggled Sunshine upstairs to our room, relieved that Florence's noisy Natasha was shut away in some other part of the house.

I planned on waking Alex and explaining everything, but I didn't have a chance. Alex wasn't there. Neither was Amber. Alex's clothes, luggage, shampoo, and toothbrush had also disappeared. A terse note on my pillow announced that she was going to stay with Dinky. She said she had already made alternate arrangements for a ride back to Seattle, so I shouldn't worry about how she was getting home.

Damn!

Which is how I spent yet another romantic night in Ashland, sleeping in a bed with a damp old dog. Sunshine had impossibly bad breath, and she commandeered more than her fair share of the queen-sized mattress. I don't know about Sunshine, but I slept like a baby.

In the morning, I waited until everyone was at breakfast in the dining room, then I slipped Sunshine downstairs and outside. After a walk on the grass, I put her—muddy feet and all—in the backseat of my rented Lincoln, where she had the good sense to lie down immediately and go back to sleep. Nobody was the wiser, no thanks to tattletale Natasha. She barked like crazy the whole time, but no one, including Florence, understood what all the fuss was about.

I tried calling Alex at Dinky's, but she refused to talk to me, so I went over to the Ashland Hills to consult with Ralph Ames. As usual, his wise counsel was greatly appreciated. He couldn't provide any assistance as far as the problem with Alex was concerned, but he did have a suggestion about Sunshine.

He directed me to Jeremy and Kelly's new apartment in Phoenix, Oregon. It was a cute little duplex, actually, with a small but totally separate fenced yard. Once I explained the situation to Jeremy, he readily agreed to keep Sunshine with them. Because of the torrential rainstorm, we had no choice but to hie ourselves off to the nearest hardware store to locate a suitably dry, igloo-shaped doghouse.

On Thursday *Painting Churches* was onstage in the Black Swan, which meant Jeremy had the afternoon off. The weather was bad enough that by noon people at the Festival were already talking about canceling the outdoor performance in the Elizabethan that night.

I had spent part of the morning in Kelly and Jeremy's apartment and had seen the meager selection of cast-off dishes and furniture he was trying to pull together in order to have a place to bring Kelly and the baby the following afternoon. Finally, about eleven in the morning, I called a halt.

"Look," I said, "let's climb into the Lincoln, drive up to Medford, and take care of some of this stuff, shall we?"

And we did. It was a massive shopping trip. The Lincoln may be your basic land barge, but it wasn't nearly big enough for what I had in mind.

The whole time we were racing through Sears in Rogue River Mall, Jeremy kept telling me I shouldn't be doing it—but by then we were both having too much fun. We quickly advanced beyond the crib, high-chair, and car-seat stage to what-the-hell-let's-do-it. That attitude moved us into really serious shopping—as in couch and chair, queen-sized bed, towels, bedding, dishes, silverware, and pots and pans. I threw in a washing machine and dryer for good measure. In my mind, diapers and automatic washing machines go together.

A visibly salivating store manager and a platoon of helpful but wondering salespeople trailed us from department to department. When I wrote out a check for the full amount and asked if it would be possible to have the entire truckload delivered that afternoon, the store manager called my bank, verified the funds, and then said those wonderful words, ones that are always music to the ears of every cash-paying customer. "No problem," he said. "What time do you want it there?"

Jeremy and I finally stopped at a hamburger joint late in the afternoon. He took a bite from a double cheeseburger with bacon and grilled onions and grinned from ear to ear.

"Kelly's going to be surprised, isn't she?"

"Because you're eating hamburger instead of eggplant?"

He blinked. "You won't tell her, will you?"

"No."

"I mean she'll be surprised about the furniture."

"I hope so."

He took another bite. He was long and skinny. His prominent Adam's apple bobbed up and down when he talked or swallowed.

"I had a great time, Beau," he said, calling me by my first name without any prompting. "I haven't had this kind of fun with my own dad since Mom died."

I frowned. "I didn't know your mother was dead," I said.

He scowled back. "I thought I told you about that, about how Kelly and I met. In Natural Helpers."

I knew something about Natural Helpers. Lots of schools have them. They're sort of a grass-roots, student-run counseling organization. Natural Helpers activities seem to bear some passing resemblance to twelve-step programs in that kids who have a problem of some kind can go there and talk confidentially to other kids who have already dealt with similar kinds of difficulties.

In my mind, I guess I had it pegged as a quasi-Al-Anon for kids. If you're a problem drinker, it's easy to assume that all the problems in the world stem from that. I remembered Jeremy had mentioned something about Natural Helpers in passing, and I had jumped to the hasty conclusion that someone in his family must have a drinking problem.

"No," I said. "I don't think you did."

He looked at me. "My mother died of cancer," he said. "Three years ago. I got into Natural Helpers years earlier, right after she got sick. I was about to graduate from college, but I went back to my old school last year to help with a Natural Helpers' leadership program. That's when I met Kelly. We ended up talking because ..." He paused and shrugged. "Well, you know. She was going through the same thing."

Even then I still didn't understand, not right away. "What same thing?" I asked stupidly.

Tears brimmed suddenly in Jeremy Todd Cartwright's eyes. His young face filled with a look of compassion that went far beyond his tender years. "You still don't know, do you?" he said.

"Know what? What's going on?"

"Mr. Beaumont," he said softly. "I'm sorry to have to tell you this. I thought you knew. Kelly's mother has cancer. She's had it for more than a year."

"Karen?" I stammered. "She has cancer? How can that be?" I tried to focus my stricken mind on what Jeremy was saying, but his words drifted over me from far away, as if beamed to earth from a distant planet.

"Kelly's been stuck in denial, and I understand that. It happened to me, too, but I've been trying to tell her all along that it was wrong to run away, that she couldn't hide out from what was happening forever. I wanted her to go back home and face up to it, but she's stubborn. You know how women are."

But that wasn't true. Listening to Jeremy talk, I realized once again that I still don't know the first damn thing about women. Any of them.

22

If I do say so myself, it was a hell of a wedding. Kelly and Jeremy had paid for the first wedding themselves—the one that didn't happen. I figured the second one was on me. We did it on the twenty-first of September, the day Little Karen, my granddaughter, was four months old.

The wedding still had to be held on Monday afternoon, because that's still the only day the theaters are dark in Ashland and the only day when theater people could attend.

But instead of being in June, in the height of the summer tourist season, this was the end of September, shortly before the outdoor theater goes dark for the winter. The end-of-season weather was beautiful—crystal-blue skies with the sharp, fresh bite of fall lingering in the air as soon as the sun went down.

Remembering Guy Lewis' down-filled jacket, I encouraged everyone to come prepared for chilly weather, and they did. With Florence's able help, we managed to find suitable accommodations. Most of the out-of-town guests arrived on Thursday and stayed through until Tuesday with a liberal sprinkling of theater dropped into the celebration for good measure.

For me the real coup was flying my grandparents, Jonas and Beverly Piedmont, down from Seattle. They hadn't been out of town for years, and neither one of them had ever flown in an airplane before, so coming to Ashland was a huge adventure for them. Not only that, my grandfather is wheelchair-bound, so there were some real physical hurdles involved in boarding that Seattle-Portland-Medford shuttle.

My grandparents have a beloved old white dog named Mandy that had to be cared for in their absence. Given the problem, Ames found a place nearby called the Academy for Canine Behavior. According to him, it was more of a doggie resort than a kennel. That news put Mandy's traveling owners at ease.

Because of a long-standing rift in our family caused by my own out-of-wedlock birth, Kelly and Scott had never met their great-grandparents. As soon as Grandma Piedmont saw Kelly, she burst into tears at Kelly's amazing resemblance to her daughter. Once she mentioned it, I saw it was true. Kelly really *does* look like my mother. If the grandmother of the bride had any derogatory comments about Karen Louise's birthday preceding the wedding by several months, she kept them discreetly to herself.

The one most likely to voice disapproval—my scrawny, tough-minded Presbyterian forebear who had disowned and never re-claimed my mother, his own unwed daughter—also kept quiet on the subject, due primarily to the fact that he suffered a stroke two years ago. Speech, for him, is all but impossible. But he sat there in Lithia Park, with his wheelchair parked next to my son Scott, nodding and beaming throughout the ceremony, so I don't think he was very much opposed.

Given some advance notice, Jeremy's dad, Colonel Jeremy Todd Cartwright II, managed to get leave and fly home from his com-mand somewhere in Korea. He's career army. We didn't have a lot of time for visiting, but he's an interesting guy, and I'm looking forward to crossing paths with him at holiday family gatherings, christenings, and the like.

Incidentally, the minister christened Karen Louise Beaumont

Cartwright—Kayla for short—in the same park immediately prior to the wedding, which is getting things slightly out of order, but I doubt God is that much of a stickler for observance of form. At my age, I've come to believe He's a whole lot more concerned with substance.

Gordon Fraymore turned up at the wedding. Jeremy had already showed me Fraymore's wedding gift—an almost complete set of automotive tools in a red, multi-drawered tool chest.

"Jeremy's so proud of his tools he can barely stand it."

Fraymore shrugged modestly. "Picked the whole shebang up from a garage sale up in Grants Pass," he said. "He's going to need tools if he expects to keep that old van of his running."

Weddings have a way of making the father of the bride feel like an extraneous jackass. Fraymore and I had gravitated over to the side of the crowd and stationed ourselves near a punch bowl at the liquid-refreshment table, a place where I hoped to stay out of harm's way.

"How are you doing?" I asked.

Fraymore looked at me as if trying to assess exactly how the question was intended. He nodded. "Okay, I guess." He thought about it a minute and then added, "It's tough."

From personal experience, I knew that was true.

"My wife and I are going for counseling," he continued. "She doesn't know about Marjorie. Confession may be good for the soul, but I don't think it's all that good for putting broken marriages back together."

Scott came searching for me right about then. "Dad, they're looking for you. It's time to cut the cake."

I waved to Fraymore. "Duty calls."

"Wait," he said. "Before you go, I have something for you." He reached into his jacket pocket and pulled out a small white envelope, which he handed to me. It had been folded down to the size of a regular business card. "Open it," he said.

Inside I found a single key and recognized it at once—the ignition key from Anne Corley's 928.

"It must have been blown clear by the explosion," Gordon Fraymore explained. "The crime-scene guys didn't find it until several days later. I mentioned it to Jeremy. He said he thought you'd like to have it back, maybe have it framed or something."

My hand closed around the key. I probably only imagined it, but it felt warm to the touch. I didn't know what to say. "Thanks," I mumbled finally.

"It's nothing," Gordon Fraymore said. "I owe you way more than that."

With a lump in my throat, I stumbled off to attend to the picture-taking of the cake-cutting ceremony. Nobody thought anything of it. On his daughter's wedding day, the father of the bride is allowed to be a maudlin, sentimental slob.

Ralph Ames had been pleased to present Kelly and Jeremy with not one but two gifts. In keeping with his penchant for gadgets, one was an automatic-bakery thing, an appliance that supposedly bakes bread from scratch. The other was an absolutely magnificent wedding cake.

The multitiered edifice had actually arrived in Ashland the night before the wedding, naked and in pieces, driven down I-5 in a '68 Cadillac limo chauffeured by none other than Ralph Ames himself and accompanied by Mary, the wizard woman who had baked the cake and also owned the limo.

Mary, Ralph Ames' lovely new lady friend of the willowy blonde variety, presides over her own dining/dessert establishment in Seattle, a place called Queen Mary's. She agreed to do an out-of-state cake only on the condition that she accompany Ralph to the wedding so she could decorate it *in situ* as an enthralled Ralph told me with a love-besotted smile.

The cake was suitably beautiful. I was happy Jeremy and Kelly restrained themselves from smashing it all over one another's faces. That's one of those currently popular customs I personally find disgusting. By the time the cake was served, it was almost evening, and I was feeling pretty damn proud of myself. As far as I could see, the whole event had gone off without a hitch.

I have a friend down in Arizona who paints watercolors. Rhonda tells me that what makes a beautiful picture isn't the colors so much as it is the contrast between light and dark. I believe the same holds true for weddings.

There was lots of light. After three months Kelly's hair wasn't much longer than mine but she looked lovely in a gauzy veil and wearing her beautiful long white gown. I figured what the hell. Why not do it right?—and Jeremy looked slick in his white tux with tails. James Renthrow made a smashingly handsome best man, and Karen, mother of the bride, was also matron of honor. Together Dave and I walked Kelly down the damn aisle, holding her between us. When the minister asked who giveth this woman, we both answered, "Her parents do."

Put that in your pipe and smoke it, Ann Landers.

But there was also plenty of dark. In four months, Karen had lost more weight. Lots of it. Her skin was almost as transparent as Grandma Piedmont's. The latest bout of radiation and chemotherapy had pretty much destroyed her own hair, and the wig she wore didn't do her justice. Knowing now that the reason she had needed to go straight back to Cucamonga in June was because she was in the middle of chemotherapy didn't make me feel any better about some of the things I said back then. But I can't ever take them back any more than Guy Lewis could ever take back his last hurtful remarks to Daphne.

As the reception wound down, Karen and I found ourselves alone for a few minutes with the autumn chill cooling the air around us.

"I thought your friend Alex would be here for the wedding," she said.

"Alex and I run hot and cold," I told Karen truthfully. "We're in a cooling-off period right now. She didn't think it would be a good idea to horn in on the wedding. She thought her being here would make things too complicated."

Karen nodded. We stood together for some time, watching the guests starting to say their good-byes and wander away. It had been a wonderful day, but suddenly, for no particular reason, I felt terribly sad. I wanted to take Karen in my arms and hold her, I wanted to tell her how sorry I was about everything, but I didn't. Couldn't. It wouldn't have been fair to either one of us, and it sure as hell wouldn't have been fair to Dave.

"Why wouldn't you let anyone tell me about it?" I asked finally. "How come I had to find out from Jeremy?"

Karen shrugged, the knobby bones of her shoulders clearly visible under the sheer material of her dress. "You'd already been through so much with your mother," she said quietly. "I didn't want you to have to go through it again."

I did hug her then. I held her because of all the good days we once had together and because of the kids and because, no matter what, we were grandparents. Dave came up about then, his face haggard and questioning, hopeful and worried sick, all at the same time. The hug ended, and I handed her over to him. I couldn't say a word to either one of them right that minute. Dave and I are indeed veterans of the same war. In more ways than one.

Alex tells me that within the next few weeks they should come close to having a solid accounting of the monies that will come to the Seattle Rep on an ongoing basis from the Guy and Daphne Lewis Trust Fund. On the other hand, the Oregon Shakespeare Festival was the primary beneficiary of the Marjorie Connors Trust. Her estate was found to include a surprisingly large amount of cash, most of which, I believe, came from her systematic blackmailing of Daphne Lewis.

In effect, both the Festival and the Seattle Rep are reaping handsome long-term financial gain due to the labor and generosity of Guy Lewis, the much-maligned king of the chemical toilets. It is my sincere hope that the next time Monica and Alex go to war, the theater-development game won't prove quite so deadly.

I talked to Kelly a few days ago. Sunshine is fine and adjusting fairly well to living in town. Kelly is excited about the remodeling they're doing on a house we bought down there. She's managed to walk her way through a complex tangle of zoning rules so that by the time the season starts up again next spring, the remodel should be finished and she'll be able to have a day-care center right there in her own home. She wants to be able to take care of kids for the people who work at the Festival, but she'll also be available for occasional playgoing parents who need a reliable place to park the baby or babies while the grown-ups get a dose of the Bard of Avon.

Ralph has been in and out of Ashland twice in the last two weeks, crossing the *t*'s and dotting the *i*'s on the financing package, changing it over from a bridge loan to a regular mortgage. When I helped Kelly and Jeremy buy the house, the price was more than right because the place was almost in ruins. The transformation since then seems truly miraculous.

One thing that's helping keep costs down is that we've had to hire out only the major electrical and plumbing work. Jeremy and Kelly both have put in plenty of sweat equity by serving as general contractors. Their friends from the Festival, especially Jeremy's sidekick, Romeo, are doing all the finish work themselves. The work crew, the people responsible for the physical labor, will move in when the work is done. Kelly is keeping track of all their hours. They'll be credited with a dollar amount off their rent once they all move in. They'll also be using Marjorie Connors' system of sharing chores. It's a good deal for everyone involved, including the major investor.

Ralph tells me that between donating dollars for ex-gang member scholars and running a hostel for impoverished actors, my investments may be becoming a bit too diversified, but he told me I didn't need to start worrying about money quite yet. I had to write a sizable check for the difference between the insurance settlement and the purchase price on my new, special-order Guard-red 928. I wrote it, and the check didn't bounce, so I guess financially I'm still okay.

I took Gordon Fraymore's suggestion. The key to the old 928 is framed in a shadow box lined with red velvet. A guy at a place called Ace Frames over in Kirkland fixed it up for me. I keep it on the table beside my leather recliner.

The last time Ralph was in Ashland, I asked him if anyone down there had heard from Tanya Dunseth. He said no. Over Fourth of July weekend, she took Amber, the few clothes she had left, and her diaper bag, and disappeared. Someone said they saw her out on the freeway, hitchhiking with the baby, heading for California. A search of Marjorie Connors' Suburban had provided enough information about the blackmail of Daphne Lewis to prove that Marjorie had acted alone. Consequently, when Tanya disappeared, no one bothered to go after her because by then it was clear that other than using fake I.D. she had broken no law.

Ralph and I have talked about Tanya several times since, wondering if we should make some attempt to find her. Martin Shore's first wife, Tanya's mother, died years ago. As her father's only child and heir, Tanya is due a small inheritance from his estate. The problem is, Tanya obviously has no interest in Martin Shore's money. She probably regards it as dirty, and I can't say that I blame her.

So Ralph and I continually debate the issue. Usually, we're in agreement that tracking Tanya down would be a bad idea—the wrong thing to do. Occasionally, one or the other of us wavers; then it's up to the other one to hold the line and talk him out of it. So far we've always decided against it.

I wonder sometimes where Tanya is and whether or not she's all right. Knowing what we know now, I believe it's fair to assume that Tanya Dunseth is certifiably crazy. She has spun some very complex webs as a device to shut out the terrible truth of her pathetic upbringing. Roger Tompkins called them "wheels within wheels." They're so confusing, I'm sure Tanya no longer has any idea what's truth and what's fiction. So yes, she probably is crazy, but she's certainly not a danger either to herself or to anyone else, including her daughter.

I imagine she's settled in someplace far away where she has reinvented herself and where she has written a brand-new set of roles for Tanya and Amber, although those most likely are not the names they go by anymore. And the part she's playing—the one for which she's best suited—is, no doubt, the one she created for herself without any role model in her own life—that of a good mother and parent.

So what if she's crazy, maybe even a little more so than most?

God knows she has far more cause to be crazy. She's had far more to overcome.

And every time I think about poor Tanya Dunseth, I try to send a good show-business thought in her direction, wherever she may be.

"Go with God, Tanya Dunseth," I say to myself. "Break a leg."